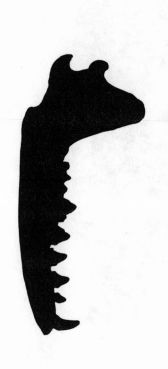

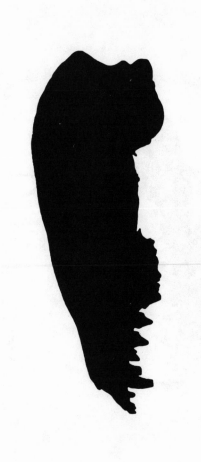

ELIZABETH
KILCOYNE

WAKE tHE BONES

WEDNESDAY BOOKS
NEW YORK

First published in the United States by Wednesday Books, an imprint of St. Martin's Publishing Group

WAKE THE BONES. Copyright © 2022 by Elizabeth Kilcoyne. All rights reserved. Printed in the United States of America. For information, address St. Martin's Publishing Group, 120 Broadway, New York, NY 10271.

www.wednesdaybooks.com

Designed by Jonathan Bennett

The Library of Congress Cataloging-in-Publication Data is available upon request.

ISBN 978-1-250-79082-8 (hardcover)

ISBN 978-1-250-79083-5 (ebook)

Our books may be purchased in bulk for promotional, educational, or business use. Please contact your local bookseller or the Macmillan Corporate and Premium Sales Department at 1-800-221-7945, extension 5442, or by email at MacmillanSpecialMarkets@macmillan.com.

First Edition: 2022

10   9   8   7   6   5   4   3   2   1

For Papaw, who gave me the stories, and Elliot,
who gets them next

WAKE THE
BONES

CHAPTER ONE

A symphony of survival wound its way through the emerald tobacco fields of the Early farm. The dead things sang their harmony in the mid-July heat, loud enough to drown out the cicadas' screams. By the roots of a sycamore tree, half a jawbone waited in the dirt for Laurel Early to find it. It was a good jaw. It had held on to most of its teeth even after the gums peeled away and beetles stripped it of its flesh. She rinsed it in the shallows of the river running alongside the fields and tucked it into her bag as she continued her walk, looking for more bones to add to her collection.

The jawbone had belonged to a fox, but when he laid his head down and failed to lift it again, he left his jaw and every other part of him up for grabs. What was left belonged to Laurel. That was the rule with bones. Unless you hid them in a casket below the earth, anyone could eat, break, or use them to their advantage.

Laurel was one such scavenger. She made half her living off growing tobacco and the other half off what the dead left behind. She needed the cash flow now more than ever. Her student loans would soon dry up into debt without the degree she'd set out for last fall. So, she boiled flesh and fat from bones or let them dry in the sun, then strung them onto bracelets or twisted them up in wire to make hairpins and brooches. These sold in her online store for far less than their lives were worth.

In her leather bag were two deer sheds, one three-pronged and the other with only two. She'd found them while following the narrow trails that scarred the near-vertical slope of the wooded ridge, stopping only to check on the decomposition status of a possum whose skull and vertebrae she wanted. These paths served as the only roads on the walk she took each morning, when the river was nothing more than a stream of fog, and the tobacco plants were wet and would bruise from a careless touch. Where their trails ended, Laurel used the slabs of limestone jutting out from the soil as steps toward the secluded cemetery at the top of the hill.

Laurel stopped there each morning to catch her breath before heading back. It was a hard spot to see until you were right up on it, the view from the main road obscured by honey locusts. From there you could look down and see the whole of Laurel's world: the tobacco barn high upon the hill, the equipment barn in the bottoms, surrounded by its own graveyard of skeletal old car frames and farm equipment covered by ragged blue tarps. Above it was the small white farmhouse where she lived with her uncle. She kept a cheerful-looking rabbit hutch painted a fading red in the yard, behind a slanting little washhouse. A wire fence restrained a garden heaving with vegetables. Below, six acres of tobacco fields sprawled, and beyond that, the thin arm of the shallow river cradled the property.

The cemetery's border stuck out of the ground like jagged teeth grinning atop the hill. It was an eyesore, all chicken wire and thick wooden fence posts, a rust-speckled bull gate instead of a wrought-iron entryway. Laurel loved the practicality of it, uniform with the rest of the fences and gates of the Early property. It was farm-functional, no different from the fields where the tobacco grew. It wasn't violating a sacred space when she hopped the bull gate; it was stopping by for a visit.

Buried in a concrete vault and a metal casket six feet below ground was another set of bones. These belonged to Laurel's mother and had been there for the better part of twenty years. Other bones had rested there longer: Laurel's Early grandparents, her great-grandparents, great-great aunts and uncles she'd never met, and a baby a hundred years older than Laurel, marked with a date but not a name.

Her mother's gravestone was her favorite of the grim assortment. Laurel loved the way the rain-stained marble looked sticking out of the earth, engraved simply ANNA EARLY. Laurel had traced those letters with her fingertips since long before she could read them.

"Didja miss me?" she asked, half whispering. "Well, you won't have to anymore. I'm staying home for good. College didn't work out."

The wonderful thing about having a tombstone for a mother was that she couldn't disapprove.

"That's where I was yesterday," she explained, shifting from one foot to the other. "Had to drive all the way back to Cincinnati just to drop off a library book. Set up exit counseling. Officially withdrew. Took forever, but it's done. My advisor barely cared."

Laurel dropped down to the ground to lie by Anna. She plucked a blade of grass and twirled it between her fingers. "It's for the best. I can make it work here at home. I know what to do. I'll bloom where I'm planted."

The sky was a single shade of deep blue, framed by sycamore branches. The sun lingered somewhere above her shoulder. There'd be blackberries soon enough, if a storm didn't shake them from their brambles. On days like this, Laurel could imagine staying on the farm for the rest of her life. She closed her eyes in the sleepy heat, her body solid against the patch of earth that would one day be her own. When she imagined her mother in heaven, it looked a lot like this: a Kentucky field in midsummer, perfumed with wildflowers, the blue sky above dotted with fluffy clouds and white cabbage butterflies. It was a good summer, bright and hazy with humidity. It was nothing like the summer Laurel had been born. The drought had been so severe that the soil was still parched and ashen in the fall when her mother's grave was dug.

Anna Early had been a strange woman, in a town that knew few strangers. Whatever field she slipped her fingers into always produced a good yield. She'd been damned for that peculiar streak of good luck, envied by the honest and cursed people of Dry Valley. Even Anna's parents' deaths, tragic as they were, caused more suspicion than sympathy. Folks had made up their minds about *that girl* long before she'd lost them, and when Anna's parents were buried, the wild, strange look in her tearless eyes did little to change their opinion.

Whether it was fated or the result of a self-fulfilling prophecy, Anna only grew stranger the stranger they said she was.

4

One year she barely left the farm, walking restlessly through the woods on dark, new-moon nights without a flashlight. The next year she was gone more often than she was present, leaving gaps not even Laurel could fill in, no matter how she played paleontologist with the artifacts left in the room her mother had slept in, or the stories she could pull like teeth from her uncle Jay, the only other Early left alive.

When no one knew how to do anything but farm, one bad year could bring a town to its knees. In hard times, people gorged themselves on gossip to occupy their hungry mouths. One dry year, they ate Anna Early alive. At the start of that summer, Jay found the young tobacco blighted in the fields. And before the first frost, he found Anna's body at the bottom of the old livestock well.

At nineteen years old, Laurel was only a few years younger than her mother had been when she died. She'd inherited Anna's ash-blond hair and the weight of the town's judgment. But even when she was a child, Laurel's ironweed resolve was strong. She could handle schoolyard whispers and the sometimes sympathetic, sometimes disgusted grocery-store gazes. She even learned to live with the one irritating nickname that spread across Dry Valley like the sickly-sweet scent of graded tobacco off to market in the fall.

The devil's daughter.

It was a fitting nickname. Laurel, like her mother, had strange gifts, though none so useful as a green thumb: sometimes, a bone would offer her the story of its death. A flash of teeth; a bullet rending flesh; a long, slow starvation or wasting illness. She could feel it through the dried marrow, singing out. It was a useless ability, a parlor trick, nothing so practical as buying a wart like witches from the hills could do. Nor was it a holy gift.

There was no Bible verse that brought it forth, not like drawing fire from a burn or stilling blood in a cut. There was no mystic promise, either, no way to gather knowledge of things yet to pass. She could not see the future, she could only feel the bite of the past.

Laurel reached into her bag, sifting through her finds until her fingers settled on the jawbone. It was an ugly thing, but she could see potential in any carcass. She brought the jawbone up to her face, cracking her eyes open to study its shape, looking for something to salvage. It was tense and buzzing in the palm of her hand, heavy with potential, waiting for some kind of mid-summer magic to bring it back to life.

Laurel closed her eyes to the sun's glare, letting the filtered stain of blood pumping inside her eyelids swallow up her sight. She breathed into the red. She could taste the morning in her throat, the pollen-tinged flavor of the air, the copper and salt of the dark river sand, the sunlight settling into the dust by the side of the road. Her heartbeat, a hair too fast, rattled against her rib cage.

A shadow passed across her face. Not cool, like the shade of her mother's gravestone or the current of the river. Cold as death. Her jaw clenched, rigor-mortis tight, her teeth splitting the skin inside her cheek. Her whole body went black with the taste of blood.

At once, Laurel sat up straight. Her vision turned blue, just in time to catch a vulture's wing circling out of her line of sight. The taste of river mud was thick in her mouth. It was only the aftershock of pain against her cheek that told her she was tasting her own blood and not the last memory of a fox's jaw snapping shut.

Laurel spat pink into the grass. Her heart settled back into her chest, blood warming in her veins. The vulture took another lazy lap high above the cemetery as the wind shook the trees, and her mother lay, unmoving, underground.

Laurel set the jawbone at the base of her mother's gravestone and studied it. Two missing molars, the gray stain of sediment sunk into its pores. If she picked it back up, it might be body-hot in her hand, as if still wrapped in muscles and veins full of blood. She considered leaving it there, an offering to her mother, but it was no crayon drawing to hang up on the refrigerator. It was nothing her mother's dead eyes could see to love.

She sighed, picking it up. The world stayed warm and still. The bones stayed dead.

Laurel held the jaw aloft, swinging her legs over the bull gate and onto the road once more.

CHAPTER TWO

Laurel fell into taxidermy the way most people fell into churchgoing or factory work. She looked around, found there was little else worth doing, and figured she might as well. She had a strong stomach and the space to simmer off the rancid meat that clung to bones she found in the woods. Peroxide and pickle buckets were cheap overhead. She could skin and degrease most creatures in the woods. She mounted deer skullcaps or macerated European-style skull mounts for hunters proud of bagging the big one. Her real talent lay not in animating furs, but in repurposing bone. She did not try to imitate life; she embraced the nature of death. It was probably for the best that she decided to drop out of college. She would have made a terrible veterinarian.

Officially withdrawn from college, day one. She'd have to say something soon, but she wasn't sure what. When she'd first announced her intentions to Jay, he hadn't spoken to her for two days. Not to punish or with malicious intent; Jay was simply a man who didn't speak until he knew what he meant to say. When he spoke to her next, he handed back her old pair of work gloves and said, "You're an adult now. Adults work."

Laurel's words had failed her for the better part of two weeks. She hadn't stopped Garrett Mobley when he offered to check her brakes before the long drive back to Cincinnati. She'd listened to his brother, Ricky, tease her for four days about being a college girl, too fancy to get her hands dirty, before she half-heartedly told him to shove it. She'd even let her best friend, Isaac Graves, babble about his plans to transfer community college credits to her university once he'd earned them. Before her senior year he'd be there, he'd promised, banking on a certainty she'd shattered without warning him.

She couldn't do anything about that now.

There were two paths from the cemetery back to the farmhouse. One had been paved with pea gravel long ago, but Laurel was the only regular visitor, so it had been neglected since she left for college. Following it required a wade through overgrown fescue and spiny ironweed. In the heat, it was almost easier to wander back on a deer path, slicing down a near-vertical holler, past hickory trees and Osage oranges, careful not to slip on perpetually muddy ground or wet limestone as she descended to a spot below the house, then climbed upward once more, along a steep ridge that emerged by the little white washhouse she used as her workshop.

She was there in that low place when her eyes caught on the face. Corpse-pale and bloated, with teeth twisting from its mouth, it glared at her, eyes like the depressions of a skull, shadowed and malicious. She saw horns, fangs. Her blood froze in her veins and her hair stood on end as the air in the woods stilled around her.

She blinked rapidly and realized her mistake; her mind had made a face of a twisted root ball, creating a monster out of nothing. She often did that in the woods. Shaking her cold fingers to get her blood moving, she scaled the ridge at a half run, leaving her fear and the imagined monster behind. She had work to do.

Laurel approached the faded whitewashed brick of the washhouse, boots kicking up dust on the narrow gravel path that led to its creaking door. Laurel's ancestors built the outbuilding more than a hundred years before, for laundry and bathing. The Earlys installed running water eighty years ago, leaving the washhouse unoccupied until Laurel claimed it as her private workshop.

Outside, two plastic vats held the macerating carcasses of a raccoon and a possum, respectively. The scent was putrid—salty and moist—but it was far enough away from the farmhouse and the garden that Laurel wouldn't incur her uncle's wrath. The stench acted as a deterrent, keeping away family and friends who had developed the Southern talent for idle chatter that Laurel hadn't managed to acquire. Sometimes, her uncle Jay would venture down with a deer skull he'd found by the salt lick. Or Isaac would join her for an afternoon if he had a skin that needed tanning. But they were visitors there; the washhouse was Laurel's hallowed ground.

Laurel shoved the door open with her hip, blinking away green spots as her eyes adjusted to the dim room. Mounted skulls, deer and coyotes and even a horse, leered down at the work space. The reconstructed skeleton of what had once been the family cat perched on the windowsill. Wet specimens of mice and spiders, injected with humectant fluid and suspended in diluted alcohol, lined a shelf just out of direct sunlight. Glass beads, copper and gold wire, little bones and teeth sprinkled the tables. Tufts of rabbit fur mingled with dust bunnies under the bench.

A broad, strange shadow shifted in the corner. Laurel's heart thudded in her chest as she stumbled back toward the door.

But it was only Isaac, propped up on a stool by the fireplace, one leg crossed over the other, smiling faintly at his phone. Like most of the boys in Dry Valley, Isaac changed more with the seasons than the years. As midsummer approached, the sun left a smattering of new freckles across his forehead and jawline. Farmwork bleached his dishwater hair the color of corn silk and stained his skin as red as the clay they tilled up in the tobacco beds.

"Sorry, sorry," said Isaac as he looked up from his phone to see Laurel steady herself against her desk. "I finished with my trail sets early, and I figured I'd wait for you until Garrett and Ricky came down. Didn't mean to scare you."

She'd last seen Isaac two hours before. After she'd picked him up from the apartment he shared with his father, they'd eaten a quick breakfast with her uncle before splitting off in three directions. Isaac had headed down the holler on the south end of the farm, where he set traps for coyotes.

"Sure," Laurel said, willing her heartbeat to slow as she pulled her finds from her bag. "Don't know what's with me this morning. Guess the coffee didn't kick in."

The drawer creaked as Laurel fished for her magnifying glass and the clamp to hold it. From its depths, she pulled a pair of needle-nose pliers. There was a sharp, metallic tang to their smell, muddled with the oil that Laurel applied to keep their jaws limber. "Catch anything?" she asked as she examined the bone under the magnifying glass.

"Not so much as a breeze. It was weirdly quiet for such a nice day. Think I must have left my scent on the traps, and they reckoned some big predator was after them." Isaac fidgeted, too big for the small room. He'd outgrown himself a long time ago. He held his shoulders as though he were trying to fold himself into a more manageable shape, and his steps were quiet as a child's sneaking through the house after dark. "I spooked a couple of deer on the ridgeline," he said after a pause, "and there was a buzzard watching me from the branches of that ash tree."

"Mm-hmm," Laurel agreed. "I'm gonna work on this jaw for a second before the others get here."

Isaac's phone buzzed and he flipped it over, letting out a quiet laugh as he started to respond.

The term "like pulling teeth" was not invented by a taxidermist. Compared to shimmying the thin skin off a carcass or scraping fat from a hide, pulling teeth was easy. Once the meat dissolved and there was no gum tissue holding them in place, it didn't require more than a couple of careful tugs, and Laurel didn't mind cracking the already-cracked bone.

She deposited the tooth into a stained jewelry dish with a gilded rim. It already held several rabbit teeth, and the mix of predator and prey made a pleasing contrast to Laurel's eye. "Looking good," she told the teeth, shaking the feeling of their locked jaw from her fingertips.

Isaac slid his phone into his pocket with a sigh. "One of these days, you're going to be chatting with one of those things, and it's going to talk right back. You might not bat an eyelash, but I'll shoot it out of your hands."

"You'd miss and kill me," she said.

He shrugged, but they knew that wasn't true. When they shot at something, they never missed.

Laurel fiddled the other tooth out as Isaac warned her, "Boys'll be here shortly. Garrett's been texting since they hit the driveway. Apparently, Ricky's in rare form today."

Laurel shook her head, unclamping the jaw and placing it back in her bag. "That boy. Good looks might have been his saving grace, if only God had sewn his mouth shut."

Isaac laughed. He'd long stopped trying to choose a side in the amicable war between her and Ricky, content to spectate. "He's not so bad when you're not around. Something about you and the summertime makes him act like an idiot."

Laurel rolled her eyes. "He's still acting like we're kids and all he wants from me is a slap. He's liable to get one, too, at the rate he's going."

Gravel knocked against an exhaust pipe somewhere up the driveway. Isaac cocked his head at the sound. "And here he comes so you can do it, too."

She could blame the rush of heat to her face on the stuffiness of the room. She could blame it on adrenaline, her fighting instinct riled at the thought of Ricky in a mood. Instead she bit her cheek and kept her blame to herself. "I swear, that boy is a glutton for punishment," she said.

"Of course he is." Isaac elbowed her in the ribs. "Why else would he be after you?"

Laurel flinched as Ricky slammed the truck door shut outside. Isaac watched her with a quizzical expression, and she shook her head minutely, offering a thin smile. She took a deep breath and steadied herself. She'd been twitchy all morning.

Wandering the woods should have calmed her. It should have reminded her she was safe. She was home.

Nerves. That was it. Keeping a secret had never suited her. She'd tell them, once they finished in the fields. Bite the bullet, swallow the blood, and get on with living the rest of her life.

CHAPTER THREE

There was mud under Isaac's nails again. He'd only just finished picking them clean. Every summer was a dirty one, the sort a shower couldn't entirely scrub away. Rainfall only determined whether it was dust or mud coating his skin. This summer was a wet one, days of driving rain and thunder, an aftermath of muggy air, half suffocating. He never stopped sweating. The woods provided some shade, but puddles lingered on paths and in tadpole-laden sloughs. The soles of his boots were caked with mud. His socks and the hems of his jeans were speckled with it. While Laurel worked, he'd scraped dried dirt from the inside of his wrist and onto the workshop floor. It was a lifelong battle, trying to keep Dry Valley's itchy summers from tattooing his skin.

They all had their ways of trying to keep clean. Laurel scraped her nails across a bar of soap she kept in her bag whenever she went outside and laid on baby-powder deodorant and cotton-breeze body spray before dealing with polite society. Ricky never let his hair dry entirely before dunking it back into the river or dumping a water bottle over his sunburnt skin. Garrett was the only one who seemed not to mind the stains of country living. He spent the summer elbows-deep in oil, spray paint, and radiator fluid, a chemical inoculation against the dirt of the woods.

Garrett's truck—a mid-sixties monster sporting a rust-spotted seafoam-green paint job and a loud diesel engine—was the source of the chemical scent that never left his T-shirts. It wasn't the stealthiest mode of transportation. It reeked of fuel and had a ground clearance high enough that, while Isaac had no trouble sliding onto its bench seat, Laurel had to scramble to climb in without his hand to help her. But it was the perfect truck for a summer spent in the fields and on the river. It could go the distance over the untamed terrain of the Early farm easier than anything except their feet.

"Laurel, cab or bed?" Garrett offered, ever the gentleman, leaning out of the window.

Laurel twitched a grin at Isaac before saying, "Think I'll ride in the back."

"Suit yourself." Garrett shrugged. "But might I point out if you kill Ricky, you'll have to do his weeding?"

"Well, darn." Laurel made a show of pretending to think about it as she walked toward the tailgate.

Garrett was all farm boy, with a body that showed its strength and a perpetual squint to his face, like he was staring into the sun. His hair grew out into walnut-dark waves during the winter, but for now it was cropped close to his scalp, an unfussy buzz cut maintained over the bathroom sink just to keep hair off his neck in the heat. A blistering sunburn peeked from under the stretched-out neck of his sleeveless T-shirt. Isaac had a matching one scalding his ears and collarbones from when they'd set jig poles up and down the river bend the weekend before. They wore mirrored damage, lived mirrored lives. They spent nearly all their days together. Their nights were something new.

Laurel didn't know about that. She knew about the bar, sure, the nights Isaac would borrow her car and drive into the nearest, biggest city he could find and try to lose himself. But she didn't know about the pieces of himself he couldn't seem to shake there.

Not that there was anything to know.

But he wanted to tell her something, anyway. He couldn't look at her without seeing the contact photo on his phone and all the times he'd lost the nerve to call her since she'd left for college. Maybe before she left again, they could talk.

Not that he had much to say.

Inside the cab, Garrett turned back to the road in front of him, raising his voice to be heard over the tinny sound of alt-rock on the radio. "I've been meaning to ask, where'd you go the other night?"

"What do you mean?" Isaac pulled his head back inside the cab; he'd been letting the breeze cool his face.

Garrett reached over and flicked the radio off. "The other night."

"Oh," Isaac said into the hollow silence, "I left early. Went for a walk to clear my head. It didn't work, so I drove back."

"In bed before midnight?"

"You know me." Isaac took a sip from Garrett's Coke in the cup holder. "Slept out on the porch, actually. I stayed with the Earlys. I had to give Laurel her car back."

"You didn't leave with someone?"

A trickle of sweat ran down Isaac's neck, slender as a spider. His skin itched as he fought the urge to wipe it away. He was sitting too close to Garrett's thigh. "Nothing happened. It's just noisy there. The lights are too bright. Sometimes it's too much."

Garrett settled back against his seat. "I missed you. Looked all over for you."

Isaac swilled the last of the Coke, but his throat stayed dry. "I was just out for a walk. You want me to invite you along next time? Since it worries you so bad."

"I'd like that." There was no artifice to the way Garrett spoke. He never saw any reason to say anything other than what he meant. Isaac couldn't stand it. He turned his face to the open window. The cool breeze held no relief from the midday heat.

Garrett steered down the narrow drive with his eyes on Isaac. And Isaac watched the road rather than catch himself on those bright eyes, that wide, forgiving smile. He knew what he was missing out on as intimately as Garrett knew the turns in the road he wasn't watching. Isaac could watch Garrett for hours without having to open his eyes. At his side, Garrett was all motion and heat; the scent of his cologne; of the sweat and grease that gathered in the moons of his nails and lines of his palms. Isaac was stained the same way, no matter how hard he tried to stay clean.

Garrett was a local boy. A two-mile walk down the road, within arm's reach. Something Isaac knew he could have. The flecks of scars across the broad backs of his hands and wrists were coordinates. If they pressed their hands together, Isaac could map out half the county based on where they'd been when they cooked up the bad ideas that made those scars. Setting off fireworks and fishing in the dark, campfires and clumsy pocket-knives. They'd done a lot of bleeding together.

But Isaac was reaching for something new. He needed his hands free, clean of the dirt and blood Dry Valley stained them with. It would be smarter for Isaac to stick his hand into a steel trap than to lace his fingers with Garrett's.

CHAPTER FOUR

Ricky flung himself out of the truck bed before Garrett shut the engine off, not bothering to let the tailgate down. Laurel jumped over the side after him. "Just shy of a cowpat." Ricky smirked as she straightened. A katydid landed on Laurel's shoulder, and she flicked it off with her middle finger.

Ricky stretched, wide enough that his T-shirt rode up, exposing a strip of tanned skin. He wore a tie-dyed Future Farmers of America shirt from high school and a pair of ragged jeans that must have been a hand-me-up from his brother, the way they hung low on his hips. Laurel's palms started to sweat. She wiped them against the front of her jeans. It was far too hot for Laurel to pay Ricky Mobley any mind. That boy would do anything to get her blood up.

Beyond them, tobacco fields stretched almost to the riverbank, an even array of plants as high as Laurel's thigh and lush green. In another couple of weeks, the tobacco would be ready for topping and spraying. If they got it early enough, the product would be dark and sweet, the sort that was in high demand. It would be a good year, if they could keep the leaves from damage until it was time to cut.

The work only got harder as the heat swelled and the tobacco plants grew, but Laurel and her friends were good for it. They'd been working in the fields since they were fat-legged toddlers picking hornworms off the leaves. They grew up playing in the shade at the outskirts of the woods while their parents cut tobacco in late summer. They'd scraped their names with tobacco sticks into the dusty barn floor while the tobacco was stripped and graded for sale up in Cincinnati. They marked their birthdays more by the height or scent of tobacco leaves than they did by month of the year. None of them smoked, but tobacco tarnished their fingers and ran in their blood.

"God, sun's blazing today. Wearing me out already. Could take a nap right here." Ricky let his eyes flutter shut, pale lashes against sun-tinted cheeks.

"On top of the cowpat or the bull thistle?" She meant for her disdain to shut him down before he could start, but some affection she couldn't control must have seeped into her voice.

Ricky grinned down at her like a man in a toothpaste ad. His green eyes met hers, daring her to look elsewhere. "Wanna join me?" he asked.

She didn't budge. Her cheeks were already flushed from sunburn. They wouldn't give anything away.

It was a gorgeous, heady afternoon, thick with humidity and rays of honey-colored light. The mineral scent of river water running past the fields tickled her nose like the carbonation of her cola. They pulled tools out from the truck bed and slid gloves onto their hands. Garrett shrugged off his T-shirt. His hair was spiked with sweat, and dirt streaked his tanned chest. Isaac balanced one foot on the tailgate of the truck, retying his bootlace as Ricky spat into the grass. *Gross,* Laurel thought.

The group split up once they reached the edge of the tobacco, Isaac with Garrett and Laurel with Ricky. Two workers per un-weeded field. Laurel twisted her hair into a rope and jerked it into a knot to keep it off her neck. She worked with her back to the woods, trying to focus on the dirt. She could have sworn Ricky was staring at her, but if he was, he looked away the second she tried to catch his gaze. The hair at the back of her neck prickled. She raised her hand to wipe the sensation away, hoping it was a trickle of sweat and not a yellowjacket.

Laurel worked the weeds out of the soil, knocking them aside until she reached the end of the field, marked by hovering stalks of pokeweed as thick as her wrist. The beginnings of a sunburn crept across her shoulder blades, hot and raw enough to make her itch out of her own skin.

Something warm brushed against her lower back.

"Whoops, sorry," Ricky said, withdrawing his hand. The crooked smile he offered suggested he was anything but sorry. It was too hot for him to be touching her like that, smiling like that.

"Almost done?" she asked, but she already knew. If he weren't such a good tobacco man, it wouldn't have been so difficult to look the other way while he worked. But his movements were graceful, almost second nature. He didn't make it look effortless. He didn't look like a god. He was all man, sweating and dirt-stained and breathing hard. Laurel's breath came a little shorter when she watched him work.

"Nearly so," he agreed, hooking a finger around his belt loop as he tugged his pants up. Laurel caught a glimpse of pale skin below his tan line before denim hid it away. He cocked an eyebrow as she dragged her gaze up. "Think I'll hop in the river after this. Wanna join me?"

Laurel's heartbeat knocked against her rib cage. She ignored its call. "I don't wanna get my clothes wet." Never mind that she was already soaked in sweat.

Ricky pointed to the sky. "Way this sun is, you'll be dry again by the time we're at the top of the hill."

She squinted as she examined the fields. "It's like soup out here." The sun glowed bright overhead, a drop of fire burning through the blue sky. Even still, humidity rising off the river meant that nothing ever truly evaporated.

Isaac and Garrett had finished their section of tobacco and dumped their tools in the truck. Garrett wiped at his forehead with his wet T-shirt, smearing dust and sweat across his face. Isaac's white-blond hair was streaked dark with dirt.

"Think of it as laundry and a bath in one," Ricky said. "Come on, just a quick dip. You know Isaac and Garrett are game. Do you really wanna climb back up that hill in this heat without cooling off first?"

Before she could answer, Ricky took the hoe from her hand and walked back toward the truck. He dropped their tools in the truck bed and turned to face her, hand out. "Swim with me," he pleaded.

"Fine," she muttered. "But I'm not taking anything off." She didn't take his hand, either. Touching Ricky came dangerously close to accepting destiny.

The formula for these relationships was simple. Laurel fell into its rhythm like she was supposed to do. Picking a boy from her high school class who woke before the sun and worked all day with his hands. Falling in love with his calluses and scars, picking at least one of his bad habits to tolerate: bourbon drinking, agnosticism, chaw tobacco. Next would be a church wedding, though Laurel had never been churchgoing. After the white dress and Florida honeymoon came raising kids and tobacco, hoping love would keep her looking young because work would do what it could to age her. Spending forty years married and ten years widowed. Same man, same house, same plot of land, tobacco rising and falling in the bottoms.

Ricky might have fit perfectly, except the bad habit he'd picked was constantly running his mouth. Sure, he smoked pot—if less frequently than he liked to imply—but Laurel could stand that. She couldn't stand the way he talked around an issue, teasing and deflecting and turning questions back on her. She wanted straight answers. She'd grown up around men who said what they thought instead of making her wonder what they felt. She wanted Ricky to be the solution to the questions she'd avoided asking herself since dropping out of school. Instead, he was terrible, more childish than ever when it was time to grow up.

But there were flashes where he seemed to glow with inner potential. When the breeze through the trees ran its fingers across the back of her neck and the very whisper of the grass told her to look, to listen. It was in those moments that she remembered him coming to her when they were children, with bloodied arms and a bucket full of berries from the heart of the blackberry thicket, or watched him bottle-feed a goat kid in his family's barn, every time she'd seen him tired-eyed and mud-streaked, reeking of fertilizer and blistered from work but still able to crack a smile when he saw her walking up the path. Those memories would converge around her like the swelling of cicadas in her ear until she believed, privately, that if she let him live to thirty, they might build a life together.

Then he turned and fired off, "Besides, a dip in the river might wash the stench of carcass off you," and she knew he wouldn't live beyond that minute. She'd strangle him with her bare hands.

Garrett and Isaac were already in the water when Laurel got to the bank, their clothes in a pile on the ground. Isaac waded out into the cold current and ducked his head, scrubbing at his hair with his fingernails. Ricky balled his T-shirt up and tossed it onto his mud-covered boots, already kicked aside. He pushed his jeans down his hips, waggling his eyebrows, and Laurel bit back a laugh. *So much for laundry,* she thought.

He passed Laurel by, flinging himself off the steep edge of the bank and into the river below with a loud whoop. Garrett ducked under the surface to avoid the splash and popped up a moment later, laughing as he cussed his brother out. Isaac edged toward Garrett, hooked a foot around his ankle, and yanked hard, sending him tumbling into the water. Isaac only had a second to hold his breath before Garrett pulled him down.

"Hey!" Ricky hollered, diving into the fray.

Laurel unlaced her boots and yanked away her socks, tucking them in the front pockets of her jeans. She took advantage of the boys' momentary distraction to pull them off, padding barefoot down the bank with her eyes on the sand, littered with the ragged edges of mussel shells. It was stupid to swim barefoot in a river full of fishhooks and broken beer bottles, but it was harder to kick with shoes on, and Laurel was desperate for the buoyant freedom that proper swimming provided. Sand gave way to soft silt as she stood at the edge of the river, letting the water lap over her toes, ice-cold against her scalded skin.

Isaac, Garrett, and Ricky played a boys' game that softened its edges almost imperceptibly when Laurel approached. They pulled their punches. They stood a little farther apart, each watching the other to see who would strike first instead of launching a full assault. The frothing water quieted when she lowered herself down from the bank and crawled on her belly until the water was deep enough for her to swim. The water's veins ran cold, then warm again, as she crossed them, moving close enough to push Ricky into the water. He let out a yelp, and he was under.

She planted her foot on his chest, squirting a mouthful of river water at Isaac while she held Ricky down. Her mouth tasted like mud. "Hey!" Isaac shouted, flailing backward to miss her spray. Ricky yanked at her ankle, hard enough to scratch, and she let him up, spinning to smack a wave of water at him as he breached the surface. She didn't count on Garrett's hand on her shoulder and his foot pushing into the back of her knee. She had just enough time to take a breath before she was face-first in the water.

It felt good to splash and fight, to pretend they were younger than they were, and that this kind of fighting was something they could get away with still. Nothing mattered while they swam. There was no secret she was keeping. There was only the water around them and the sand below. Eventually, they tired, and Garrett slapped the surface of the river in a wordless plea for mercy that Ricky granted. Panting, the boys retreated to catch their breath. Isaac kicked off the riverbed and floated on his back. Laurel flicked some water off her fingers at Ricky's nose.

"That feels nice, do it again," Ricky said, tilting his face toward her. Laurel splashed him across the eyes. He smacked a wave of water back at her, drenching her hair. "You up to anything after this?"

Laurel picked at a bit of dirt under her nails. "Blog post. On working with rodent skeletons. Standard maceration just gnaws right through the fragile parts. You've got to use a delicate hand. It's hard work."

"No doubt," he drawled, face too casual. Laurel had just enough time to recognize the feint before Ricky grabbed her around the waist, trying to dunk her again. She planted her foot firmly under a mossy chunk of limestone to keep him from taking her down. It was a mistake. His chest pressed against hers in a hot line as he dipped her so low her neck grazed the water. All she could see was the sun. The wet material of her T-shirt was the only thing preventing their skin from touching. She stepped away, onto the slippery wood of a submerged tree branch. Her foot slipped and she pitched backward, but Ricky grabbed her wrist before she could fall.

The look in his eyes was too soft, his hand on hers too delicate.

"Steady, girl," he cautioned.

Then he tugged her forward into the water and she smacked his arm, hard.

"I'm not a horse!" she spat, suddenly furious.

"Got a face like one, don't you, though?" He ducked as he said it, preparing for her to smack him, laughing like they were still playing.

Laurel wasn't laughing. They weren't kids anymore. Instead of living in the past, she wanted to know what her future was going to look like. It was a question she didn't know how to ask or get a chance to frame before she heard her uncle calling from the banks. Her heart sank. Here was another reminder that the time for acting like children was over.

CHAPTER FIVE

L aurel Early, get on up here!"
It took Laurel a good minute to slog out of the river and up to where her uncle was waiting. A huge man, he cast a long shadow across the banks. His face was lined prematurely with disappointment and a bone-deep tiredness that came from a life spent holding together a world hell-bent on falling apart. He had little time or tolerance for self-indulgence, and what leniency he'd had for Laurel's girlish mistakes had long since dissipated. In his eyes, she was an adult, and she wasn't acting like it.

"There's work that still needs doing," Jay said. His work shirt was half buttoned, the elbows torn and front stained with black grease. The brim of his hunter-orange cap shadowed his face, but she could see the ruddiness of his cheeks. He was as tired and hot as the rest of them, but he wouldn't go swimming midday. He'd rather drown under the weight of his responsibilities. "I've been busting my ass all morning trying to fix the fence line up the ridge and haven't even checked the ones down here, if you want a place to start. And the garden's full of weeds that could use some attention while you're splashing around like you're on summer vacation."

"Yes, sir," she agreed, shifting nervously from one foot to the other. The boys had gone quiet, all moving toward the bank as if understanding their romp through the river had ended. Maybe they were just trying to get a good viewing of the rare spectacle of Laurel Early in trouble.

"By the time I get finished, there'll still be more left to do. I was relying on y'all to help me."

"Sorry, sir." Garrett wrung river water from his boxers as he stepped up onto the bank. Ricky dragged himself out of the water onto the trunk of a fallen maple. He slipped as he pulled himself into a seated position, watching their argument unfold with his head cocked like a golden retriever's. Laurel prayed he would fall off. Maybe start to drown a little. Then she could slip off into the jewelweed and grab her jeans while everyone else was trying to save him.

"We weren't slacking, honest. Just wanted to cool off before we got back to it. It's so damn hot today," Ricky offered up before she could assassinate him with a glare.

Laurel wanted to sink into the murky depths of the water and hide in the mud with the catfish until Jay was gone. His chest puffed as his lecture picked up speed. "Every day from now till October is going to be a hot one. That doesn't mean you get to take it easy. Especially you, Laurel." She knew where this was going. She'd wanted to break the news to the boys herself, but her uncle plowed on. "If you wanted an easy time, you shouldn't have dropped out of school. Like I said, once you're out, you're an adult. Adults work."

"Yes, sir." The barest whisper, light enough for the current to carry it away. She couldn't chance a glance at the river. She could imagine their faces: Ricky's considering gaze, Garrett's poorly constructed mask of indifference concealing his shock, Isaac not bothering to hide any of his disappointment.

The fear and shame lingered after Jay got back on the four-wheeler and drove away. Laurel scrambled, not caring about the itch of dirt against her palms as she crawled up the steep bank to where her clothes were waiting.

She moved fast, but Isaac wasn't far behind. "You dropped out?" Isaac asked, voice muffled. He had pulled his T-shirt over his face as she snatched her jeans up.

No point in beating around the bush. "As of yesterday, I am officially unenrolled."

"So, what, you're just gonna—"

"What I'm gonna do is figure out my life here." Laurel brushed the sides of her feet against the grass. She pulled her jeans on as quickly as she could over her damp skin, grateful to hide her pale, hairy legs under denim.

"You wouldn't move back? To Cincinnati?" Isaac clarified.

"Why would I? Family's here, you're here."

Isaac swore under his breath as his pruney fingers fumbled over his bootlaces.

"Garrett's sticking around," she added. She pulled her socks out of her jeans pockets and yanked them over her feet, sorry to trap them back in the hot boots she didn't bother tying up again.

"Yeah, he is, and Ricky, too, but I— Why?"

"Academic probation."

Ricky whistled low under his breath as he pulled himself onto the bank but walked past her to find his clothes without saying anything. Laurel bit back a comment about the stinging nettle that had to be nipping at his calves.

"How did *you* get on academic probation?" Isaac asked. *Mouth open wide enough to catch flies,* Laurel thought.

"You fail your classes, then they threaten you with losing your scholarship—"

"I know what probation is. I'm not stupid."

Laurel wrung more water out of her T-shirt, twisting the fabric tightly in her hands. "Well, apparently, I am, so, you know—"

Isaac scoffed. "You are not stupid. You got fours across the board on every AP test you took—"

"Yeah, well, maybe your dad was right about those. They're just for people who think they're too big for their britches."

"My father," Isaac enunciated slowly, through thinned lips, "is never right about anything."

Laurel immediately regretted opening her mouth. They'd just seen Jay at his worst. Isaac's father, at his best, wasn't half as kind as Jay had been. Her shoulders stiffened with guilt, bearing down on her hotter than the sun. She tied her hair back to shake the feeling and said, softer, "Can't change the past. Surely can't change my grades. It's done, Isaac. College is over. I'm sticking around."

She thought he'd fight her more, but Isaac seemed content to leave the rest of his thoughts to silence. He zipped his jeans, dusting sand from his hands. "Well, you heard him. Fence line needs fixing. That's the way of the world, so long as we're here."

She sniffed her shirt and wrinkled her nose. It smelled of leaf rot and new sweat thanks to the wet patch growing at the small of her back. So much for laundry and a bath in one.

Summer winds and winter ice were the sworn enemies of a good fence line. A broken fence line was bad news, not only for livestock that might escape without five lines of barbed wire to hold them at bay, but for anyone on the farm idiotic enough to utter that they might be bored.

The four went down to fetch new gloves, wire trimmers, and a roll of barbed wire from the equipment barn, everything they'd need to mend any broken strands that had fallen. Laurel and Ricky sat in the bed of the truck, each balanced against a wheel well and sipping from a Coke bottle, neither able to muster up the bravery for conversation. He rested his cheek against his hand as the truck rattled down a path of packed dirt and gravel. It left a red smudge across his face when he jumped off the tailgate.

"Lord," Isaac swore as he slammed the truck door. Laurel almost choked on a sip of her Coke. A stripe of lightning had struck down the black walnut by the old livestock well. A charred line ran down its trunk, which was split nearly in half, and its two largest branches had crashed down through the scrap metal and rotted boards covering the hole.

"That doesn't bode well for the fence line," Ricky said with a low whistle as he studied the pattern of lightning spread across the tree trunk. "Laurel?"

But Laurel couldn't answer. Her jaw locked as the blood drained from her face. This wasn't a new or unexpected fear, but it was a paralyzing one when it came upon her. Most of the time, she was able to ignore that her mother's watery grave was still a gaping chasm. But to see its surface bashed open, she couldn't help but fear falling in.

"It's okay," someone said by her ear. Ricky, concerned, studying the greenish tinge of her face. Judging whether or not she was going to puke. He put his big hand on her shoulder and pulled her into a squeeze. The pressure of his body against hers brought her nerve endings back to life. Laurel stepped away and shook out her fingers, which pricked like pins and needles. "There you go," he said, "there you are."

"Here I am," she agreed, offering him a smile she could only hope didn't tremble.

He took her by the elbow and led her back toward the barn. "We'll try and clear the branches out, let Jay know the boards caved in. Then we can fix the fence line. Why don't you go into the barn and grab some supplies?"

Laurel nodded mutely, turning away from the well at last. *Don't look, don't look,* Laurel thought as she ducked under the length of chain keeping the barn door half closed.

"Garrett and I could probably just fix it, without you or Jay having to think about it again," she heard Ricky offer from the door.

Don't touch it! Laurel wanted to yell. Her jaw was still stiff with fear. Rationally, they'd be fine. They did more dangerous work every day than nailing a couple of new boards across the surface of an old well. And it would be a welcome relief to go back to pretending the well wasn't there, to escape into the woods with a roll of barbed wire and work until she was too tired to be scared.

In the dusty silence of the barn, she could catch her breath, blinking as her eyes adjusted to the dim light filtering through the roof slats. She clenched her fists and released, rubbed her jaw, and tried to shake that old fear and its hold over her. All of this talk of growing up and she'd frozen like a child. How stupid. She'd picked this place to live. She knew what graves it came with. These weren't new ghosts.

She plucked a few sets of gloves and the wire cutters from a shelf, steeling her shoulders as she prepared to march back out to the truck. As she ducked under the chain, she heard Garrett say, "What even bleeds like that?"

"I've been here all morning, didn't hear a single shot," Isaac answered in a low voice. He said something Laurel couldn't make out.

Ricky let out an exasperated huff. "You can't not tell her, she's going to see—"

"See what?" Laurel asked, dropping the wire cutters in the truck bed.

"Just hold on, Laurel," Isaac said from where they knelt, the line of his mouth grim, "it's not, bad, per se, but it's weird—"

"It's blood," Ricky interrupted. "A whole wash of it behind the well. Like something laid here and bled to death, then stood up and left." He added in a rush, "You don't have to look, but it's there."

Laurel exhaled, eyes on the grass and not on the gnarled fingers of the black walnut branch reaching up at the sky. "I'm not scared of a little bit of blood," she said, and stepped toward the well.

Where they studied the ground, it was sodden with dark blood. Not like a patch beneath an animal with a bullet wound, more like a bucket had been used to drain the life from a creature and spilled. Laurel reached out her hand and Isaac flinched back, probably wondering if she could sense something they couldn't— but her fingers only came away wet. She knew no more than what the boys could read from the blood on her palm.

"That's fresh," Garrett said. "Like, right out of the vein fresh. Like, I should be holding the knife fresh."

"Fucked up," Isaac said, shaking his head. "This isn't right."

For herself as much as the rest of them, Laurel gathered her nerve and wiped the blood from her hand onto the well. As she stood, her eyes caught on another wet patch. "There's more."

"No," Isaac said, just as Ricky said, "I reckon you're right."

"We'll catch whoever did this if we follow the trail," Laurel murmured. "Is anyone armed?"

Garrett nodded and went to retrieve his pistol from the glove box. Isaac hovered, expression uncertain. "If someone's poaching, we should call Jay."

"Why?" she snapped, aware she was irrational with fury but not caring. "Why should we add another task to his busy to-do list? We're adults, like he said, and there's four of us to one of him so we're better equipped, anyway."

Isaac rolled his eyes but said nothing. He glanced between Laurel and Garrett and seemed to realize his chances of hanging back were limited. "Fine," he said, "fine, let's follow a trail of blood into the woods. There'll definitely be something good waiting at the end of it."

"That's the spirit," Laurel cheered, swallowing down a knot of fear as she stepped neatly around the puddle of blood and onto a trail leading down the ridge.

CHAPTER SIX

T he trail of blood didn't stop at two bright puddles by the well. Every time they thought it might have dried up, there was a new lashing of it, bright, arterial, clotted in the reeds. "Nothing bleeds this much and walks away," Isaac muttered with a frown. "I don't care how much adrenaline propels it."

"Does it seem drier to you than the patch by the well?" Ricky asked Laurel, kneeling in a patch of pin-oak leaves to examine a splash of red.

Almost as if they were following the trail backward, the wash of blood dried and lessened as they went deeper into the woods. "Are we going in the wrong direction?" Garrett asked.

"Let's hope we're heading away from whatever killed this thing," Isaac grumbled.

They were nearly half a mile down the ridge when she smelled it, beyond the metallic tinge that lingered in her nostrils. The hair at the back of Laurel's neck prickled, standing on end before she could pinpoint the source of her sudden fear.

"Oh, God in heaven!" Garrett groaned, throwing a hand over his face.

The sweet smell of the woods—all leaf rot and tree sap—scattered, swallowed up by the musky stench of carcass. Stronger than the antler-velvet smell of old blood spilled was the briny smell of rancid meat and sulfuric gas. It filled the back of Laurel's throat like bile until she thought she might gag. The smell was so thick as she approached the edge of the clearing it was like she could see it.

There were small clearings like this pockmarking the thick woods of the farm, a good place to sit and watch wildlife or nap in the shade. But this spot was a crime scene. In the heart of the clearing, a morbid mandala of old bones pointed like an accusatory finger at a dead deer lying in the grass.

Behind her, Ricky let out a string of swears, shutting up when the scent of rot gagged him. Garrett took one step back, and another. Isaac pulled his T-shirt off and tied it around his face like a bandana. She could hear his muffled swearing.

The bones weren't natural. It took Laurel a long stare to place what was off, before she realized with a wash of terror. "Those bones, they're *mine*."

"Laurel," Ricky said, cautious, "those are animal bones."

Laurel shot Ricky a withering glare. "I didn't mean they were *my* bones, you idiot. Look, these here. I bleached them. They're from my discard pile."

A piece of rib, a round ring of vertebra, a busted jaw. Laurel recognized them all. She bent gingerly to lift a cow's fractured tibia from the dirt. Her fingertips brushed its surface and suddenly she was choking on a hedge apple, the sickly yellow smell filling her nostrils until she fell to the ground and it swallowed her up. It was a story she'd heard before. The bone was more than a month old, one of the first she'd picked up after coming back for the summer. She'd been thrilled to find it. But she'd been forced to abandon it after a failed attempt to degrease it with oxyclean left it too brittle to work with.

"What about the deer?" Garrett asked. "What'd you have to do with that?"

From scent alone, Laurel could assume a couple of days had passed since the deer first fell, legs folded in on itself as though it decided to hunker low in the grass and sleep through the sunny part of the day. A huge tear in its tissue heaved with flies and its body was bloated with gas. A pale tongue lolled from its gaping mouth, its dark eyes glassy and bloodless. The heat of the sun had brought every carrion eater and microorganism into a frenzy of activity. Laurel remembered the buzzard she'd seen circling overhead that morning. She hadn't realized it had a destination. Another turkey vulture took flight as Laurel and the boys approached. A third stayed behind to pull a piece of flesh from the deer's hollowed-out ribs.

"This isn't the bleeder," Isaac said, and when she didn't respond, he added, "Laurel, I said—"

She'd heard him. But she was far away, narrowed in on the details of this death. Laurel couldn't sanitize this kind of rot with her solutions and soap and salt. This was decomposition the way nature had intended, the way the woods taxidermied. Not with a sharp knife or maceration vat but with time and heat and hunger until nothing, not even the memory, remained.

Laurel circled the edge of the clearing, studying the deer. A black strip of old blood splattered the grass underneath the fatal gash, the exposed flesh drying in the midday heat. Its neck lay at an improbable angle, the lifeless face tilted toward the canopy of trees.

"Killed, but barely eaten," she observed. "Jesus. What did this?"

Ricky lifted his hand from his nose and mouth just long enough to speak without breathing. "Some fucked-up scavenger hunt we followed."

Laurel shook her head, holding up a finger. "No, this is lucky. Will one of you help me hang it up?"

"Hang it up?" Garrett spluttered. "No. Hell no, I'm not going to touch it."

Isaac said, "I'm with Garrett. That thing is fresh enough to peel paint. I'm out of here."

"It's a doe. Can't weigh more than a hundred pounds. I can't lift her myself, but I can't risk some scavenger running off with the body. I can make a few hundred bucks off these bones."

Garrett turned on his heel. "You do what you gotta do, but I'm out."

"I hang out with you all the time, living dead girl," Ricky blurted. "I ain't scared of a little rot."

Ricky stepped forward and stood in front of the deer, steeling his nerve to actually touch the dead thing. His eyes squinted against the smell of rot, so ripe that it overwhelmed every sense. He covered his mouth with the crook of his elbow.

"Can't lift it one-handed," she teased, stepping over to lift the other shoulder. The doe was easier to hang than she expected, light in spite of its dead weight. She managed to avoid exposed bone as they lifted it up. The sick, liquid rub of old, sticky blood against organ nearly made Ricky drop his side, but they managed to drape the top of her chest across a low walnut branch. As soon as they did, they bolted for the safety of the hill above the carcass.

"Not a full skeleton," Isaac said, pointing. "Her bottom legs—"

"What?" Laurel spun around. The bottom half of the doe was in tatters, entrails nearly brushing the grass below the tree, old blood spilling from the gaping wound. But it wasn't just blood and entrails. Sprigs of greenery, flower petals, and long stems of grass poured from the doe, falling to the forest floor in bunches as though she'd been intentionally stuffed. *Tansy,* Laurel thought, *and nettle leaves.*

"What the hell?" Laurel wondered aloud.

But none of the boys were looking. They ran.

Garrett swore as he tripped over a rock and caught himself on the trunk of a sapling. "Come on, Laurel, let's get out of here!"

The four sprinted up the hill, as far from the deer as they could get. With each breath, the rot cleared from Laurel's lungs, but she couldn't shake the fear from her heart. Death did not scare her. Intentions did. There was no coincidence of nature that could have felled the deer in that spot or stuffed its belly with falling flowers, no natural disaster washing old bleached bones into formation around its corpse. Someone wanted her to find it.

CHAPTER SEVEN

C hristine Maynard worked at the Dry Valley C-Store, the only restaurant left in town. It wasn't a proper one, with menus and cloth napkins, but a hot-bar deli in the back of a gas-and-grocery convenience store where you could fill your tank and pick up a lotto ticket, a bucket of chicken, a gallon of milk, and enough beer to get you through a weekend in between factory shifts. Besides the courthouse and the jail, it saw the most traffic of any building in the county, and yet the tip jar had remained empty since she'd started her shift.

The store smelled like mop water, freezer burn, and frying oil, but it served passable fried chicken and potato wedges. Most of the sides, macaroni salad and mashed potatoes and green beans, contained some sort of cubed ham. On Easter and during family-reunion season, Christine and the owners' high-school-aged daughter filled big plastic tubs with to-go food made of grease and mayonnaise. In the high heat of summer, the restaurant's traffic was light enough that Christine could serve as cook, cashier, and waitress and still have time to let her nails dry between customers. The bottle of polish sitting by the cash register today was a holographic pink.

She liked the work. Management was decent and she was guaranteed a shift meal. The couple who owned the shop were also Maynards, technically. They were of no blood relation that Mrs. Maynard could trace, though likely they'd hired her to make the business look like a family operation. Mrs. Maynard had offered Christine a look at their Ancestry account, but Christine was certain she'd find no names she recognized. Christine's line of Maynards, crooked and broken, did not live with genealogy in mind. They buried their roots and cremated their relatives.

Her own parents were scattered on a hill back east that had long since been stripped. If any memorial had been erected to mark their short time on earth, neither she nor findagrave.com knew of it. She and her granny had already relocated to a shotgun house four miles from Pikeville two years before her parents' demise, their initial burning in a single-wide trailer at the hands of a frayed electrical cord and their second, direct cremation performed by a mortician at a funeral home in a county she'd never visited. She'd woken her granny up the night it happened to complain about the chemical smell of melting plastic. Four days later, a coroner called, having finally located next of kin.

Christine had always been privy to visions, scents, and impressions. She knew things before she should, about babies and broken marriages and the number of jelly beans in a jar. She could read a passage from the Bible aloud and use it to stop bleeding or draw fire from a burn. She'd caused a man to break out in hives just by looking at him. "In other words," her granny had once remarked, "you're a woman."

In Dry Valley's words, she was a witch.

As such, she was not welcome to worship with the Baptists or the Nazarenes and was not even welcome at the more liberal Methodist church the next county over. People in Dry Valley argued the finer points of religion from time to time, but as a whole believed the Bible ought to be used in an advisory capacity only.

Other things bothered them, too. She kept a garden but not a house. The trailer she'd lived in for the past six years was serviceable but not pretty, and definitely not homey the way it had been when her granny was living. She was fat and pale with a pinched face, dark eyes that reflected judgment like a mirror, and thick, unruly hair that grew an obscene shade of red. She was unlovely, yet still prone to vanity they felt was undeserved. That alone gave them self-appointed rights to disapprove of her. The witching gave them rights to hate her.

For all her precognition, Christine had never figured out why her granny had moved them to Dry Valley to die when Christine was just old enough to avoid being a ward of the state. The two had been all over small-town Kentucky. They'd even spent a memorable year in Louisville, where Christine thought their luck had changed. But the mountains called them back and sent them away again. She'd met the sugar-lending sort and the sundown town sort alike, and few had been as mean-mouthed and close-minded as the sort of people she could find hanging around Dry Valley. Maybe it was something about the land, the gorgeous, gentle slopes of the knobs and the rich soil ripe with magic. Or maybe the curse the townspeople suspected caused their bad luck had simply caught her granny in its grips.

Christine didn't care what anyone thought about her, but she was subject to their innermost opinions nonetheless. Not only did they affect her comings and goings, but sometimes she caught snippets of them playing on a radio frequency she could only hear in fits and starts. Today she was attuned to a particularly stressful channel. Shouting louder than conservative talk radio and more filled with apocalyptic predictions than the fuzzy wailing of a Baptist preacher, the forecast of her second sight predicted bloodshed.

The visuals were heavy-handed, subtle as a shriek in her ear, and they pursued her, relentless, up and down the pacing path she took to fill catering orders and slather mayonnaise on sandwiches. The image overlaid across her eyes like the mesh of a screen door. Entrails slid onto earth, flowers withered in sunless shadow, brown grass erupted into patchy scorch marks in a dying field. Blood dripped into the banana pudding, soaking the grave—no, the vanilla wafers. In the slow hour between the breakfast and lunch rushes, she dipped a mop into bleach water and watched the river pour forth from its ends as she wrung it out.

Most people could beg off migraine mornings like this one. Christine wished she could lie down and let these visions crystallize into dreams behind her eyelids. She'd let them have their say if only they'd let her have her eyes back. But her shift ended whenever Mrs. Maynard came to let her off, and that might not be for another five hours. She was in no rush, each hour adding to a thin paycheck she'd have to waste on getting the gutters fixed before summer storms rotted out her walls. Besides, Christine relied not only on the meager income and the spare change that sometimes found its way into the tip jar if an out-of-towner low on fuel found their way to the C-Store, but on the shift meal and the leftovers they couldn't sell, when her dollar wouldn't stretch far enough at the Save-A-Lot to feed her. Luckily her appetite was shot to hell today, so she could save money on hunger.

Christine counted down another hour before her answer walked through the door. She smiled politely at customers as she peeled a roll of quarters open and found a fingerbone instead. Her vacant grin held as teeth bobbed to the top of a vat of boiled peanuts. When the bottle of holographic nail polish she'd bought dripped blood red onto her nail, she murmured, "That's quite enough," but managed to apply an even coat that dried glittering pink. "That's better," she told it, examining her work.

Christine capped her nail polish a second before the shop bell jingled. In came the Mobley boys followed by Laurel Early and Isaac Graves. Christine wasn't overjoyed to see them. Garrett and Ricky Mobley were scared shitless of her, and their fear made them obnoxious. As a courtesy to him, she did not think much either way about Isaac Graves. Worst of the four was Laurel Early, who reeked of destiny and uncontrolled magic. There was not a lot of destiny to be found in Dry Valley. In concentrated doses, it gave Christine headaches.

But it explained the bloodshed, at least. The devil's daughter, home at last, with no idea of what waited on her land. If there was a curse on this town, it was wrapped up in her legacy and coming at her faster every day. Each omen Christine had seen that morning sang out the same answer; it wouldn't be long before it caught up to Laurel Early.

CHAPTER EIGHT

Garrett and Ricky snickered when they entered the C-Store, elbowing each other in the candy aisle and howling like ghosts. It took Laurel sidling up to the counter to realize why: Christine Maynard was behind the register, and the Mobleys didn't like her. They didn't trust her. They thought she was a witch, and they hated that she didn't seem to mind the accusation.

Their dislike of Christine made Laurel's palms itch. She wasn't certain that she was a witch herself, a term she'd always thought required some intent, or a worldview she'd never maintained. Even so, she'd inherited power and a deadly reputation from her mother. If they knew even the paltry things she could do, would they freeze her out? Maybe the only reason the boys withheld the stinging judgment from her that they applied to Christine was they'd been shaped from similar clay, whereas Christine had been forged counties away. She didn't belong.

Whatever their reasons for hating Christine, they were not serious enough to keep the boys from ordering lunch from her after a morning in the fields. Garrett selected a drumstick and some mashed potatoes while Ricky picked up a greasy piece of tinfoil-wrapped pepperoni pizza. Laurel ordered a hot ham and cheese and tossed a packet of potato chips onto the counter to stuff inside the sandwich. When Isaac ordered chicken livers with a side of stewed tomatoes and a big piece of corn bread, Ricky made a gagging noise. Laurel didn't think that was entirely fair given he'd willingly purchased a piece of pizza that if tested for *E. coli* would immediately bring the restaurant count in Dry Valley to zero.

"What?" Isaac blurted when even Garrett laughed at him. "I'll have you know they're a delicacy."

"The only reason anyone ever convinced themselves chicken liver was a delicacy was that their other option was starvation," Garrett said, cracking open a Mountain Dew as they settled down at a Formica table, their Styrofoam plates heaped with food.

"They're a great source of iron!"

"Which must be of great relief to a man whose diet is mostly wild game and Coca-Cola," Ricky said, rolling his eyes. Laurel grimaced as he bit into the pizza. Orange grease dripped onto the plate below.

"You're at risk for type-two diabetes, maybe, but no one ever bled to death on a diet of venison," Garrett assured him. "Too much iron for you to worry about anemia."

"And lead, too, by the time Isaac's finally brought one down," Laurel teased, miming firing several rounds into the menu Ricky held up to shield himself.

"Oh, hush," Isaac snapped. "One mishap, one time—"

"Christmas dinner that year was smoked duck stuffed with jalapeños and a healthy helping of buckshot!" Laurel said, tearing into her bag of potato chips.

"Don't talk to me about good food while I'm eating bad food," Ricky groaned, taking another bite of his pizza.

"No one made you order the pizza!" Garrett and Isaac protested in unison. "I specifically told you not to eat it," Garrett added.

"Food all right?" Christine asked them, looking down at her feet instead of at their plates. The frayed shoelace on her tennis shoe was untied, and her pink nail polish had already chipped halfway off her thumbnail.

"Yes, thanks," Laurel said, trying to look her in the eyes because no one else would. Christine gave a nod before wandering away.

"That pizza's just her trying to poison you," Garrett drawled. Isaac's eyes danced with amusement, but at Laurel's quelling look he said nothing.

"Think those bones are some sort of weird witchy curse she cast on Laurel's farm?" Ricky stage-whispered back.

It would have been bad enough if they only hated Christine, but they were scared of her, too. It was sort of like the dead deer they'd been laughing about since the sun had warmed the fear from their bones after they emerged from the woods. It was easier to mock what frightened them than admit they were afraid.

Still, it wasn't fair. Maybe Christine was still the weirdo she'd acted like in high school, three years above Laurel and mean as a copperhead. But weren't they supposed to put those years behind them, in the interest of getting along in the same small town for the rest of their lives?

Laurel opened her sandwich and shook half the bag of chips into it. "No one's going to curse my farm. They all think I'm curse enough." She bit in, potato chips crunching deliciously against melted cheese. "Still, it looked almost ritualistic."

"Well, I doubt we've got genuine satanists performing mid-day rituals in Laurel's woods. Statistically, I mean, we barely have Catholics," Ricky reasoned.

"Who would take the time to steal from your discard pile and kill a deer they didn't even dress without a serious reason behind it?" Isaac asked.

Like teeth yanked from a jaw, the bones in Laurel's discard pile had not been where she'd left them before she went to college. Oftentimes coyotes, foxes, vultures, and raccoons would drag choice scraps out of the holler, but this clean-out was too pristine to have been an animal's work. The hollowed-out places where bones at the bottom of the pile were once embedded in the earth ached with the loss of them. There was only empty space and yellowed grass left behind.

Laurel wiped her fingers with one of the precious few paper napkins Ricky hadn't used to blot the grease off his pizza. No matter how she washed her hands, she hadn't felt clean since she'd touched that pool of blood by the well. "So, what does that leave us with? Some kind of poacher?"

Ricky guffawed. "Yeah, that looked a lot like poaching."

"I'm considering all our options," Laurel said. "You're innocent, though I'm loath to ever describe you as such. Isaac hasn't had the time, and Garrett's not a shithead. I don't have any other friends who'd try to pull a prank." She ticked off ideas on her fingers. Ricky offered her a finger of his own.

"Maybe it wasn't friendly," Garrett suggested, shaking the remains of Laurel's potato chips into his mouth.

Ricky rapped his knuckles on the table, leaning in. There was no laughter in his eyes. "Too personal to be a poacher, too threatening to be a friend. This is someone fucking with you."

Laurel frowned. "I haven't been home long enough for anybody to get mad at me."

"Fine. A poacher, then," Ricky said. He picked at a hangnail, peeling back the dead skin to reveal a strip of fresh pink underneath. It was the only part of his hands the dirt hadn't reached. "A poacher who doesn't even eat what he kills. Who thinks, 'I'm going to make a mess on purpose and hightail it away from the scene of the most needlessly complex crime ever executed before the blood so much as dries.'"

"The blood was fresh," Isaac reminded them, "but the deer wasn't."

"You don't think—" Garrett said suddenly.

Isaac cut him off, following a trail of thought Laurel couldn't force herself down. "If they'd dumped it in the well, we would have seen blood on the branches we were moving."

Laurel shuddered, trying not to think of something, *or someone,* her mind supplied, bleeding out at the bottom of the well the way her mother had. This was her fear, painted across the very landscape that belonged to her. Ricky was right. This wasn't a prank. This was a threat.

"Laurel?" A voice at her shoulder made her pause. She turned to see Christine holding her busing tray, ready to clean up their mess and free their table.

"What can I do for you, Christine?"

Christine set her tray down hard. "You're not looking for a poacher. Your farm's not a target for revenge. It's haunted."

"I beg your pardon?" Laurel blurted. "Haunted" was a ridiculous word that conjured up images of agritourist traps. Ones that reeked of spoiled hay and petting-zoo muck, all pumpkin patches and corn mazes full of face-painted teenagers. Not her home.

"Not this again, Christine." Ricky sneered the words. Laurel flinched, startled by the ice in his voice. This was no teasing tone. This was Dry Valley's fear sharpened to a knife blade, wielded against someone else the way it had been wielded against Laurel all her life.

But Christine didn't back away from its cut. Instead she smiled and flicked her fingers at him as if flicking off a burr. Ricky went pale. He stumbled out of the diner without another word, his brother hot on his heels.

"What the hell did you do to him?" Laurel's hands came up defensively, curled into fists.

"You think I can curse him without a word but don't believe in a haunting you've already seen?" Like a magician demonstrating sleight of hand, Christine repeated the movement at Laurel. Nothing happened.

Christine picked up her rag and began to clean the table. "I didn't have to do anything. There's enough fear in that boy right there on the surface. You barely have to say 'boo' and he'll die of fright."

Laurel sighed. "I don't believe in curses. I don't believe in hauntings. It's all just fear and frustration and guilt. You've lived in Dry Valley long enough to know this. They turn it on you, too."

Christine smirked, drumming her nails on the black-speckled Formica tabletop. "Now you're getting it."

Laurel said nothing. She didn't understand. She couldn't fit herself into a Dry Valley where Christine Maynard, with a tired, hard look to her eyes that glinted sharp as a switchblade, had answers to offer her. Laurel didn't like that mirror-bright gaze. In it, she saw herself looking back.

In the long moment where Laurel remained silent, Christine either changed her mind or gave up. "Or not. Take it or leave it or come running back when you believe me. But I've got to bus this table, and the sooner you get gone, the sooner my headache goes away." She dismissed Laurel with a flick of her dishrag, an unmagical gesture that nonetheless made Laurel want to escape the bleach-water-and-grease smell of the diner and the ghosts in Christine's eyes.

"I'll see you around, Christine," she muttered without intention.

The bell on the door almost swallowed it up, but she thought she heard Christine say, "I'm sure of it."

The boys were ready to leave when she emerged. Garrett yanked open the door to his truck, nearly pulling it off its hinges. "Don't listen to her. She thinks she's some kind of witch. What's worse, she's lazy."

Ricky agreed, sliding into the passenger seat. "Seems she's made up an excuse for her work this spring. A stupid one." His face was still pale.

"While you were away, Jay hired her to set tobacco," Isaac explained. "She showed up just once, and her work ethic was . . . nothing. She was pale and sweating a couple minutes in, eyes darting around like she was seeing things. Left at lunch and didn't come back. The next day, every plant she'd set was withered dead in the ground."

Laurel rolled her eyes, resisting the urge to flick her hands at him. "You've never seen plants die? And you've been working tobacco for how long?"

A bit of color had returned to Ricky's face. "She was junk

sick, I'll bet you anything, like half the county. Rather fake a broken back, take a pill and a government check, than get out and do some actual work."

Laurel wasn't willing to fuel any more gossip about cursing and haunts. "I've never heard that about her. I've heard that when you hire her, she's good for it."

"The point is, Laurel, she was hired to replace you, and she couldn't even do that right." Ricky grimaced as soon as he said it. Laurel looked down and counted cracks in the asphalt until the flush in her cheeks subsided.

"You're lucky she didn't actually curse you." Garrett tossed a look over his shoulder as he slid his key into the ignition. "She's that piss-and-vinegar kind of witching. That weird shit they do up in the mountains. Blights your crops and kills your wife, spiders crawl out of your bathtub and into your mouth."

Laurel snorted. "You sound like a fucked-up country song."

Isaac put a hand on her arm, tugging her away from the truck. "You weren't there, Laurel, you didn't see it. Best stay away from whatever she's involved in."

"Dare to resist drugs and alcohol," Ricky called with an ugly laugh. He pulled his head back in the window as Garrett started up the truck.

Dry Valley's hatred was a cruel campaign of whispers, that haunted like a wraith and not a poltergeist. There was no need for shows of force or threats like the deer in Laurel's woods. They didn't run people out of town on rails anymore. They faked pity, they passed judgment. They sneered a lot like Ricky Mobley just had, and over the years, that water torture was enough to drill a hole through the heart of anyone.

Laurel held a picture of Christine Maynard in her mind: red

hair, pink shimmery nails, double-knotted sneaker laces. She looked tired, sure, but in that run-down, shift-work way, not in a hollowed-out, heroin sort of way. But Laurel couldn't deny it: there was something weird about the tired edge to Christine's gaze, strange as the dead deer in the woods and every bone pulled from the ground.

Haunted.

CHAPTER NINE

Laurel's mother came to visit, and the skulls on the wall tittered with laughter every time she spoke. Everything in the washhouse was alive. Even the skeleton of the cat she'd taxidermied purred in her lap. She ran her hands over its spine, eliciting another rumble from somewhere inside its hollow body. That was how Laurel knew it was nothing more than a dream; she could touch it without feeling how the cancer closed in all those years ago. Its bones clinked together as it vibrated from the pleasure of being touched by someone living.

"You should open the window," Laurel said. "With the fire going, it's stuffy in here." She wasn't sure if her mother could feel the summer heat. She looked alive enough, an echo from a Polaroid taken when she was about twenty-two. Serene smile and hooded eyelids, the same thin hair that hung from Laurel's head.

"It won't help," her mother observed. "There's no breeze tonight."

Laurel yawned, stretching out in her seat. There was something about the cat on her lap, the dim glow of the fire, and the alien quality of the shadows dancing across the walls. It made her tired somehow, even though she was already asleep.

Laurel's mother bent down to slip the lid off a cast-iron kettle that was suspended over the open flame. She pulled a piece of root from a muslin bag and drew the blade of one of Laurel's sharpest carving knives across its rough surface. The wood peeled from the bark in curlicues, releasing the smell of root beer with every scrape. "Sassafras. Blood purifier. Good to drink once spring arrives. Has spring come yet?"

"And passed." Laurel settled back against her chair as her mother shook the last of the scrapings from the blade. Her tiny hands with their short, dented nails made the hilt of Laurel's knife seem huge in comparison. "We're past midsummer."

"The tobacco?" her mother asked.

"It's coming along. We'll top and spray, soon enough. It's not a bad year for it, weatherwise."

"But the soil's not cooperating."

"You can't know how the soil is when you don't even know the season," Laurel objected.

Her mother laughed. "I know the soil. It sleeps on top of me. Do you know how to harvest sassafras?" She wiped the blade against her thigh.

Laurel searched among the detritus of herbs and pressed flowers that stirred whenever she consulted her mother's memory. The answer eluded her. "If I want the taste, I can buy root beer for spare change up at the store."

"You should know how to do these things for yourself, Laurel." There was a flat tone of annoyance in her mother's soft voice. "I'd teach you, but—" She gestured with her hands. *I'm dead,* the skulls echoed. "You've got to get under the soil to understand. You've got to dig the answers out of the ground."

"Are we still talking about the sassafras?"

"We're talking about the soil," her mother corrected. "The soil, the earth, ultimate purpose of everything. Run your roots through it. Stamp it down with your living wanderings. One day, you'll fall down and feed it."

Laurel's mouth twisted. "What a pleasant thought."

"I know all about how pleasant it is," Anna said mildly, in a tone that left Laurel cold. The cat shifted in her lap, as though she'd disturbed it. And the skulls tittered, in on some joke that Laurel was not.

"It's made of everything, and it knows itself—knows everything, I mean." Anna stammered a little, as though working through a difficult translation in a language she did not speak fluently. "It does not struggle. It wins any war against all that walks above. You'd do well to know it before it knows you."

An hour passed in an instant then wound back up as tight as it could. Her mother poured the tea into two cups. Laurel dimly recalled them as the same cups that sat atop the armoire in her bedroom. Curls of bark settled at the bottom, leaking pink as they fell.

Laurel took a sip of the tea, the color of thinned blood. Another memory, blood in water, spilled from her thoughts and was gone before she could catch it in her hands. She drank deeply. The taste was all summer, spice and a tang of underlying, earthy sweetness. The air smelled like root beer and the stagnant, dusty scent of Laurel's profession. "You should at least open the window."

Laurel's mother shook her head. "Windows keep things out. I don't mind if the heat stays in."

"But I do!" Laurel said. The cat in her lap shuddered to its feet, disturbed by the volume of her voice. It leaped nimbly onto the workbench, bones clicking. There were no joints left to sustain the force of the impact. She wondered if it ached when it landed.

"Your uncle thinks he knows everything about what's in the woods. And he might. But he doesn't know what's coming. He can't see it, walking around aboveground. That's why you need to listen to the breathing of the soil. It will protect you when you need it."

Laurel drained her cup. The splinters of sassafras at the bottom might have spelled out her fate, but to her, they were illegible. "From what could I possibly need protection?"

Laurel's mother stared out the dark window, her eyes taking in something Laurel could not see. "Someone's trying to reach you."

CHAPTER TEN

L aurel's eyes opened to the glow of her phone screen as it buzzed on her nightstand.

I need to borrow your car.

It was going to be one of those nights. Isaac had them as often as twice a week since she'd come home. He'd ask for her car without telling her where he was taking it. In the morning, it would be sitting in her driveway with a full tank of gas, and Isaac would be asleep in the backseat. If it was a warm night, he might make it as far as the front porch swing, like his courage stopped him before he knocked at the door. Every time he smelled of whiskey.

She knew where he went. There were only so many places he could go. Seventy-four miles northwest, just across the state line in downtown Cincinnati, sat the plain brick facade of a bar called Connect. If it weren't for the rainbow flag hanging outside and the people smoking out front, it might have been the headquarters of some cheap office or a political campaign. Laurel had heard about it at college but had never bothered to go inside.

Laurel accepted that Isaac had a need Dry Valley couldn't serve. To fill it, he chameleoned himself to blend in with the people of southern Ohio, flattening his accent in order to sit and drink with a bunch of city kids and rural transplants who needed the same thing he did—a place to be himself.

Something wrong? she asked. She'd picked him up more than once only to see the red blossom of a fresh bruise across his cheek or peeking out from under his shirtsleeve.

Can't sleep. Too quiet.

Quiet's not the worst thing in the world.

Whatever. Get dressed. Wear something nice and I'll take you with me.

Done, she replied. He'd never offered to take her before and questioning it would only make him rescind his offer. She knew him well enough that if he was damaged, she would see the source of it. Maybe she could fix it. One thing was certain: She couldn't fall back asleep with that dream still haunting her.

Isaac's leg bounced up and down. He was all frenetic energy, had been since he jumped off the curb outside of the dim little upstairs apartment he shared with his father and threw himself into the passenger seat of Laurel's car.

He switched off the radio and filled the silence with the static blare of his voice, talking endlessly about nothing in particular as the highway blurred around them. Laurel could barely get a word in. After a while, she stopped trying, content to nod and say "for sure" whenever he paused for breath. He talked like this sometimes when she picked him up from the apartment, words spilling over so fast he could barely spit them out of his mouth, like someone who'd come in from the cold rubbing his limbs to warm them up. She'd listen until he sounded less blue.

Guilt pressed into her shoulders, a knife blade that her uneasy dreams had done nothing to dispel. She and Isaac had lingered in town until nearly sundown, both putting off going home because of different fears. When she'd finally pulled into the driveway, the first stars glinted in the blue sky. Jay was at the house, cutting up a tomato from the garden. He hadn't said anything more about the fence line and she hadn't been able to muster the strength to tell him about the well. They sat in silence, with the TV blaring, eating BLTs with bitter Bibb lettuce and licking grease from their fingers. He'd bid her good night not long after *Wheel of Fortune* ended. She'd sat there, tracing the grain of the table like a maze. By the time she'd resolved to knock on his bedroom door, she could hear him snoring, bone-tired from a day of hard work.

Isaac didn't stop chatting until she parked the car in front of the two-story brick building. Even then, it was a mere pause before he said, "I didn't realize you knew where we were going." They had bars like this in a lot of cities, but not Dry Valley.

"I went to college here," she said with a shrug. "Long enough to know where you've been going. I just never went in myself. It's twenty-one and up, isn't it?"

Isaac nodded, glancing distractedly at the line queueing up by the doors. "You're going to wander around back until you see some people smoking. I'll get you in from there, smudge my stamp onto your hand."

"How are you going to get in?"

He flashed an ID with someone else's face on it, winked at her, and disappeared.

Laurel went around the corner and leaned against the brick of the building, fiddling with her phone. There was Wi-Fi in the building, so she could load her email and handle orders from her shop while she waited. Two girls talked between cigarette exhales, close enough to breathe in the smoke but too in love to mind. A tall person in teetering heels smiled at Laurel. They offered her a cigarette with a voice as rough as the crystallized sugar in an old jar of honey.

"Suit yourself, sweetheart," they said when Laurel declined.

At that moment Isaac stepped out the back door. He brushed a kiss over the person's cheek, straining a little to reach. Laurel noticed that his lips didn't quite touch their skin, preserving the gorgeous arch of blush that fell over their cheek. They greeted him by name.

A beat of awkward silence lingered. Laurel might not have caught it at all if it wasn't Isaac's first quiet moment of the night. But he smiled, brushing the back of his hand over Laurel's, and said, "This is my friend from home."

So initiated, Laurel followed Isaac into the bar, close enough to eclipse his shadow. Inside there was a din of noise that confused her at first and comforted her seconds later. The pulse of bass-heavy music cocooned her, muting everything. A U-shaped bar stood near the front entrance. Behind it, two bartenders mixed cocktails out of strong, clear alcohol and a rainbow of colored syrups, poured shots of well whiskey, and sent cans of beer sliding across the veneer surface of the bar.

"Want anything?" Isaac called. She shook her head. She'd never been much for drinking. She got herself water in a little plastic cup from a serve-yourself station and watched the thrum of people moving past. Most ignored her, but some smiled, friendly enough. She tried to stretch an answering grin across her face, but it fell flat. It had been weeks since she'd been in the city. Strangers made her feel claustrophobic. Once upon a time, Isaac had been worse than her about people he didn't know. But here he nodded back, his smile genuine. She supposed they weren't strangers to him.

Isaac sidled up next to her as he sipped something dark from a plastic cup. The light made the shadows on his face stand out. Without the flush of hard work or the thin sheen of sweat glowing across his cheeks, he looked paler. Tired. He leaned in to murmur, "It doesn't seem like it, but it's quiet tonight. On the weekends, there's more college boys."

"*Mm,* college boys." She pursed her lips, unimpressed. "I've met a few. Didn't like them much." Feeling bold, she added, "Do you?"

Isaac laughed. "They're all right. Better dancers, at least." He brushed a long strand of hair out of his face. He hadn't cut it in a while, and it had begun to curl up at the ends. But hair aside, he was neater than she'd seen him since their high school graduation.

"You dance?" She tried to picture it, the flurry of his long limbs tangling as he tried to move to the pulsing beat from the speakers upstairs.

Isaac shook his head, grimacing around another swallow of his drink. "Not often. If you want to, we could?" he offered, but she blanched at the suggestion.

"Unless some nice boy's given you lessons since I've been gone, I'd rather not risk it."

He smacked her arm lightly, posturing offense, but added, more confessional than sly, "I've learned a thing or two since you left."

She tried not to show her surprise, but she leaned closer. "Really? With whom?"

He shrugged and finished his drink. "Couple people, here and there. Nothing serious. Sneaking around with no place to go, there's not much future in it."

Isaac rarely spoke about the future. She wondered what it looked like when he thought about it, the endless expanse of winters and summers, dirt and sweat and work. How bright the sunlight, how heavy the rainfall. Where he stood in the fields. Who he stood there with.

Laurel let the question die on her lips. "So, you came here often while I was at school?"

"I did." Isaac studied his drink, swirling the ice cubes in his cup.

"I wish I'd known when you were down. I might have come and seen you."

"You and I escaped from the same place. I didn't want to think about home while I was here," he said with a shrug. "I should have called, though."

"*I* should have called," she insisted, hastily. There was guilt in the slump of his shoulders, and it was blame they carried equally.

"We don't talk enough," Isaac said. "We should fix that."

"We should," she agreed. "Wait, is that Garrett Mobley?"

He stood at the door, ducking a little in order to let the short bouncer stamp his hand.

Isaac's face reddened. He wouldn't meet her eyes, examining the rainbow halo of Christmas lights against the brick. "Garrett plays pool here sometimes. He, we—we both play pool."

"Together?"

"Sometimes." Isaac took a gulp of his drink, trying to finish fast, mouth twisting as the whiskey burned his throat.

Garrett stepped up to the bar, pulling his well-worn leather wallet out of his back pocket. He slid his debit card to the bartender. He'd turned twenty-one not long ago, hadn't he? She'd missed his birthday in favor of studying for the spring midterms she'd failed anyway. She'd watched Ricky's Snapchats from the library, heart aching over blurry bonfire videos, listening to their accents broaden as the three boys put a heavy dent in a jar of clear. Drinking illegally to mark the first birthday any of them could drink legally. Laurel thought of Ricky's face, washed out by the flash of his phone camera.

"Wish you were here," he'd drawled, saluting her with the jar.

She'd be there next time. She wouldn't miss a birthday again.

Laurel opened her mouth to say hello to Garrett, but Isaac put up a hand, the scars on his fingers visible even in the dim lights, and said, "Look, Laurel, I'm sure he doesn't want to be bothered."

Garrett ordered a beer and turned to scan the crowd. As soon as he saw Isaac, his face lit up, and the grin only broadened when he saw Laurel standing beside him. "Laurel Early! Now this is a surprise!"

Laurel pulled him into a quick hug. "Can't get away from you, huh?"

Isaac snorted, but if Garrett heard it, he ignored it. "Want anything? My treat."

"I'm good." She raised her water, and he tapped the neck of his beer against her plastic cup.

Isaac shifted, looking around the room. The restless energy that had manifested in endless chatter still simmered under his skin, but it was like he was biting his tongue to hold it back. "Nice to see you, Garrett," he said quickly, and shot off for a booth by the pool table.

Laurel watched his shoulders tense as he retreated. She gave Garrett an apologetic shrug, careful not to spill her water as she followed after Isaac. Garrett waved to show he didn't particularly mind and took a sip of his beer, turning to speak to the bartender.

By the time Laurel caught up to Isaac he was halfway to the booth. She took a fortifying sip of her water and caught his shoulder. "What was that about?"

"Nothing," Isaac lied, knocking her hand away as he slid into the booth.

Laurel realized she'd stepped onto what she thought was solid ground only to break the floor underfoot. Her ears burned with embarrassment as she settled in across from him. "I wouldn't have asked. It's just that I thought I could. I didn't mean to freak you out."

"You're not— It's—" He took a breath, but it did little to relax his shoulders. He glanced at the bar. "I'm not sure what to say."

"Thought you wanted us to talk more," Laurel pressed, keeping her voice gentle. Isaac took it like a knife.

"What I want is another drink," he muttered, but didn't move to get one, instead shaking the ice in his cup, looking for trace remains of whiskey.

She took the cup from him and popped an ice cube into her mouth, beaming around it as he made a face. "Are you waiting until Garrett leaves the bar to get one?"

"No," he said, fast enough to mean the opposite. He flicked her arm and got up, pausing to let her ruffle his hair. It was as good an apology as they ever gave each other. "I'll grab you another water while I'm up."

"Don't worry about it," she said. Garrett was making his way toward them, balancing two waters in one hand and his beer in the other. She stood to intercept him, taking a water.

"Thanks," he said. "How long are y'all here for?"

Laurel shrugged. "Haven't been here long, but he's in a weird mood, so who's to say?"

Garrett's expression was amused, complicated by something she didn't quite understand. "Long enough to play a game of pool?" he asked.

She shot a glance to the bar, where Isaac was fidgeting, bored and a little anxious waiting for the bartender's attention. "If there's no one else expecting your company?"

"No one nearly so interesting as you," Garrett said with a laugh, fishing some quarters from his back pocket.

Laurel with a pool cue was more akin to a jouster than a shark, but she did her best to beat him. Garrett agreed to let her break, the only part of the game she actually enjoyed. She didn't have much finesse, but she could send things flying. She bridged her hand and let the cue fall parallel to the table, knocking it as hard as she could into the cue ball. Garrett called stripes, and for a while, they just played. Her friendship with Garrett was one of easy silences and friendly competition. He was more patient at fishing; she was nimbler when it came to cleaning them by the campfire. Sure, he was beating her at pool, but she could outshoot him blind with a rifle.

Garrett took a long swig from his beer, draining and setting it at the edge of the table. He abandoned the shot he had lined up, pointing toward Isaac's profile with the edge of the cue. "I must have spent half of high school watching him, wondering what he'd look like when he got older. I couldn't quite fathom it, you know, his face all settled like that. Mature. But he looks good here, doesn't he?"

He did, talking to a woman in a long sequined gown who he seemed to know. He wore a neat teal T-shirt tucked into his best jeans, dressed nicely for a man who'd never cared what he looked like, hair clean of river silt and combed for once. It was strange how little she'd seen him in public since they'd left school, but with other people to cast light on him, he shone a little brighter, smiled wider, threw his head back when he laughed. The jolt of nervous energy that kept him on his toes just seemed like animation from this far away.

"Sure," she said, raising her cup to Garrett's empty beer bottle. "The future looks good on him. You gonna take that shot?"

Garrett nodded, cheeks flushed as he settled back into the game. He eyed up the cue ball and took the shot, focus drifting up to Laurel before the ball hit the pocket. "So, you're home for good?"

"Looks like," she agreed. There wasn't a lot of future left for her to wear, only the sweat and mud she'd been made out of. The same stuff was packed under Garrett's nails. He was the only one of them who'd never even threatened to make it out of Dry Valley. He liked its seasons and patterns, thrilling to the things that bored Ricky and made Laurel feel claustrophobic. He liked the porch-sitting and tolerated the politics because he hadn't yet found anything he liked as well as standing in the river watching a sheet of rain falling around him.

That, and there was Isaac. In a bar full of people, dazzling light, and swelling sound, Garrett couldn't keep his eyes off

Isaac. It didn't interfere with his pool game, or if it did, Laurel was a bad enough player that she couldn't take advantage of his distraction. But his focus guided his movements, the tilt of his head, and the point of his feet, like magnetism, toward Isaac.

Laurel didn't put much stock in fate, but she wanted to believe there was weight in the coincidence that aligned these two to find each other before last call in their slowly emptying town. She wanted to believe that same fate ran electric through the wire tying her to Ricky, and that somehow, even though he was miles away, her body and his moved toward each other in the night. When she had woken in her dorm room each night, and the compass of her heart pointed home, had it been pointed at him instead?

"Laurel," Garrett said, loud, like he was repeating it. "Earth to Laurel. You scratched. That means it's my shot."

"Dammit," Laurel swore without heat. She studied the pool table, the colors that remained. It would take a miracle to beat Garrett now, and she wasn't interested in conjuring one up. Isaac returned, hovering at her shoulder with a frown as he looked between them. "You wanna take over this mess for me?" she pleaded, poking him in the ribs.

He scratched his nose, mulling over the proposition. "Looks pretty hopeless, honestly."

"Wanna play winner?" Garrett offered.

Isaac shook his head. "Not unless Laurel wins, and that seems unlikely."

The sparkle of laughter died in Garrett's eyes. "All right," he said simply, considering the table. He placed the cue ball on the table and took his shot, pocketing the last ball and winning the game. Laurel tried to catch Isaac's gaze, but it was trained studiously at the floor; Garrett racked up the balls and put his cue away.

"I'll see you later," Garrett said to Isaac. "Laurel, it was a pleasure." He let Isaac hold his silence and walked away.

CHAPTER ELEVEN

Laurel's hand flitted over the radio dial, flipping through ads for cereal and preachers screaming scripture in order to find something to fill the silence. She settled on a palatable, inoffensive channel, some mix of *the best hits of the eighties, nineties, and today!* Isaac stayed quiet through one song and another, cheek pressed against the window. He was only feigning exhaustion, she thought. In the dim reflection of the glass, his eyes were wide open.

She knocked the dial on the radio, slipping it out of focus. "Oops," she said, angling her head to check her blind spot before she merged into the next lane. "Will you get that?"

Isaac switched the knob to the left, coming to rest on an alternative rock station he preferred, and dropped his face back to the window. Whatever he was thinking, he'd drown it out under the music before she ever heard it.

She didn't want that. She wanted him to talk.

"Isaac, I think Garrett is in love with you."

She wasn't sure how she'd expected Isaac to react. She hadn't expected him to burst into laughter.

"Why, yes, I'd managed to parse that one for myself, Laurel, but thank you for the heads-up."

"When did you find out?" she asked.

"I had my suspicions last fall when he sat me down and told me as much." Isaac's voice was full of the dry humor Laurel hated. It sounded like defeat.

"He told you?"

Isaac nodded. "He's about as subtle as that truck of his. If I'd have listened closer, I would have heard it a mile off."

"You never told me."

"That's because it wasn't a conversation I planned to involve you in. It was one between him and me, and it wasn't one that went very far." Isaac laughed again.

Laurel could have smacked him. "Explain."

Isaac shrugged. "What's there to say? He told me he was in love with me. I told him it was a side effect of having lived a whole life crammed into the same shoebox and that he'd get over it."

"Harsh."

Isaac shook his head. "Like I said. He doesn't do anything halfway. He took the rejection fairly well. I actually thought he'd changed his mind right there on the spot. It wasn't until later that I realized he had no plans to stop. He just thought he'd let me know." There was a soft sort of fondness in his voice despite his words. "By the time I figured that part out, he'd had another couple of months to really work himself up about it, and there was no convincing him otherwise."

"What chance does he have to get over it?" Laurel asked. "It's not as though there's a whole host of eligible bachelors in Dry Valley, least not of your variety."

"We just left a whole bar full of them."

Laurel ignored him. "It'd be convenient if you two fell in love."

"Don't I know it," Isaac said to the window.

"You ought to at least give it a shot."

"He thinks I should. He thinks things are simple like that. He's wrong, and so are you."

"Why?" she snapped. "Why would it be so bad for you to have something worth keeping in this shithole town?"

But Laurel knew why. She'd known since she came home. She'd smelled it in the air. She stopped in front of the yield sign and didn't move even after a car had passed, flashing its lights at her.

"You didn't have to yield there," Isaac pointed out. "It took that man half a minute to show up after you'd pulled up to the sign."

"When are you leaving?" She hadn't meant to ask. She wasn't for certain that he was. But Isaac reached over and turned the radio off. Then she knew.

"This winter," Isaac said, "after New Year's. I want to finish out the year, see the tobacco sold off before I leave."

Laurel had to keep herself from slamming on the accelerator. People wrecked their cars having conversations like this. It was one thing to let Isaac move away from Dry Valley and another entirely to let him fly through the windshield.

"Good timing. We won't need you as much on the farm then."

Isaac let out a sigh of relief. "I figured it's the best time, since—"

"Except," Laurel continued, "you'll still be needed as far as I'm concerned."

"Kevin doesn't want me sticking around much longer."

"I don't care," she spat, "about your father. Fuck him. Since when does it matter what he thinks?"

Isaac huffed, breath fogging the window. "I'm not you, Laurel. For all they call you the devil's daughter, you've got no idea what it's like to be raised by one."

Laurel pressed her foot back onto the pedal. Any response she could cook up to that would sound whiny in comparison. She had a dead parent but never a dangerous one.

"I didn't mean that," Isaac said after a moment.

"I don't mind honesty from you every now and then."

"That's not fair either." He slapped his hand onto the dashboard.

"I didn't intend for it to be," she countered. "So, where are you going? Cincinnati?"

"To start with. A girl who graduated with Garrett is living up there, says she'll take me as a roommate. Month-to-month it for a bit. After that, I'm not sure. It doesn't snow in California."

Laurel snorted at the idea of Isaac wearing flip-flops on a beach somewhere. "You wouldn't last a day in California. It's too dry for your tastes, and you hate anyone you've ever met who's so much as vacationed there."

Isaac's mouth quirked into a smile. "I might grow to like it."

"*Maht cud yew?*" Laurel mocked, broadening her accent so the words stretched along the curve of crumbling road leading to the farm. "Let's see how well they like you with an accent like that."

A shallow creek bed ran alongside the road, shining oil-slick wet in the darkness where the moonlight caught its current.

Isaac's hand tugged his hair, spiking it upward like he'd been hit with a bolt of static electricity. "Look, I can't stay here. You know I can't. You've known it all our lives."

Laurel hummed. She was going thirty-five on a road she usually wouldn't take at more than twenty. Hardly anyone else was on the road this time of night, but sometimes teenagers would joyride around the back roads. But at that moment, it was hard to care about a car wreck.

"Are you still taking me back to your place?" He stared out at the dark woods lining the road as though he'd just noticed where they were. A curl of fog clung to every dip in the road, swirling low around Laurel's tires like a ghost as the Buick cut through it.

"That was the deal." Laurel spoke in a clipped tone as she turned in to the driveway. Gravel flew. There was a mile's worth of it between the mailbox and the farmhouse. The sooner she closed that distance, the sooner she could put Isaac in the living room and ignore him until morning.

"Laurel, cut the engine and talk to me."

Laurel gave up, slamming on the brakes so hard that the velocity of her anger shoved her into the steering wheel. She killed the engine, and they sat in the dark, not speaking. Barely a sliver of moonlight filtered in through the walnut leaves. Laurel undid her seat belt.

"What's there to talk about? You're leaving. You've got no other choice apparently, so why argue?"

He laughed. He actually laughed at her, his dry laugh, like he couldn't believe her gall. "You chose to leave, and you chose to come back, and I had no say in either of those decisions, did I?"

Laurel smacked her hand against the dashboard. "As I recall, you were encouraging me to leave!"

Isaac watched her shadowy reflection in the glass but wouldn't meet her eye. "I had an idea, stupid and vain as any other fantasy I've ever had, that I might join you up there. I just wanted to get my shit together first."

Laurel laughed back. She couldn't help it. "I thought I had mine together and look at what happened to me. I wasn't ready. At my best, I was barely getting by. I was lonely. I was always sick, and every time I left the dorm room, the world closed in on me. I stopped going to class entirely there at the end, once I'd decided I could just go home. I couldn't have stayed, waiting for you to get it together."

"Well," Isaac said into the cold quiet that followed, "just because you couldn't stay doesn't mean I'm not going."

Laurel was too tired to keep fighting. She reached for the key in the ignition. "Whatever, it doesn't matter. Let's just—"

"No," Isaac said. "You wanted me to talk." But he didn't talk.

Laurel sat, stone-faced, resolutely ignoring the struggle playing over his face, wondering if he'd break before the sun rose. In the silence, the woods whispered around them, a voice of quivering leaves and the quiet breaths of animals in the dark. Right as she was about to give up, the dam broke.

"I've kept my toes to one side of the line when it comes to how I act. Everybody who knows, knows I'm one of the good ones. I take it elsewhere; I don't cause a stir. Only I'm gay all the time, not just on the weekend. That's Garrett's game. He can play it alone. I'd like to live seven days out of the week."

Laurel took a long exhale, hoping the right words would follow her breath. They didn't. She searched for something to say anyway, knowing full well it would do no good. Part of knowing Isaac was accepting that the lonely parts of his life were off-limits and only warming the places she could reach. Garrett

Mobley held a part of Isaac she could never understand, and he seemed not to know how to handle it with care. "If he wanted you to pretend to be something you're not, he wouldn't be in love with you," she said.

The hood of the car clicked, still hot from the engine. There were no streetlights on the lonely stretch of gravel drive before them. The glow of the stars couldn't reach them through the roof of the car. Laurel felt rather than saw Isaac shake his head in the dark.

"Asking me to stay here is asking me to pretend," he said. "The best people can do around here is tell me they don't care. I don't want to be absolved. I want to exist."

"That's fine. Exist where you please, like you won't have to bite down on your accent and change the subject whenever anyone brings up animal rights, and act like you've never shot a gun and you startle at the sight of a Confederate flag hanging off some dumb fuck's tailgate. But when you're forgetting all that, and being the good, palatable Yankee liberal everyone expects, you can forget me and all the other ugly things you've been to fit in where you're from."

"Maybe I'll have to do that," Isaac shouted, reaching for the door handle, "but at least I won't have to be here to watch you fight down shame every time something reminds you that you failed out there."

A branch snapped outside.

"That's my point, Isaac. If I couldn't make it out, what makes you think you can?" Laurel snarled. She turned the key, and the lights flared. They caught on something big and dead. Blood shadowed a mouth that almost seemed to leer. Empty eye sockets stared straight ahead, fixed on Laurel and Isaac.

CHAPTER TWELVE

W hat the hell is that?" Isaac shrieked, his hand slapping against the dashboard as he recoiled.

In the driveway stood a scarecrow of bones. On closer inspection, it had a deer skull for a head, the long jaw hanging slack against its throat. The skin had been partially cleaved from its face; sightless, cloudy eyes were sunken in their sockets. Its yellowed ribs held no organs, and stringy tendons draped loosely around its pelvis. Dried sinews threaded its legs and were stained black with blood. The slit-open smile showed every tooth in its mouth as it gaped at them.

Deer are herbivores, Laurel thought dimly. *That's what those teeth mean. They belong to something very stupid, something that eats grass and stands there with its mouth hanging open, watching death chase it down because it can't bite back.* But in its hands were the sharpened points of coyote claws, meant for tearing flesh.

She could see black sky through the back of its throat. It was more than just skeletal structure, carefully reconstructed by an archaeologist in some sterile museum. There was some hideous creativity to the jigsaw-puzzle pieces of predator and prey, come together in a macabre dance. Laurel, who categorized bones blind, could not identify what some of it had been in life.

Many myths had trickled down from the hills. There was the catawampus, a giant panther that prowled through the night. The moral was this: Stay out of the woods after dark. And there was another creature like the one she saw before her: an unholy stack of bones ready to eat children who strayed too far from their mothers' sides. Rawhead and Bloody Bones.

The bones shifted deliberately, animating a body that should not have been able to move. Its hulking mass moved to hunch over the bloated carcass of a deer by the side of the drive, arms sunk deep into the decaying flesh. The carcass made a squelching sound as the monster's clawed appendage pulled a shattered piece of rib from its depths. It lifted the rib, scraping the shattered edge against its worn, walnut-stained molars as though using a toothpick to dislodge a piece of flesh from between its teeth, and it looked at Laurel and Isaac, staring through dead flesh.

The creature's arms were stained to its shoulders with dark layers of blood. It lifted its clawed arm, bending the joints in its fingers one by one as though waving at them. Then, as if to clear its vision, it raised those fingers to scrape away one of its useless eyes, like it could see her better from the hollow pits of its skull. Bile rose in Laurel's throat.

The deer skull cocked at a strange angle for a second, considering. Then the creature pressed against the earth and pushed itself onto its hind legs. Vertebra after vertebra, bone touching bone with no flesh to mute the sound as it rose to its feet. It stood as tall as the trees lining the road. It took a step toward them.

Laurel meant to reverse back up the driveway. Instead, her trembling hand knocked the car into drive. Her foot slammed the accelerator, and the car jolted forward.

Bones broke. The grinning skull crunched against the glass of the windshield. Laurel's head slammed against the steering wheel as the front of her car splintered the trunk of a cedar tree. The body of the vehicle rocked back and forth as metal pinned bone to wood. White pain spread across her body, the origin hard to pinpoint. Her hand, her head . . .

"Laurel." Isaac's voice was urgent as he scrambled to unbuckle her seat belt. "Come on, come on—"

She groaned. Her stomach, her chest, her *head* . . .

"We've got to get out of here." Isaac shoved his hand under her armpit as he tugged her body out of the driver's seat. "Come on, get up."

A horrible scrape sounded from outside the car, and the vehicle began to roll backward. With supernatural strength, the creature shoved the Buick away from its body. Isaac braced himself against the dashboard as the rear of the car crashed into an oak.

"It's getting up! How is it doing that?"

Laurel whimpered. Her hands lay a million miles below her. Beside her, Isaac reached for the door handle.

"We've got to run. I can't get it open. Laurel, help me!" The creature stood, moving faster than it had before. Its blood-soaked claw reached for Laurel's door.

The lock popped. Isaac shoved the passenger door open with one shoulder as the creature's claws scraped the cracked-open window on Laurel's side. She recoiled from the layered stench of putrefaction. The thing might have been reanimated, but it had not stopped decaying, and some of the lingering flesh seemed older than other parts.

"Gun," Laurel breathed, a hand over her mouth to keep away the rot. "There's a gun in the glove compartment, Isaac. Grab the gun." Isaac pulled the .380 from the glove box as he dove out of the passenger door. "One in the chamber, three in the magazine, pull the trigger—" Laurel slammed her knee into the open glove box as she slid out of the car, wincing as another firework of pain sparked across her vision.

Isaac's foot slipped on the gravel path, and he caught himself, clutching the pistol grip so hard his knuckles went white. They were too loud, too living, all breath and aching bodies. The click of bones was the only sound they heard signaling the creature's approach.

"Shoot it!" she screamed, her vision spinning as she bounded down the gravel driveway, nearly tripping on the uneven ground in front of her, She could twist an ankle easily, running like this, but what they were running from was far more dangerous.

Isaac lifted the gun to aim it but couldn't seem to pull the trigger. His eyes were wild and the pistol shook in his grasp. "I can't get a clear shot." He swore. " I'm not even sure what the fuck I'm supposed to shoot at."

"Center mass, dammit," Laurel said shrilly. The gun jumped in Isaac's hand as he fired off a shot that missed its mark by a mile. "What is wrong with you?"

"There's nothing in its rib cage to hit!" Isaac panted.

"Fine, here, give it to me." Isaac shoved the gun into her grip.

She wished she had a rifle. It was a little less than thirty yards away by her estimation. It would be a miracle if she hit it at this distance, but she had to try.

Laurel played with death every day. She knew its calling cards. This creature defied every last one of them. It moved quickly, like a living animal, in spite of impacted ribs and an entire arm dragging against the ground. Its bulbous skull grinned widely as it bobbed forward, brushing against the lowest branches of the canopy.

Whatever possessed it seemed to know what living looked like and mocked it. There was no trace of the clinical and careful assemblage of a skeleton or the wholesome feeling of heat and breath in a creature's body. It was a nightmare walking through her world.

Laurel pulled the trigger. The shot flashed like lightning, echoing through the night. Her ears rang. The creature didn't flinch.

She missed.

Laurel never missed.

But Laurel never shot indiscriminately into the dark. Laurel didn't run for her life, clutching her pistol and hoping her eyes would adjust to the dim moonlight before a jutting rock tripped her. Laurel didn't retreat when something invaded her home, her personal holy ground. She fought.

She turned, steadying her stance, feet apart, one hand on the grip of her gun and the other wrapped around her fingers. She aimed, ignoring the throbbing pain in her head, the tremble in her trigger finger.

She fired. She hit the monster between its empty eye sockets and knocked the skull from its neck.

She didn't stick around to see it fall. She turned and ran.

"Did you kill it?" Isaac called over his shoulder.

Laurel shook her head. "Not sure. Can you kill a skeleton?"

There was no sound behind them beyond the whisper of wind through the woods. When she dared a look over her shoulder, there was no movement other than some bird flitting from one tree to another in the dark. It was surely dead, but whether or not it was still chasing them, Laurel couldn't say for sure. Her head throbbed with every footfall.

The lights were on in her house at the bottom of the hill. Too late she remembered her uncle Jay, who had a primed response to the sound of shots fired in the middle of the night waiting by his bedside table.

"It's us, don't shoot!" she panted, falling onto the lawn.

Jay stood by his truck, hunting rifle pointed into the darkness, a look of grim determination on his face. "Laurel, Isaac, get in the house," he barked.

He didn't lower his gun until Isaac stopped in the glow of the floodlights at the side of the house, his hands on his knees as he gasped for breath. "Oh, Laurel. Your head. You're bleeding."

Laurel brought her hand to her forehead. Her fingers came away red. "Oh," she echoed, "I guess I am." She sank to her knees.

CHAPTER THIRTEEN

J ay was yelling when Laurel awoke. She blinked as the yellowed ceiling of their living room swam into view. The novel
Jay had been reading sat spine-up on the coffee table in front of
the couch. He'd probably been napping there before she'd roused
him, firing her gun at something she wasn't sure she'd killed.

"So, y'all thought—what? Help me out here, because I'm
having trouble understanding." Jay snapped his fingers. "You'd
drive the car into a tree rather than parking it down the hill?
Did the thought of driving it another mile back from Cincinnati at nearly four in the morning exhaust you that much?"

"No, sir," Isaac muttered. He stood still in the center of the
room, his eyes focused on the grain of the floorboards.

"And then what? The walk home got boring so instead of
calling me to fetch you, you just fired a warning shot, so I'd
know you were home?"

Isaac didn't say anything. Jay was broad as the front of a Mack truck and loud as its horn. He'd been planted in wide-open fields and grown unimpeded by the limits of closed-off spaces. There was no violence to him, no sadistic bite, but Isaac's fears were caught in patterns his thoughts couldn't dispel. He'd learned well from his time in the small apartment, where his father's temper exploded like a bottle rocket in close quarters. He was anticipating a blast that wouldn't come, hoping it wouldn't fire at him if he said the wrong thing.

Laurel had grown up unafraid to shout back, fearless of fists because she'd never felt them. She and Jay had been battling since she could first form words. She wasn't afraid to use hers. "We didn't intend any harm, honest." She struggled to sit up. "Accidents happen."

"Good morning, sleeping beauty!" Jay said. "Wasn't sure if we had to get you to a hospital with that head injury."

Laurel tried not to groan as she raised her fingers to the shallow cut on her head. "I don't think I have a concussion."

Jay snorted. "You're gonna damn well wish you had one by the time I'm done with you. What's with your happy trigger finger?"

Laurel was tired of lies and half truths, of missing things because of what other people failed to say. She was tired of secrets. "We saw a ghost."

Isaac's head snapped up. Shocked out of silence, he mouthed, *Ghost?*

Laurel agreed it was a sterile term for whatever the creature had been, but she wasn't sure what else to say. "Monster" sounded more juvenile, like a haint under the bed that a child might cry about. She didn't want Jay thinking of her as a child when she needed him to take her seriously.

Jay reached for his truck keys. "Come on, Isaac. We have to take Laurel to the hospital. Unless you drove drunk?"

Laurel blanched. "It's not like that. Christine Maynard said it, but I didn't believe her at first."

Christine? Isaac mouthed, and Laurel knew she was losing. She talked faster. "But then we saw—we saw—" She wasn't sure how to say what it was she'd seen. She could identify raccoon and deer and coyote claw, but the sum of those parts was a creature harder to classify. "Bones," she finished lamely, defeated.

Jay shook his head. "Bones?"

"Mom!" Laurel said suddenly. "I've been dreaming about Mom. I think she was trying to warn me. She said something was trying to reach me, and its hands—"

"Your mother?" Isaac asked. Not even he was following, and he'd seen the thing.

"You talk if you think you can do better," she snapped at him.

"Laurel, sweetheart," Jay began, his voice soft and serious. She could have died at the pity in his voice. She shouldn't have said anything. She definitely shouldn't have brought up her mother.

They'd had this conversation once before, when ghosts were just trick-or-treaters in the church parking lot with sheets over their heads. Some kids on the playground hadn't known the false hope they were sowing within her, playing a game where a potion they invented could bring the dead back to life. When she'd brought it up at supper that night, her uncle, with his prematurely lined face, had offered a smile that was even more rare back then than the ones he offered now.

As gently as he could, he'd said, "The dead don't come back to life, Laurel. They go to heaven or hell, or maybe somewhere in between that we haven't heard of yet, but they don't come back. When they're gone, they're gone."

No one had prepared Jay for a world in which he lost both parents in two years, then his older sister soon after. Death had stained Jay Early's young life, leaving him with a child to raise while he was still growing up. He'd thought learning the hard lesson early would serve Laurel well, and it had. She'd never before doubted the finality of death. She'd long ago dispensed with ghost stories.

Jay stood with his hands shoved in his pockets, staring at the floor. "You can't do this anymore, Laurel—playing with bones until they haunt your waking life. Find another hobby."

Laurel wanted to protest, but there was no fight in her. It had drained away when she saw the sadness in his gaze. She'd spent her whole life trying to be an easy child. He deserved that for being the best stand-in parent he could. When had she grown so ungrateful for the effort he'd put into raising her?

Jay shook his head, as finished as her. "Clean up that cut."

"Yes, sir," she said.

Laurel thought that was it, but Jay gave another sigh and said, "Laurel, I'm going to take your gun. Whatever you think you saw, what you did was irresponsible. Someone could have died. You can have it back when I think you're ready, but it's clear you're not. I bought it for your protection, not so you could shoot in the dark."

"Yes, sir," Laurel repeated, and a shock of fear rocked through her, as strong as when she first saw the monster standing in her headlights. There were enough guns in the house that if she needed one, she could get to it, but the LCP was hers, an extension of her arm when she needed something that would hit whatever she aimed at. She couldn't stand the thought of being defenseless after being attacked.

But her uncle took the gun off the coffee table, no doubt to store it in his bedroom safe. She watched him walk away, trying to slow the quick, shallow pants of panicked breath in her chest.

Isaac didn't move until Jay left the room. Then he lowered himself onto the couch. He seemed content to focus on taking his boots off, starting from the bottoms of his laces to loosen them. First the left, then the right. Laurel couldn't decide if he was pretending that she wasn't there or if he was so intent on falling asleep that he'd forgotten her.

"Be right back," Laurel whispered. Isaac nodded, still working on his boots.

The tap was old and smelled of iron when she turned the hot-water knob. It ran rust red for a few seconds before clearing up. Laurel soaked the washcloth in the basin and rubbed a bar of soap onto its fabric until she saw bubbles. She scrubbed away the gunpowder residue on her fingers, the dirt on her wrist and knees from where she'd fallen, the streak of mud across her cheek, the gummy trickles of blood emanating from her head wound. With the blood cleaned away, it wasn't nearly as bad as she'd expected, though the bruise wouldn't be pretty come morning. She kept scrubbing until the water turned murky with soap, blood, and dirt.

When she came back into the room, Isaac was staring at the moons of his fingernails. He brought his hand to his nose and sniffed. "Ugh, cordite. Bet you're worse. You actually shot at it."

Laurel wasn't sure what to say. "I'll call Garrett in the morning about the car."

Isaac reached for the hem of his shirt and yanked it off, folding it neatly on the arm of the couch. Arranging his limbs, he settled his head against the flat feather pillow he'd been given. "I'll call him for you."

"Sure," she agreed.

Isaac turned his face in to the couch, trying to block out the light. Laurel switched it off. "Good night, Laurel," he said into the dark.

"Good night," she echoed, and went to lie down.

If Laurel closed her eyes and let her hearing drift out of focus, the white noise of crickets under the house could help her fall asleep. But if she lay awake listening, it started to haunt her. The percussive whisper of a chorus of bugs rising and falling like breath in the trees, the hollow, eerie hooting of owls talking in the darkness and out of sight. Each individual sound fell slightly out of place.

Her mind measured the distance between a coyote's howl and her front door. The dark around the house suddenly seemed too complete, and the papery whisper of a cricket's legs rubbing together sounded like a pattern of footsteps moving ever closer. Part of living in the middle of the woods was knowing when not to listen too hard. She'd snap her fingers or sigh, any human noise to break the spell she'd cast on herself. But it was hard to move with the weight of fear on her chest.

Laurel watched the spiderwebbed cracks of the ceiling, wondering if they'd open up and pull her into them. The shadows in the window barely shifted as the wind blew. They were just branches, shaken in the wind, casting skeletal outlines in the dim moonlight. Laurel closed her eyes to them. From there, it didn't take long for sleep to overtake her.

CHAPTER FOURTEEN

I t was hot in the washhouse and some odd hour, either sunset
or sunrise judging by the orange glow of the room. The air
was humid and smelled herbal, a welcome reprieve from the
reek of rotting flesh. Another breath and the scent of crushed
clove and black pepper tickled her nose. At first, Laurel thought
her mother was cooking, but the bubbling pot in the hearth was
full of wheat paste.

Laurel's mother pressed dried flowers against the milky
windowpane, trapping them against the glass with a brush full
of paste. Laurel thought of the dried flower-petal remains on
her bedroom window. Those petals were nearly two decades old,
all their sweetness and color long since soaked up by the sun.
Laurel loved how it was something her mother had done for
enjoyment. She liked to think that once her mother had been
like her, young, with selfish blood thrumming through her

veins. Maybe she'd wanted a little beauty for herself and made it before dying in an ugly way, broken and drowned at the bottom of the old livestock well.

"I did this for the windows of your nursery," Anna said, gluing a fresh petal to the washhouse window. "I was going to do the rest of the house, but I didn't have time before I died."

Laurel was the only one who laughed. The skulls on the wall stayed quiet. She tried to cover the sound, acting as though the pepper in the back of her throat made her cough. "You might have had more time for floral arrangements if you hadn't thrown yourself down a well."

"I never intended to die."

Laurel was still too awake to believe her mother, but dreams didn't last long, so she let it go. Anna reached for a dried sprig of tansy.

Laurel leaned over her mother's shoulder. A plate of herbs and twigs sat on Laurel's worktable. Laurel vaguely recognized the china pattern from one of the saucers stored in the cabinet by the front door.

"Tell me what these are," her mother said, sweeping a hand over the dried flowers.

"Looks like fleabane." Laurel's hand hovered over a clump of fuzzy-headed flowers she'd once mistaken for a ragged variety of daisy. "And plantain grass. Stinging nettle." She motioned to a stalk that grew along the riverbank. "What looks to be violet leaf?" she said, a question in her voice. As a child she'd loved to weave chains out of the delicate purple flower. When weeding she was grateful for how easy it was to pull their rhizomes out of the ground by hand. She'd never paid much attention to the leaves.

"And ragwort, along with some curls of birch bark, boneset, holy basil," Anna said. "All to hold back evil. Remember that."

Laurel pinched off a piece of plantain leaf with her fingernail. "Plenty of these plants are natives. I can find them all over the farm. Yet it seems like evil's sprouting up everywhere I turn."

Anna nodded. "Faster than Japanese honeysuckle, and even harder to get rid of. But there are some places it has trouble growing. The riverbank, where the stinging nettle makes its home. Around the birch trees and the black locust. There are patches of land that the ground marks holy for itself."

A memory tugged at the back of Laurel's mind. "There was tansy in the deer carcass. Nettle, too."

Anna merely licked her finger and pressed another flower to the windowpane. "To imitate the pattern, you just have to pull in the right elements and glue them to the window, like so. Or to a door. Sprinkle them across the soil. Use them where you need them."

She took the plantain leaf and brushed paste over it, flattening the edges against the windowpane.

Laurel's eyes were drawn to the orange light beyond the glass. "That's not the sunset."

"No," her mother agreed, "it's not."

"What is it?" Beyond the shadows, orange flames roared, licking the bones of the woods beyond. Laurel's view—the house, the woods, the barn up the hill—was washed in bloody light. Laurel pressed her fingers to the glass. They came away blistered, but the burning didn't hurt.

"The end of the world."

Laurel opened her eyes to darkness. Her feet brushed against the cold floor as she struggled to stand.

Isaac rolled over when she entered the living room, his face pressed into the seam of the couch. She heard him shifting rest-lessly as she filled a glass with water. The water was cool and sweet, almost enough to wash the ashy taste of the dream from her mouth. She set the glass down on the counter and turned to walk back to her bedroom, trying not to disturb him.

"Laurel?" Isaac's voice was muffled.

"Yes?" she whispered back.

"Are you okay?" It didn't seem like he'd meant to ask—not in those words, not in the tone of voice that reminded her of a time when they were children and the shadows were cast by monsters they could fight. He rolled over to look up at her, and she was struck how, even smoothed by the dim moonlight through the window, his face wasn't as young as she remembered. He looked grown. She supposed they both were.

"I'll be all right, I reckon," she answered. "What about you? Are you okay?"

Isaac shifted back toward the seam of the couch. "I'll be fine. Don't worry about me."

"I always worry about you." She reached down to run her fingers through his hair.

Isaac let his eyes fall shut. He shifted closer to her touch, already drifting back to sleep. "You're in worse shape than I am. And your car, Laurel . . ."

"Oh, hush. I'm scratched at best. Cars can be fixed. You've seen what Garrett was able to make out of that shit pickup truck. My corpsemobile will be back to stinking up the place in no time."

Isaac snorted, his eyes fluttering open. "That's a shame."

Laurel scooted him over, sitting in the space he left her on the couch. She tucked a bit of the blanket around his chin, thinking. "I don't know how I'm going to get my gun back."

He shrugged under the blanket. "Should've lied."

Laurel untangled her fingers from his hair. "You're better at that than I am," she murmured.

Isaac looked up at her, unrepentant. He caught her hand in his, rubbing his thumb across her palm. "Be as mad at me as you want. I'll miss you, but I won't regret leaving."

She squeezed his hand and let it drop. "Do you think it's still out there? The ghost?"

"Monster," he corrected, barely a whisper.

"Whatever it was. Do you think it's alive?"

"I don't want to think about that thing at all before the sun comes up." He turned in to the couch, pushing her off. "I'm beat. Try to get some sleep."

She paused in the doorway. His back was to her again, face hidden in the cushion. All she could see were the near-white tufts of his hair. "I don't know if I'll forgive you if you leave."

Isaac was silent long enough that she thought he might have fallen asleep. A floorboard under her foot creaked as she walked away, and she heard him whisper, "I won't forgive myself if I don't."

CHAPTER FIFTEEN

A living carcass; an effigy of a man dripping with the skins and sinews of dead animals, its arms soaked in putrefied blood. Too tall to be human. Too dead to spring to its feet and give chase, and yet somehow, it had. Isaac had described this thing to Garrett over the phone, every other sentence packed with qualifiers: "You won't believe me. I don't believe me. I must sound crazy."

He did sound crazy, but Garrett made a habit of believing Isaac, so he decided to believe this, too. It was a stupid habit given that Isaac lied all the time. But there were plenty of lies that Isaac needed people to believe in order for his life to work. *I'll be fine to go home tonight; he's probably passed out anyways. I tripped on a root in the woods, and that's how I busted my lip. I'm not in love with you, so I can leave this shitty town behind without regret.* Rather than trying to parse out the truth from the lies,

Garrett had chosen a long time ago to take everything Isaac said at face value.

A monster made of bones was a hard lie to believe.

Stepping out of his truck onto the gravel end of the Earlys' driveway, Garrett tossed a careful glance over his shoulder. It was half past nine in the morning, and the sun was still on simmer. Dew sparkled on the grass. The aura of fog from the river was faintly visible from a high point on the hill, ghosting its way past the edge of the property and upward toward the Ohio River. Down in the quince trees, black-capped chickadees and delicate bluebirds twittered, squabbling over minor territorial disputes and black oil sunflower seeds. Vultures circled above, black specks in the clear sky. Life and death were the only tenants left on the Early farm, but they weren't a set of neighbors on speaking terms. There was no room for a shuffling corpse in the blue of morning.

"Morning, Garrett," Jay called from behind a sack of fertilizer he was carrying.

"How are you, sir?" he asked.

Jay shook his head, laughing. "Another day in paradise," he said as he hoisted the sack of fertilizer into the back of the four-wheeler. "If you're looking for Isaac and Laurel, I think they're down at the lower barn looking for something to fix the mess they made of Laurel's car."

"I'll start there," Garrett said. "Thanks."

The equipment barn was an old weathered building painted the same flecking black as the tobacco barn atop the hill. Every license plate belonging to an Early dating back as far as 1941 hung on the wall. It housed two red tractors; the four-wheeler, when not in use; a riding mower; the brush hog; and the tobacco wagon. The far wall was lined with oily rags, stained coveralls, red toolboxes dirty with gray grease and orange rust. Outside, junk cars and equipment that had fallen out of fashion in the last century had rusted in the rain. When Garrett began the long process of restoring his truck to the beauty it was today, Jay had told him he could help himself to any part in the junk cars he thought he might be able to use. "Better you than the mice," Jay said.

The Earlys' old equipment barn wasn't anything like his garage at home. It smelled more of dust than the metallic tang of oil, more like rust than the sugar-sweet smell of antifreeze and radiator fluid. The lighting was too dim, and the floors were too soft for his taste. But he liked it well enough, especially when Isaac was around. The summer Garrett turned seventeen, Isaac had found plenty of excuses to make his way down the disused path that led to the shop. He'd always claim he had business to attend to but instead would pull up a stool and linger for hours, talking theory about traps but forgetting to set them. Garrett loved his truck with all his heart. It was a needy old thing, always on the verge of breaking down. It had given him an excuse to spend all summer with Isaac at his side.

When Isaac wasn't down there, however, Garrett didn't hang around long. It wasn't the lonely graveyard of vehicles spread outside the barn that bothered him. He belonged among the rusted-out skeletons of wrecked cars and old plows that no longer ran without draft horses to pull them. But the location was a bad one. Veins of ice-cold springs lay just under the earth, sprinkling the land aboveground with cold spots that stopped him dead in his tracks every time. A person could only spend so much time alone there before the cold spots scared them off.

As he stepped onto the lot, a chill crept over his skin and the gaze on the back of his neck turned hostile, calculating. He looked around, trying to pinpoint its origin.

By a lightning-split tree lay the Earlys' old, disused well, once boarded over, then piled so high with scrap metal and broken appliances that it was impossible to approach it. Now it gaped like a wound in the yard. Garrett couldn't look at the old barn wood underneath a snarl of rusted barbed wire without thinking of a body below.

When he was young, his parents had scared him and his brother away from a similar cistern on their property with the ghost story of a child who'd drowned in its depths. Comparing notes with the other kids at school, he found that everyone with a disused well or cistern on their property had a similar tale—a headstrong little girl, a stupid little boy had been playing near a well against their parents' wishes and fell into a hole too deep for their body to be recovered. A sacrificial storybook character who died so that living children wouldn't make the same mistake. The only child who didn't have a fairy tale to tell was Laurel Early, whose mother had been pulled from the depths of the well he now looked at.

Living with Laurel for a friend robbed the fear from ghost stories. Her family had lived them all and unmasked most of the monsters of rural living. If one or two still survived, though, they'd haunt a place like this.

"Y'all down here?" he called out.

"Over here!" Isaac's voice rang out from the other side of the barn. Garrett turned the corner to find him perched on the tailgate of an old water truck, his hands in his pockets. He had his head cocked a little to the side, and the smile on his face was easy, wide with possibilities. Like being seventeen again, hearing the roar of an old engine for the first time after so many sputtering false starts.

Garrett knew he was stupid. He lacked his brother's ambition and Laurel's precognitive ability to stay out of trouble. He talked plain and rarely read. His accent was so thick it smothered his words and stuck to his vowels like the motor oil under his fingers. Any talent he'd developed was slowly carved from years of mistakes—little planning, little foresight. A lot of doing things wrong. "Hey y'all, watch this!" and the crash that came after.

Garrett was a hick. He wasn't like those boys from Ohio, the ones at the bar who bit their lips to keep from laughing when he spoke. When he wanted something as wildly as he could, he wanted the things he'd seen before: a reliable truck, a kit house with a green tin roof, fiberglass fishing rods, and an ATV that he could really get stuck somewhere in the woods. He couldn't see a future outside of the world he'd been born into, and rather than dreaming up anything bigger, he dreamed of things he knew he could one day have.

For one summer, he thought he could have Isaac Graves. But he'd forgotten the first rule of the world he lived in: People left all the time. Especially if they had a shimmer to them brighter than the work and years spent under the sun could beat out of them. They used it to light their way out of town.

And they didn't come back.

If Garrett hadn't been so stupid, he might have known how to spare himself the heartbreak. He might have known how not to want something he so obviously couldn't have. But at the end of the day, he was just another creature who couldn't tear his eyes away from something bright.

Isaac's feet barely made a sound as his boots hit the dusty ground in front of the water truck. He walked toward Garrett like he was the only person he'd ever seen, like he'd been at that spot all morning, waiting for Garrett to stumble along and find him. He was all clean lines, the slump ironed out of his posture. He was nothing like Garrett. He was becoming a man who lived in a world into which Garrett couldn't dream himself.

But Isaac's voice was soft and strange against Garrett's ear as he stepped in close, too close, close enough to cross a line he'd sworn he'd never cross. "I know you. I know what you want."

Isaac leaned in and kissed him.

When Garrett allowed himself to daydream—he rarely did—Isaac didn't talk. There was nothing he needed to say. No words to tangle until they ended up twisted far from the truth. No attempt to let Garrett down easy or to break his heart. It was just kissing. A kiss a lot like this one.

Isaac pulled away. In the blurry distance between them, his face was strange. Too many teeth, too many shadows. Garrett's stomach ached.

"You're hungry. I see it in you. I've got it in me." Isaac's lips curled into a smile, and he pressed his fingers against the pulse point in Garrett's wrist.

Garrett froze. His body went cold with shock as if he'd fallen through the piece of rotten barn wood and into the well below. His neck prickled, and his lips went numb, radio static buzzing through his head and his fingers.

Something was wrong. Where was Laurel?

"Laurel?" Isaac echoed the question Garrett hadn't asked aloud. He stood, too thin and a little too tall, suddenly at full attention. "Laurel Early?"

"I thought she was with you," Garrett whispered, bewildered. It was all his voice could manage. The man he had just kissed was not Isaac. He was unmistakably someone else. Too pale. In his mouth were straight, white teeth, and when he beamed, Garrett could see each one glistening like polished metal. Garrett cringed away from the smile, horrified to think his lips had been anywhere near it.

The man who was not Isaac sniffed the air. "She's not here, but she's close. I'm going to find her," he said, rounding the corner faster than a man could walk. By the time Garrett caught his breath enough to try to stop him, there was no one to follow.

CHAPTER SIXTEEN

The morning was not yet hot, graced by the afterglow of mist off the river, which kissed the canopy of trees. Mushrooms blossomed up the trunk of a dead ash tree lying on the slant of the hill, orange and jelly-like, alien in the midst of powdered mold and rotting wood. A squirrel jumped from red oak to maple branch, chiding Laurel for making noise as she wandered toward the lower barn.

The hill rose high at her side, fractured by deer trails and pockmarked with slabs of limestone that thousands of years of rain had unearthed. Wild honeysuckle clustered in sunlit patches. An old stone fence, coated in moss, wound down the far side of the road. Mint-green lichen streaked across stone and tree trunk alike. Deep holes dotted the base of the fence where creatures—ground squirrels and chipmunks and fat black snakes—made their homes in the shadows. A buzzard hung in the treetops, lazily overlooking the bottoms for signs of something dead to eat.

Through the water maples and white oaks on the shore, Laurel could make out the tea green of the river, its surface glassy and peaceful. The air smelled of sweet william and leaf rot, a Hades-and-Persephone dichotomy of new life and recent death. Laurel tilted her head to the sky, breathing it in.

A shudder ran through her.

At first, Laurel thought she'd crossed over one of the springs that hollowed out the ground underneath the old road. It was a sensation she'd gotten more than once lately. The feeling that someone's eyes were on her.

A man stepped onto the path, maybe fifty yards ahead. He wasn't in camouflage, nor did it seem as though he was trying to move stealthily, but it was still difficult to pinpoint exactly where he had come from. There was only one road down here, and it ran right by her house. Unless he'd crossed the river and come up through the fields, she couldn't imagine how the man had gotten where he was without her seeing him first.

He didn't have the shifty slouch that Laurel had seen on the men known for stealing farm equipment and slippery elm bark. There was nothing defensive in his posture. He might not hurt her, but Laurel didn't trust her odds if she had to sprint away. She sized him up. Her clothes were better suited for dashing up a deer trail. It only took one nimble leap to give her the upper ground on the ridge as she closed the distance between them.

"Excuse me," Laurel called. She kept her voice friendly but shifted her empty holster forward on her hip. "You must be lost," she told him, giving the smile she reserved for the rare stranger she encountered. "The road's back that way. By a mile. And a river. And a lot of barbed wire. Were you hiking nearby?"

"Laurel Early?" the man asked. His voice sounded as though he were calling Laurel up to sign forms at the DMV, but it made her blood run cold. She brought her hand to her cell phone.

"I don't know you, but I do know my uncle's coming along right behind me," she lied. "He's got a shotgun, and he's had a hard morning. I suggest you turn around and head back to where you came from. I don't particularly care where that is."

The man smiled blandly. "But I love you!" he said. He turned his head, and his vague features shifted slightly on his face. The sudden wrongness of him at that angle hit her like a whiff of something big and dead, rotting in the stagnant summer air.

There had been scattered moments in Laurel's life when she stared into the woods and thought she saw a face made of leaves and tree branches staring back at her, its features grotesque. She would stare and keep staring, like pressing down on a bruise, until her brain puzzled out the illusion and she could dismiss the monster.

But Laurel didn't want to stick around and wait for this man to turn back into a tree branch. She ran.

She made it two steps up the deer trail before a root snarled out of the hillside, tripping her. Like an abrupt yank of a fish on a line, Laurel found herself suspended high above her body, unable to see anything but the hideous, perfect blue of the sky above. Her knees hit the ground hard somewhere far below her. The pain was a distant pulsing, a warning siren sounding.

It was as though she were falling up into everything she could possibly want. Every desire sated; every thirst quenched. Perfect, terrible tranquility came over her. *Death,* she thought. She knew what it smelled like, how it withered a body into dirt. *But this is what it is.* She lay there, sticky and glutted, muscles pinned by the oppressive weight of pure satisfaction. Somewhere far below, her heart was beating triple time, fast enough to burst. But all Laurel could see was light.

The next thing she knew, she was empty once more. Breathing hard, like she'd been flung back to earth. Laurel found herself on her hands and knees, grounded by the sharp stab of a piece of limestone against her palm. Her head pulsed with pain. Her mouth was too full of saliva. Bile climbed from the pit of her stomach to the back of her throat, and she retched, spitting acid into the dirt. The scent of vomit filled her nostrils, and she gagged again, rolling off her knees and onto her back. She choked, coughing hard as she tried to fill her lungs with air. The man smiled from his place on the road, as if waiting for a child to finish a tantrum.

Laurel wiped the spit from her mouth as she scrambled onto her elbows, crawling as far from the man as she could. A root scraped the back of her neck. She willed her feet to carry her, but she couldn't seem to stand.

"That was me courting you," the man said in his reedy voice. There was something a little too flat in his intonation. Like a voice you'd hear on television. There was static in the sound. "A taste of how I love. I want inside your body, Laurel Early. I want to eat you up. If you won't give me what I want, then I'll love you to death. I'll love you till there's nothing flesh and blood left. I'll gnaw the bones of you until they splinter and break."

An instant later he was close enough to grab her. His fingers clawed her shoulders. His breath on her face was as cold as the wind off the river but reeked like the stockyards, shit and rotten blood. "I'll let you lie here like the grave and think on your answer, but I'll be back soon enough for your bones. Have them laid out easy, where I can crawl inside, or it'll hurt when I have to peel you open."

The weight that pinned her fell away, as though someone had removed a knife from between her shoulder blades. He had vanished. She wasn't sure how long she lay there, breathing in the sickening stench of her vomit and trying to reorient herself with the limiting curves of her body. The ground was solid beneath her, a little too hard and speckled with sharp rocks that dug into her skin and reminded her she was alive. There was a buzzard circling overhead, but he had no interest in her today. Even from that high in the air, floating on a current in lazy circles, he could tell the difference between death and terror. Laurel was not yet to his taste.

She heard heavy footsteps coming down the road, a voice somewhere above her. "Laurel?" The voice was not Isaac's, like she had expected, but it was familiar.

"Ricky?" She struggled to lift herself off the ground, turning over on her back.

"Wrong brother." Garrett knelt above her, breathing hard like he'd been running. His hand went to her pulse, her hair. She must have appeared more corpse than girl. She wanted to arrange herself, be more presentable, less ugly in her victimhood. But she couldn't manage to get ahold of her muscles. "Jesus, Laurel. Christ. What—"

She wasn't sure what to tell him, what excuse she could give. She had on the right kind of shoes for running, the right kind of outfit for getting away. She knew the land and had the upper hand. It wasn't a very believable crime scene. Especially not in her home, where she should have been safe.

He lifted her from the ground, trying to prop her into a sitting position. She leaned a little too hard against him, then realized she reeked of vomit. A thin trail wetted the front of her shirt. She tried to pull away, but he held her closer. She felt lead weights hanging from her wrists and ankles as he scanned her body for trauma, lifting her hands and legs to check for bruising. "What did he— Did he?"

Laurel shook her head, and he pressed her face against his T-shirt. She could hear his breath and the heartbeat in the hollow of his chest, but dull and steady. "It wasn't like that," she muttered. Words failed her again. "I was choking. He held me down with— I couldn't breathe."

It was clear Garrett wasn't listening. To him she was delirious, no doubt, traumatized. "Which way did he go?"

She reached a hand to his face, yanking it down so she could look at him. His eyes were as green as Ricky's, but she'd never seen them in quite that shade of fear.

Her voice caught in her throat, rough from vomit and terror. "Don't go after him," she whispered.

"Do we need to go to the hospital? You look like hell," Garrett said, wiping the dirt from her face.

"I'll be okay," she said, smiling a watery grin, trying to sound reassuring. She was aware that she was scaring him to death. "C'mon. Help me up. Let's get back to the house, get Isaac, and get out of here."

Garrett glanced at the woods behind her as he helped her to her feet. "Do you know where he is?"

Laurel frowned and pointed down the hill. The core of her chest went cold at the expression on Garrett's face. "He was supposed to go to the barn and wait for you while I went to grab a key . . ."

Garrett shook his head, his lips pressed into a thin, worried line. "I thought I found him, but it wasn't him."

"There you are!" Isaac's voice rang out too loud over the silent road.

It was all too easy to fall back to her knees. She would have, if Garrett hadn't been holding her up. He nearly dropped her as Isaac came around the corner.

Isaac pulled a green metal wagon they'd played with as children. It held a length of chain and two old wine vats sealed with fresh white linen. "I went to move those vats in the equipment barn to get at the chain behind them. Only I couldn't. They were full of wine. I remember we'd made some year before last, but I'd thought we'd finished it before Laurel went off to college."

She'd never seen the vats sitting in the wagon before. Something was wrong. Her heart, stuttering in her chest, struggled to make sense of it. Her lungs threatened mutiny. Isaac looked at her colorless face and frowned. "Laurel, what happened?"

She shuddered. The whole woods shook with her.

CHAPTER SEVENTEEN

C hristine wasn't much for props. She didn't care for cards: oracle, tarot, or Zener. She'd been a deft hand at gin rummy, but no one who hadn't been raised by their grandmother knew how to play, and she wasn't much for support groups, so she'd let the skill lapse. She'd never caught a vision in any one of the glass garden balls for sale in the Walmart Garden Center. Spirits she spoke to tended to bypass the Ouija board altogether and reach down her gullet instead, letting her do the talking without getting to pick the words. It was mannerless and crude, as well as completely unsuitable for slumber parties. So was Christine.

Sometimes she fantasized about quitting the C-Store and setting up shop as a genuine commercial psychic. But it was a recipe for disaster, and she needed no intuition to tell her that. She was unskilled in the subtle art of suggestion necessary for that line of work. She was far better at bodies and the frank information they provided. Palmistry wasn't too hard if she had to sell something. Blatant statements like "You've got cancer" were far easier but more difficult for a client to hear. "You're pregnant" was a breeze, but someone could buy a test from the mini pharmacy hanging off the C-Store counter faster than Christine could get the words out, and by that point, usually they already knew.

People wanted their diagnoses from doctors and their cures from a witch. Christine had never been good at curing what she could catch, so she kept quiet. She dished out fried potato wedges and banana pudding against doctor's orders. She sold kratom to hands that trembled with the need for something stronger and ibuprofen to a man who grimaced around an abscessed tooth, afraid, even though the dentist who'd drilled through his mother's teeth for Medicaid money had long since retired. She sold a pack of condoms to a teenager, knowing one would break and the girl would be back in for a pregnancy test before fall.

In between, she sold ham biscuits for a funeral and a tub of coleslaw for a baby shower, doled out candy bars and sandwiches and baked frozen pizza to wrap in tinfoil. The clock above the door neared noon by the time a man wandered in to stare morosely over the hot bar before grabbing a pack of Tums and an Ale-8 bottle from the cooler, looking green-tinged and nervous. Christine made him drop the money on the counter. She didn't need to catch whatever stomach bug he was carting around. She was sick of other people's bodies. Her own was too real, the aching lower back and the bone spurs she'd gotten from too many miles walked in bad shoes. She wanted to escape it all.

The clock struck lunchtime, and a throat cleared above her.

The elderly man with a starched, pressed collar and a suntan from the rocking chair he sat in outside most weekdays. She'd been refilling his coffee all morning, but as the A.M. switched to P.M. he switched to Coke and a pimiento sandwich, holding up her line for half a minute trying to sweet-talk his way into a political conversation she wouldn't rise to. He pawed some change across the counter. None of its remainder found its way into her tip jar.

When Christine looked at him on open-eyed days like this, it felt like wearing prescription glasses that weren't hers. Her vision blurred and doubled; at once she took in the sight of Dry Valley as it was and Dry Valley as a hard layer of acid whitewash would have it be. That perspective dissolved Christine and the extra holes pierced in her ears, then moved on to her neighbors whose bright laughter and rapid, fluid Spanish lit up the evening cicada song from their deck until the stars came out. It scoured out the parish priest who came to pick up supper for a family to whom he was administering Eucharist in Kenton's Lick. Soon it even turned on its own and stripped away Isaac Graves's bruised shoulder and Laurel Early's buried mother, a scald hot enough to leave scars. It flooded whole neighborhoods in Dry Valley, boarded up windows, and washed families out of the state, while its waves lapped serenely at his ankles, rocking the chair he sat in, soothing him.

"You take care, sir," Christine said, sugar that mollified his tongue but couldn't temper the venom in his eyes. She could feel it wearing holes in the soles of her shoes.

When the last of the lunch crowd left, she locked the door and went out for a smoke. She crammed herself into the space between the freezers that held bags of ice. The back of her ponytail pressed against the bricks. It was not much cooler here than it was on the asphalt, but it was private, and the heavy hum of the freezers cleared her mind of unwanted visitors. These smoke breaks were her preferred method of meditation. She fished a blue Bic lighter out of her pocket and lit up a cigarette, repeating a mantra of *fuck this* over and over in her mind until her thoughts emptied.

She took a deep drag and stuck a finger into the hole she'd worn in the toe of her shoe, testing a theory she'd been working on for most of her shift. As suspected, she'd busted another pair of tennis shoes. She'd been too tired to glue the tear when it was still small, and now the sole was hanging halfway off. She'd have to buy another pair, an expense she'd wear out another pair of shoes just trying to pay for. *Fuck this, fuck this.*

Transcen-fucking-dental.

She was too in-tune today with the insights the world had to offer her. She was always perceptive, but today no psychic shield passed down by her grandmother or white-witch ritual to protect her empathetic nature seemed to do jack for her. It was as though somebody had their fingers prying open the lid of her third eye, forcing her to see everything. She could just feel the press of a hand on her brow bone, fingers digging into either side of her eye sockets. No pain, but pressure. Her vision blurred, dry eyes watering as she struggled to blink.

Someone was holding her eyes open.

Christine swallowed a lump in her throat and spoke around her panic, keeping her voice so low no one could pick it up over the hum of the freezers.

"If you'd please take a step back, I'll be able to see you better."

It was a polite request. Best to start polite and escalate from there. If she had to, she'd get rude. But she didn't have to. The pressure receded. Christine blinked once, twice, letting her vision clarify.

Laurel Early sat in one of the white rocking chairs.

No, not her. Laurel Early was a living, red-faced thing who reeked of a time still to come. She radiated the future. There was no future for the ragged corpse on the rocking chair, dripping water onto the asphalt.

"Anna," Christine tested. The corpse grinned, not to show that she had teeth—indeed, she did not have all her teeth—but to show she had a skull. It was hard to watch the wet, sagging skin across her face stretch as her mouth moved, but Christine did not turn away.

Christine offered her own placid smile, clamping down on thinking, *That thing just touched me.* She suppressed a shudder. She'd have to wash her hands before returning to work. "Can I help you?" she asked, unable to shake the customer service in her voice. Against the wall with a ghost blocking her exit did not seem the safest place to pierce the veil, but there she was. She'd might as well finish her cigarette.

If she were a professional medium, she might say something about moving into the light. That seemed like a good television-show solution to spirits. But if there was a light available to anyone, it didn't shine at the end of any tunnel meant for Anna Early. There was only more dirt.

"Laurel," Anna cried out, shouting to be heard from far away though she was close enough that Christine could smell rot. She had a wet voice, thick with sediment and disuse. Christine could feel the wrongness of her body, snapped spinal cord and missing teeth, badly angled broken bones and a drowning's worth of well water soaked into her gray dress. But above that,

Christine could smell the acrid, animal-sharp scent of panic. It was a strange juxtaposition from what she usually smelled around spirits. The dead had nothing left to fear except the fates of the living.

"You're the haunting," Christine whispered, awed. She'd never seen a ghost like this before. Spirits left impressions, scars. They didn't reach out for more life after they'd died.

Anna nodded, then shook her head, as though puppeteering a marionette. "I'm not alone," she said, desolate. "You heard his voice. You know what he wants."

Christine tried her best not to think about that disastrous spring setting tobacco on the Early farm. She hadn't lasted a day. Tobacco work was always hard, the honest, bone-seeping sort of hard that promised dreamless sleep at the end of the day. This had been nothing but nightmares. As soon as she'd stepped onto the property, a niggling voice like a minnow's bite hung around her ear, whispering filth and promises and magic like she'd never heard before from any spirit. It begged for her hands. It begged for her bones. It begged for her to cast off the thin charm she could feel pinning it to the land. It didn't dissipate with the mist off the river but grew louder as the sun brightened, until it rang through the hollers, nearly knocking her to her knees. The only time she managed to quiet it was when she called it by name.

Devil.

Silence fell over the hills like a shadow. The wind stilled in the trees, and the river froze flat and smooth as polished glass. Christine could taste the end of the world at the end of that word, all ash and snow packed against her teeth.

Then, it smiled at her.

She hadn't waited around to be caught in its teeth. She already knew she was prey. For all the disdain of the Mobleys and Jay Early's disappointment, she wouldn't return. She wouldn't be hunted.

"Help her," Anna begged, reaching her vulture-picked fingers out in supplication. "It wasn't enough that it killed me. It wants to destroy everything I've ever touched, everything I created. It's coming for her, biding its time until it's strong enough to swallow her up."

"I don't see how this is my business," Christine balked. If there was one thing people in this part of the country frowned upon, it was trying to mother someone else's child. Particularly given that the child in question was now an adult and had never been mothered before. Christine was barely an adult herself. She'd rather work a double every day this week than spend an hour in Laurel Early's business.

"You're the only one for miles with the eyes to see. She doesn't know what's coming," the ghost pleaded.

Christine eyed Anna over her dwindling cigarette. There was very little fire left in her. She flickered and blurred with the effort of maintaining a shape so far from the bones that once shaped her. If it got ugly, Christine could take her, force her into the light or back into the dirt. She kept her voice cool. "I won't go back there. I'm sorry, but any grave dug there belongs to you."

A warped mirror, Anna's smile twisted back on her. Christine could see her tongue, wet and gray, through a hole in her cheek, poking out from between her teeth like a crawdad hiding under a rock. "You will," she promised.

"Is that a threat?"

If it was, it was not one Anna was strong enough to hold. She faded even as she spoke. "I have to do something to drive it away.

You see what she can't. You understand what she won't. Speak to my daughter for me. Tell her—"

Devil.

Anna didn't have to speak it for Christine to feel it knocking around in her head long after Anna disappeared. She leaned over her knees to stub out the cherry into the red plastic ashtray she'd positioned at her feet. A gesture of punching back in. She had many more weary hours of work to go before she could even think about what she'd seen. She could only pray that Laurel wasn't feeling peckish today.

CHAPTER EIGHTEEN

Laurel sat on a picnic table under the red mulberry by the Mobleys' house waiting for Garrett's prognosis on the state of her car. He'd towed the Buick behind his truck for her, its crushed face bobbing in the rearview mirror as they drove toward somewhere presumably safer than the safest place she'd ever known. Isaac was on his way to their back fields to find Ricky. She had been told to "stay put and eat something, for God's sake."

Next to her, a glass bottle of Coke with an ice cube stuffed down its slim neck fizzed merrily. She hadn't touched it since Garrett had opened it for her. It was kind of him to press it into her hands, telling her to drink, but she could barely get her throat to swallow her own spit, much less cloyingly sweet pop. He'd also given her the better part of a tube of sour cream and onion Pringles and half of a dry bologna sandwich he'd made himself. Before they'd left on a summer RV trip to visit their oldest daughter in Savannah, Mr. and Mrs. Mobley had given their two sons a debit card and some vague instruction on how to fend for themselves. Laurel couldn't be sure sandwich making had been covered under those instructions. Perhaps it should have been.

He'd spread out the Walmart bag he'd used as a lunch sack and turned it into a place mat on the picnic table. "Gotta get your strength back up," he'd told her. She hadn't taken a bite.

He'd been kind, but not helpful. It was a Southern dysfunction, a misinterpretation of the acts of mercy. Southerners read "feed the hungry" and decided that course of action was best applied to anyone who suffered. If it was good enough for the hungry, it ought to be good enough for the naked and the afflicted as well. Even while burying the dead, Southerners were more likely to brandish ham biscuits and bake loaves of sugary friendship bread than buy flowers for the grave. So, Garrett brought a sack lunch to a haunting, and Laurel ached too much to eat it.

Her knees stung when they rubbed against the denim of her jeans, a reminder that her skin had been cut. There was sweat at the nape of her neck. She was uncomfortable. She was alive.

She heard the sliding door open but didn't turn to the house. Garrett shuffled his feet along the gravel driveway to let her know he was coming back. The picnic table shifted with his weight as he sat down across from her, reaching into the Pringles tin to pull out a handful of chips.

"Two tires out. The front's dented and scratched up something awful. There's some blood across the interior, but I think it might be yours."

"The thing we hit didn't bleed." She tried to make it sound

like a question, but the exhaustion in her voice made her incapable.

Garrett agreed around a mouthful of chip. "From what Isaac described, it didn't sound as though it had the physical capability."

"You believed him?"

"I always believe him."

"That's a fool's mistake," she muttered, too bitter to take a bite of the chip he offered her.

Garrett's self-deprecating smirk was a statement in and of itself. "He told you he's leaving."

Leftover anger shocked through her like a punch to the gut. "How are you okay with this? If he goes, he'll stay gone."

"Good. He should go." Garrett pushed the can of Pringles back to her. She didn't bother taking any.

She watched his expressionless face for any twinge of regret or fear. If there was any indication they were discussing something that mattered more than the weather, she couldn't parse it. "He said you were in love with him," she prompted.

Garrett shrugged. "You love him, too. Your folks, my folks. We all love him."

"But there's a difference, isn't there?"

Garrett's eyes flicked up to hers. He held her gaze just long enough to let her see him, then dropped it back to the picnic table. "When it comes to a decision between having Isaac here or keeping him safe, what choice would you make?"

Laurel held her silence. She didn't want to answer, but it was all the answer he needed.

Isaac returned, Ricky a half step behind him. Ricky, pink with exertion and flecked with grass clippings, wiped a hand across his brow. "How's she looking?" he asked.

"She'll live," Garrett replied. It took Laurel a second to realize they were talking about the Buick. "I can install the new windshield and fix some of the damage to the body."

"How much is that gonna set me back?" she asked, bracing herself.

"Pay me for parts, and we'll call it even."

It wasn't right, but she didn't want to argue about it. The song and dance of kinding yourself out of someone else's kindness was usually second nature, but she couldn't get her body to move through the steps.

Isaac slid next to her at the picnic table. "Make room. You gonna eat that sandwich?" She shook her head. He picked it up and bit into it, frowning. "Could use mustard."

"Will one of you come help me lift these damn things?" Ricky called from the back of the truck.

Laurel had forgotten that Garrett and Isaac had decided to bring the vats. She hadn't been able to say anything to convince them not to. Her power was diminished. She'd been hurt. They'd made decisions for her. Now there they were, a shadow marring the afternoon light of the Mobley farm.

Garrett grunted as he and Ricky settled one vat then another onto the table. "Feels like they're full to the brim."

Ricky examined the linen seal with wary fingers. "The seal is fresh. Couldn't be more than a year old. I don't know if whatever's in them is any good, but I'll either bottle it or dump it."

"Dump it." Laurel spoke up, finding her voice under the rubble of fear in her chest.

"Are you okay?" Ricky asked, looking closely at her. His hands came up to hold her jaw, his face so close his breath grazed her skin. His attention startled Laurel. They'd seen each other in all states of scraped up. He'd seen her worse than this, but she didn't want to shake him off.

"I'm . . ." She trailed off. They were all watching her. She swallowed, mouth dry. "Don't worry about me. I'll be right as rain in a couple of days."

"Looks like it's bruising up around that gash on your head. Concussion?" He hovered over the wound. She tried not to flinch away from his fingertips, so close she was afraid he might brush against the torn skin and hurt her. He smelled like toothpaste and Irish Spring soap, clean sweat and hard work.

Vomit gelled the ends of Laurel's hair together. The smell of panicked sweat had escaped her deodorant. She leaned away from him. "Don't think so. I don't want to drive the half hour to the hospital to find out for sure. My mind is clear," she said, even as her heart slammed against her rib cage, hard enough to sprain.

"Swelling's not bad." He tilted her face back and forth gently.

"I slept fine last night," she murmured.

"I bet you'll be okay, then." His touch lingered on her skin long after his fingers left her face.

Garrett cleared his throat. "Let's check out these vats already."

Ricky reached into his back pocket and pulled out his multitool, pinching the edge of one wine vat's linen seal. "Be right back."

When Ricky returned, he had four jelly jars tucked into the crook of his elbow and a ladle from the kitchen in his other hand. "Shall I do the honors?"

"I don't want to touch it," Laurel said.

"Shouldn't drink with a head wound anyway."

The seal peeled off the vat like a scab. Laurel pushed herself back against the tailgate of the truck, ready to dash off if the man somehow emerged from the vat like a genie made of toxic sunshine. But the air stayed still and quiet.

Ricky sniffed, leaning over the first vat. "It's a fruit wine. Blackberry, maybe. It's fresh."

Laurel's heart sank. "There weren't enough blackberries last year to throw a cobbler together, much less two vats of blackberry wine."

"Fuck this," Garrett muttered under his breath.

"I don't think we should—" Laurel started, but Ricky tipped the vat forward. Dark liquid splashed into a waiting jar, sprinkling the other three jars as it dribbled forth from the vat's ceramic mouth.

"Cheers," he said, and downed the shallow sip of wine in one gulp. Laurel shuddered as the dark liquid disappeared behind his pink lips. He held the wine in his mouth for a heartbeat, considering. Then, his expression shifted. He spat hard onto the asphalt.

Red.

He dropped his hands to his knees, coughing the dark liquid onto the asphalt. Laurel was reminded of the way tuberculosis revealed itself in old films, pale girls delicately spitting the omen of their doom into virgin-white handkerchiefs.

When he looked up at her, his face was pale as paper.

"Blood," he hissed, voice hoarse. "That's not wine. It's blood."

"Whose blood is it?" Garrett asked, stumbling backward away from the vats as though they were radioactive.

"How the hell would I know?" Ricky swore.

"*Is it your blood?*" Garrett asked.

Before Ricky could answer, the jar he'd thrown to the ground popped, sending confetti of glittering glass onto the gravel. Laurel was given only a second of warning to duck down before the vat in front of her exploded. Shattered ceramic flew in all directions. Like pop cans at target practice picked off one by one with a BB gun, the jelly jars shattered, one after another, spraying the driveway with glass.

Laurel lay flat against the gravel driveway under the truck, watching as wine seeped into the dirt under the picnic table, sticky red. It wasn't wine anymore, if it ever had been. Her memory of it sloshing in the glass seemed tainted, as broken as the vats littering the ground. It was blood, gallons of it spreading into the yard. Like the blood by the well, it pooled on the ground, fresh as if someone had just sliced open a vein.

Isaac was halfway up the mulberry tree, his hands on his forehead covering a gash that nearly matched the one on Laurel's head. Garrett curled in on himself under the picnic table, his hands covering his eyes. Blood leaked from the tabletop onto his hair.

Ricky lay on the ground, still.

CHAPTER NINETEEN

Ricky," Garrett snapped, pulling himself out from under the picnic table and picking out a piece of glass from where it had embedded itself in the back of his hand. "Come on. Get in the house."

But Ricky didn't move. Laurel's heart took a long, careful pause between beats and only resumed its activity when his hand twitched.

Ricky muttered something unintelligible into the ground. Garrett grabbed the back of Ricky's collar in his huge hand. He hauled his brother up to his feet, straining with the effort it took. Ricky struggled, limbs a little limp, skin still pale, as if all the blood on the ground had spilled out of him.

Ricky stumbled and Garrett grabbed him again, shaking his shoulder. "Stand up. All of you, come on, let's get into the house."

No one moved until Garrett shoved Ricky toward the house. "Go!" Isaac slipped from the trunk of the tree and hit the ground hard, pushing himself up with his hands. Laurel crawled forward, gravel digging into her belly, until she was out from under the protection of the truck and in the open air. Once she struggled into a standing position, she ran for the safety of the Mobleys' house.

They stood on clean carpet in the air-conditioning and the artificial glow of a lamp—all except for Ricky, who slumped down onto the couch when his brother released him, head on the armrest, like a marionette with his strings cut.

Laurel struggled to catch her breath. "Are you okay?" she asked, kneeling down to examine him for the unseen wound that had broken him. There was blood on his clothes, cuts across his skin. She ran a careful hand across his ribs, the outsides of his thighs, his chest, behind his head, waiting for him to wince, to hiss with pain. To hint at something broken.

A weak hand came up to bat her away.

"I'm fine." He wasn't. "I am." He couldn't be. "Laurel, stop."

"What happened to you?"

"What the fuck do you think?" he muttered, expression dazed. His fingers trembled. "It was blood, in my *mouth*."

Laurel withdrew her hands, realizing how badly she'd misunderstood. She thought the tremble in his fingers was from pain. But as he took another unsteady exhale through lungs that seemed as whole as the rest of him, she realized it was fear that kept him frozen, strong as the fear that had pinned her to the path. Somehow, their twin terror was worse than the thought that he might be bleeding out.

"Laurel." The tone of Garrett's voice had not yet softened, and he stood stiff and apart from the rest of them at the mouth of the hallway, vibrating from lack of purpose. "You'd better go wash up in the bathroom. Isaac and I can use the sink in here."

He did not offer instruction to his brother. Instead, he turned to the paper towel dispenser by the sink and began pulling sheets. He soaked a giant wad in the sink and placed it into Isaac's hands. Laurel wanted to wipe the blood from under Ricky's eyes. But she turned to deal with her own wounds.

Shimmering shards of glass fell from her scalp when Laurel shook her hair over the bathroom sink. She ran a washcloth across her face. A speckled constellation of burst capillaries across her left cheek was sure to blossom into a bruise to match the one on her forehead. On top of that broken skin was a glaze of blood. Her jeans were speckled with it, and her shirt was soaked through, sticky against her back as she blotted the blood away with the washcloth. She needed a shower.

She took off her damp clothes and stepped into the spray of water without waiting for it to warm. The water stripped away some of the blood and old vomit from her hair and across her skin, running pale pink into the shower floor. She thought about the curling tendrils of sassafras tea in her dream. It stayed with her long after the water ran clear.

By the time she'd dried off and pulled her clothes back on, Ricky was up from the couch. He'd sponged off the blood and had on a clean shirt. He still looked pale but moved with determined efficiency to make up for his earlier slip, picking through his hopeless cause of a room in search of clean clothes for her and Isaac.

Ricky's bedroom was a mess. He had plenty of books, recently read, but none sat on the shelves built to hold them. His wardrobe and his carpet were one and the same. His dresser drawers jutted like steps up to a surface cluttered with deodorant cans, crumpled papers, and fishing tackle. There was a deer's skullcap mounted on the wall, Laurel's work but Ricky's kill. Hanging from one of the antler points was a pair of boxer shorts with a St. Patrick's Day shamrock print. Ricky snatched them up and tossed them into a corner, where they just missed the overflowing laundry basket he'd been aiming for.

Tacked into the drywall was a tapestry of green pot leaves, a relic from Ricky's high school years that never failed to make Laurel smile. He'd bought it from the mall on one of their few school trips to Cincinnati and had served a whole week of detention for letting it wave out the school bus window.

"Virginia creeper," she said, pointing to the tapestry. Her voice was weak, but the joke felt good. There was no way she'd survive another blow like this if she couldn't laugh.

"Legalize it," Isaac agreed solemnly, nudging Laurel as he came up behind her. She reached back for his hand and gave it a squeeze.

"Man, listen," Ricky said, relief in his voice as he assumed the familiar role of the jokester. "You can give me all the grief you want, but in five years when it *is* legalized, we'll all be farming it."

He dug through his drawers for clean T-shirts. The air in his room was thick with the scent of incense and Old Spice body spray, smoke and an underlying bodily scent Laurel wanted to hate. It was clear he'd never put much stock in dusting or bleach or washing his sheets.

Laurel reached behind her head to start braiding wet strands of hair. Ricky shook out one of the T-shirts, emblazoned with another pot leaf, and offered it to her.

She crossed her arms over her chest. "No, thank you."

"Be that way," he said, tucking it back in the drawer. The next one he pulled was a Seether shirt, cut-off sleeves and seams slit halfway down the length of it.

"I don't understand why you boys ruin perfectly good shirts doing that," Laurel complained. She could have worn the shirt as a dress if it wouldn't have exposed half her bra in the process. "It's not as though you've got such bulging biceps that you need the extra space."

"Actually," Isaac said in a low voice, "I think that shirt is Garrett's."

Ricky inspected it more closely. "So it is. Tell him to start doing his own laundry if he doesn't want his shirts mixed up."

Isaac took what was left of the shirt from Ricky and stripped off his stained one. "I reckon I'll have to throw this away." He held it out to examine the blood splattered from sleeve to sleeve. Some of it was his, Laurel noted, watching him pick a piece of glass out of a nasty cut above his elbow.

"I've never had to launder a bloodstain this big," Ricky said, studying his own wasted shirt.

"Cold water. Hydrogen peroxide," Laurel recited, rote. "Hot water sets a stain. But it won't all come out. And if Jay sees my clothes covered in blood, I don't even know what he'd do. Better to burn these."

Isaac balled his shirt up and tossed it on top of Ricky's. "They're not actually evidence of a crime," he said.

"They might be." Garrett stepped into the room. He held a washcloth against his face. His hair was spiked with water. "We've got no idea whose blood that was."

"Or what it belonged to," Isaac agreed, "given the amount of dead shit that's turned up on your farm recently. All that blood by the old well."

Ricky looked green. "Please, I swallowed it. I don't want to think about it."

"Ricky," Laurel started, but he held up a hand.

"I mean it. Will this shirt work for you, princess?" The shirt Ricky offered her was one she also owned, a kelly-green 4-H shirt that clearly hadn't gotten much wear since he'd left high school.

"That's fine." She snatched it from his hands and ducked behind his half-open closet door to peel off her shirt and slip on the new one. It was a little tighter across her chest than the one she owned; he'd been even skinnier in high school than he was now. But it would keep her covered, and it smelled enough like him that Laurel couldn't bring herself to mind. She tossed Ricky her old shirt, and he caught it one-handed.

"We could have a trash-fire party," Garrett suggested.

Ricky balled up the shirts and the bloodstained washcloth Garrett had flung at his head. "Only it'll be dry, since I'm off wine for the rest of my life. I can't imagine it'll be much fun."

"We've got beer somewhere," said Garrett.

"No way am I breathing in the smoke of whatever the hell that was," Isaac insisted. "I've seen horror movies. People are always sucking in a cloud of ghost smoke right before it takes over their bodies and makes them murder each other."

Laurel remembered Isaac's earlier words. *Not a ghost. A monster.*

A creature made from bones, skull bobbing above the pines and stolen claws stained black with blood. A pale man in the road, vague face and mouth spilling pointed teeth, demanding she turn over her own bones to him. Whether it was one creature or two, it wasn't anything she'd ever seen. It stood there like a snag in the current of life and death, catching her thoughts every time she turned them over. Eyes watching her from the woods. Blood seeping into the gravel road. "Haunted," she whispered to herself.

"Beg your pardon?" Garrett asked, so politely it was evident he had not heard.

"Christine Maynard said it first. You said not to listen."

Ricky looked at a pile of books in the corner of his room to avoid meeting her eyes. Isaac examined the hem of the shirt he was wearing.

"Is that mine?" Garrett asked him, voice light. That was enough to turn Isaac's expression guilty.

Laurel rolled her eyes. "I'm done ignoring her, and y'all are done ignoring me. I want to go find her."

"Doesn't she live up on Baldridge Hill?" asked Isaac.

"Yeah, but her trailer's trashed." Ricky gave a snort, stretching out across his bed. He still had his shoes on, Laurel noticed, wrinkling her nose at him.

"Trust me," Garrett added, "if they've got the hours to spare, she's working them up at the store."

"I thought she was lazy as well as a goddamn witch?" Laurel raised her brows at him, and he made a pained face back.

"She's at least one of the above, but I reckon you're counting on that."

Laurel stuck her hand out. "Give me your keys."

Ricky let out an undignified noise, curled over his knee, and heaved with laughter.

Garrett gaped at her. "You're kidding me. You already wrecked one car. You're not getting my truck."

"You would have wrecked, too!" Laurel protested. She wouldn't let him look at her like that after she'd seen the fear etched on his face. She refused to withdraw her hand. "Besides, you taught Isaac to drive in your truck and didn't seem to mind that."

"I could drive," Isaac suggested, holding out his hand. Garrett looked back and forth between them, bemused. "Unless you want to come with? Sure she's dying to see you."

Garrett tossed him the keys.

CHAPTER TWENTY

The heavy slam of a truck door woke Christine from her trance. She'd seen nothing of the future behind her closed eyelids and was instead envisioning what a morning off might look like somewhere sandy and far from here. A cup of coffee and nowhere to go was a luxury she'd be unlikely to catch any time soon. A cool breeze seemed even less likely. The pavement baked even as the sun began to set. She pulled herself out from the space between the freezers, tugging her shirt down over her stomach as she stretched out aching limbs. Laurel Early strode across the parking lot with Isaac Graves trailing after her, his shoulders hunched. Laurel offered Christine a winning smile.

"Isaac Graves! Nice to see you!" Christine called, giving a cheery wave. He stumbled at the sound of his name, looking up with a sharp glance at Laurel.

Laurel didn't catch it. She paused at a rocking chair with a hand shoved in the pocket of her jeans, country convivial. She hadn't come to fight but there was a lot of fight in her at the moment. Laurel seemed to channel that energy into pointed politeness. "Was wondering if you could enlighten me as to a couple of things we spoke about earlier."

Christine could play nice, too. She smiled, wholesome. Downright neighborly, in fact. "Gladly. Been expecting y'all. Won't you come in?"

As she shouldered the door open, Laurel remarked, "I heard you could do things like that. Know things without reason."

Christine ducked behind the counter, peeling some polyethylene gloves from a packet next to the napkins. "I had a reason. I spoke with your mother earlier."

Isaac slumped into one of the tables closest to the hot bar, resting his foot on the opposite knee. Blood splattered his jeans, sprayed across them like he'd slit an artery. They hadn't been gutting fish, but there was a sickly smell on the two. A scent she'd smelled before.

"You spoke with her?" Isaac echoed, an eyebrow raised.

"After a fashion." Ghostly fingers pressed into the skin around Christine's eyes. *Only a memory,* she reminded herself. She rubbed her eyelid before she could think about it. Her fingers came away smudged gray with eyeliner and crumbling mascara.

Laurel leaned over the counter. "What did she say? What was she like?"

Christine thought of the flesh sliding across Anna's face, the way she moved, the waterlogged pain in her voice. "Soft," she decided. A smile lit up Laurel's face, real and warm. Christine let her take a moment with the thought. She washed her hands in the sink behind the counter, counting to twenty as the antibacterial smell of the soap washed away the memory of wet corpse.

"Do y'all want some of this mac and cheese? I'm about to dump it. It's a little burnt, but it'll feed you."

Isaac exchanged glances with Laurel. "Sure, we'll take a couple plates." Laurel agreed, something complicated and guilty in her expression.

Christine obliged, dropping dollops of macaroni and cheese onto two Styrofoam plates. "She had a message for you. She wasn't entirely clear." Christine looked at the graying shadows under Isaac's eyes and considered the spread of the hot bar. "These potato wedges are getting cold. I could probably rustle up some chicken, too."

Laurel looked a little ill, but Isaac said "Yes, please" and so she thanked Christine for the offer. Christine didn't say anything more for a second, wondering if she could get away with getting rid of the corner edge of the banana pudding. In the time it took her to decide she couldn't, Laurel decided Christine was being recalcitrant.

"What would you do if it was your mother trying to speak to you from the dead?" she begged, earnest. Christine rolled her eyes, warding off sentiment with a flick of her wrist.

"My parents aren't dead," Christine lied.

Laurel tilted her head. "I thought you lived with your granny for a while." Isaac covered her hand with his, a warning, but Laurel shook it off.

Christine set the two plates in front of them and presented some prepackaged plastic utensils. "I always lived with her. My folks are carnies. Juggling and shit. Travel around a lot."

"Oh, yeah? Where are they now?" Skepticism poured from Isaac's expression. Of course he'd come with Laurel to talk to

Christine. He could spot a lie better than anyone else in Dry Valley.

"Burning Man," she said. Isaac shook his head, murmuring "Christ," but Christine pointed a paper-wrapped straw at him. "Where's your mom at?"

Isaac cast a mournful look at the tiles. "I don't know. She denied my friend request."

Laurel's eyes widened, but before she could say anything, Christine cut her off. "Look, I realize our existence demonstrates a need for Planned Parenthood in Dry Valley, but you've got bigger problems on that farm than a lack of parental supervision. Do y'all want pop with that?"

"Water's fine," Laurel said, right as Isaac said, "You got Coke?"

"Two Cokes?" Christine held up two fingers. Laurel shook her head. "Coke and a water coming right up."

"Look," Laurel spluttered, "we didn't come here for supper; we came here for answers." Isaac looked wounded, a hand resting protectively at the side of his plate like she might try to snatch it from him. Laurel shoved her plate over to him, standing up from the table to pace. "I don't know if it's escaped your *heightened senses,* but we've had a bit of a day, and if you've got answers, you owe them to us."

"Owe you?" Christine dropped all pretense of politeness. "I don't owe you or your mother anything I've got or anything I can do. That's the landed fuckin' gentry for you, ain't it? Asking other people to work for nothing, die for free. You want answers? You get what I give you, then you'll get your ass out of my store."

It wasn't her store. It belonged to Maynards who had her name but little love for her, who probably had more blood relation to Laurel's ancient family than to some redheaded stranger from the mountains. But it was hers until her shift ended, and she wasn't going to let Laurel Early disrespect that hard-earned scrap of belonging.

Laurel seemed more than willing to take what Christine offered and run, but Isaac spoke up. "Christine's right. I don't know what you're involving her in, but I do know it's blood-soaked and bad. The only thing you're offering her is a share in trouble. Not everybody wants to do what you want all the time."

Guilt crossed Laurel's face again, but Christine knew it had little to do with her. "What do you want?" Laurel asked.

Christine thought hard about what Laurel Early could offer her, what it might be worth to hold a huge favor over an Early's head in a place where names had power. *Friendship,* a voice in her head that sounded like Granny's whispered. She dismissed it swiftly.

"I don't want a damn thing from you," she said. Laurel opened her mouth, but Christine held up a finger. "I just wanna get you out of my hair."

Laurel crossed her arms over her chest. "Go on."

"There's a devil wandering your hills. It's hungry, for the earth, for the air, for the people walking above. For everything." Christine sat down next to Isaac, and she explained, as best she could, the events of that spring, unable to suppress a shudder at the sharp memory of that voice, that whisper of insect wings in her ear. "It fixated on your mother and it's fixated on you. Your mother is burning herself out trying to reach you before it does. It's not like spirits are commonplace. You can't just pick one up in any graveyard. She's got some serious postmortem adrenaline going if she reached out to me."

"She's been speaking to me, too," Laurel said. She told Christine a convoluted story of dreams, laughing skulls on the wall and flower petals against glass holding back a burning earth.

Christine did her best to comprehend. She was better with living bodies, and there was no breath in Anna Early's ghostly voice. She'd picked up nothing from the cold skin of Anna's dead fingers digging into her skull. "She knows more than she's letting on, or more than she can say. I'm sure that devil's interfering. She must be fighting like hell just to reach you."

"Is she in danger?"

"You're in danger."

Isaac set his cup down, but Laurel shrugged off Christine's words. "What can I do about that?"

"I don't know. I'm not fortune-telling, just telling facts. Wanna do this official-like? Give me your hand." Laurel looked as though she might say no, but Isaac tapped her wrist. Laurel sighed and settled her hand facing upright in Christine's out-stretched palm.

Christine jerked back. The acrid, sweet scent of flesh burning filled her nostrils. A penetrating cold like salt on ice blistered the skin of her hands, chasing up her forearms along the blue pattern of her veins. Hastily she wiped her arms against her jeans, cleaning the image away in a sweep of gray ash that faded when she blinked. Her mind held the pain longer than her skin did.

Laurel let out a bark of a laugh, all shock and no humor. "Well, that can't mean anything good." She hadn't seen what Christine did, but it couldn't have been hard to glean the effects of her attempt with Christine's chest rising and falling so rapidly. The ground shifted beneath her. Ice water flooded her veins.

"That wasn't you. That was a fingerprint left on you," Christine said between gasps. There wasn't enough oxygen in the room. "Give me a second." Laurel passed her the water she'd barely touched. Christine drained half the glass in one go.

"I know what it feels like," Laurel said as Christine set the glass on the table before lifting it and gulping down the rest.

No wonder she barely touched her food, Christine thought, shuddering, as she drained the water.

If Christine were kinder, she might have offered some comforting platitudes. She could kill a monster. She could vanquish a nightmare. But Anna's ghost flickered at the edge of her vision, mouth open in a silent scream. "She said it killed her," Christine remembered.

The electric buzz of refrigerators and fluorescent lighting kept the silence in the C-Store from swallowing them all. Finally, Christine could breathe.

"She killed herself," Laurel said, voice flat with disbelief.

"Magic killed her," Christine said more firmly, and took Laurel's hand again.

Laurel flinched but didn't try to take her hand back. Christine wasn't certain what she was looking for, just that she had to look. In spite of herself, she was hunting for hope. A strong life line indicating that Laurel had the fortitude to do hard things, a smattering of psychic triangles or magical crosses that promised power resting on the mounts of her fingers. Her fate line was deeply ridged. Her money line was as light as the ones on all the other hands Christine watched grappling for change at the bottoms of their purses.

All indicators, all potential. Nothing she hadn't smelled on Laurel the moment they first met. "Poor. Powerful. A bit of a bitch. Entitled to your things."

Laurel rolled her eyes and tugged her hand away.

"I could've told you that." Isaac snorted.

Christine shook her head. *These kids.* Laurel, with her fire and her future, ready to save herself with no idea of how to do it. Isaac, so bruised under his own skin that wearing it around their town felt too tight. Anna was right. There was no one around for miles who could look after them. There was no one else who could understand what they were facing.

Another glance around the gas station to make sure. But no, it was as Christine had suspected: She was the adult in this room. *Fuck.*

"So, what should I do?" Laurel asked.

"We already tried shooting it," Isaac added.

Christine templed her fingers, pressing them to her forehead like the barrel of a gun. "Right, okay. To fight something magic, you'll have to use magic." *Obviously.* What an eloquent summation of a serious problem.

But to Laurel, clearly, it had not been obvious. She looked paler than she had before. "You said it killed my mother?"

Christine thought about Anna Early's gray, pruney fingers spread in supplication. The potential her palms held was worn away by the well water she'd drowned in; Christine wondered how similar they had been to her daughter's hands, back when she'd first touched the magic that would eventually end her life. "She was willing to die to stop the devil from doing much worse than killing her. Do you love your home that much?"

Laurel looked at Isaac. "Of course," she said.

"Then you understand."

Laurel studied her palm as though she'd never seen the skin there before. Perhaps she hadn't. Infused with potential, veins of magic pulsing under the surface, waiting to be tapped. No wonder a devil wanted to drain her.

"How do you do it?" Laurel asked.

"Magic?"

Laurel nodded. "I know what it feels like, when it happens. But it's always been something that happens to me. Something I'm given. How do you take it?"

Christine considered this. She understood too well, the feeling of being given something she did not want. It had taken her years to understand how to thread it through her fingers and do more than just wish something so. But it was one thing to do it and another to say how. "Generally? I want something badly enough."

That wasn't entirely true. Christine wanted things, when she let herself, that magic couldn't manifest so easily as all that. New shoes. New opportunities. New ways out. If magic had ever given her any of that, she'd forgotten to ask for a glowing sign illuminating it. Maybe she didn't have the energy to want it that much. But she had a garden that flourished without her having to so much as weed it, light that illuminated her home without the electric company knowing a thing about it, and just last week, she'd felt the pop and hiss of a tire half a mile down the road, after flipping off a truck that had slowed down to harass her. It was easy to want things. It was harder to explain how to want them into being.

Finally Laurel nodded, still staring at the upturned curve of her palm as though she could feel something resting in her hand. Her fingers closed around the memory, reflexive, before she shook them out. "I thought I already had everything I could have."

Christine stood up from the table, clearing the plates of food Isaac had decimated. "If you want to make magic, you'll have to make it yourself."

"*How?*" Laurel asked again, half desperate.

She was so tired of prophesying. Her mouth was dry. Her eyes hurt. She looked at Isaac Graves, who looked back as though surprised she could see him. "Get out of here," she said, meaning it. "I don't care how. But you're going to leave this place alive, and I don't want to see you around again after."

The words burned a little on her tongue, lashing out and wrapping around his ankle. He started, wrong-footed in spite of himself, and to Christine's surprise, he stood.

"Fine," he said, "we'll leave."

Laurel followed, after shooting Christine a long, searching look. Christine spread her arms, trying to show her that she'd seen all there was to see. But maybe Laurel had seen something after all, because she shook her head and let the door shut behind her with a clang.

Good, Christine thought, weary, looking around the store at the mess she still had to clean up before she could close her eyes. She hoped they wouldn't come back.

CHAPTER
TWENTY-ONE

B y the time Laurel and Isaac returned to the Mobleys' farm, the trash-fire party was well underway, grim and silent. Garrett set the fire in an empty oil drum, stoking it high with dry apple branches and scrap wood from an old chicken tractor. The sweet smell of woodsmoke wasn't enough to mask the stench of burning rayon/cotton/polyester blend, but from where Laurel stood a few steps away, its glow was pretty. The firelight was the best place for thinking, but Laurel didn't want to think.

She missed the sunlight, the way it made the fields and the people in them glow. She turned thoughts of rot and bone to thoughts of flushed pink skin and want warmed through her. She wanted Ricky. Not the quiet, moody man he'd become in her absence but the boy he'd been, loud and wild enough to drown out any darkness creeping into her thoughts. Back then, he'd plug his aux cord into the tape deck of the Buick and let her drive from dusk until dawn to a soundtrack about beer and weed and girls who were far meaner than Laurel had ever been to him. He let them play with no more accompaniment than his drumming on the dashboard, occasionally pausing the song to let her know when the best part was about to come on.

But the Buick was out of commission, and there was no music. Every once in a while, Garrett would glance at his phone like he was thinking about turning something on to fill the quiet. Even the sound of the furious rock he preferred, all bass and distortion blaring through cheap phone speakers, would have been welcome over the silent stars, but it seemed he couldn't pick the right soundtrack for the end of the world. He stared into the quickening night with the rest of them.

Laurel saw a window of opportunity as Ricky struggled to his feet and wandered away from the fire, back toward the house. "Gonna get some water," he muttered, staggering a little under the spell of firelight. She let him start on his way and jogged to catch up when he was halfway there, just out of hearing range of his brother and Isaac. She reached out her hand to tap his shoulder.

"I want to talk to you," she said.

He caught her hand in his fingers, turning it palm-up. The ridges of his calluses scraped against the tough skin of her hand. He skated around a new blister on her palm, one she'd barely noticed beyond the normal sting of sweat-in-wound that marked the high heat of summer. Funny, she was nearly numb to the feeling now, but the blisters were still there. They bubbled up under calluses that caught splinters and sliced open under a pocketknife's kiss. Her hands held on to scars.

Laurel thought of the secrets Christine had read in her palm, a relative stranger with only enough time for a quick glance. How much more would Ricky know if she let him truly see her, even in the dimming light? Before she could think about it, her hand slipped out of his grasp.

He smirked as she pulled away, looking as though he'd won a bet with himself. "No, you don't." He turned from her and continued to the house, sticking his hands into the deep pockets of his jeans.

"Yes, I do," she insisted. Under the tension and twisting fear he was holding inside his mouth, there must be a part of him that wanted her. She could feel it without touching him. If she let her hands linger on him, there was no telling what she could make him do. He was here, he was alive, sunlight-warm wherever their skin touched. Couldn't he just make it easy for her?

He didn't turn around when she grabbed for his shoulder, simply stepping aside so her hand glanced off. "Go talk to Isaac some more."

"Isaac's leaving." She hadn't meant to blurt it out, but she wanted to say it before someone else could bring it up. It was easier to hear from her mouth than anyone else's.

Ricky shrugged, shoving open the door to the house. One of the dogs on the couch gave a huff of acknowledgment as Ricky stepped into the kitchen. He paused to kick his shoes off on the linoleum floor. "No, he's not."

"He said he is," Laurel insisted, sliding in behind him.

Ricky picked a jar from the cabinet and filled it with water at the sink. After a moment's thought, he filled one for Laurel, too. "It's like I told Garrett: You two are in an upset about something that won't happen. He's got a dream, and he's dragging everyone along with it, but that's all he's got. He's not getting out of here. If you didn't, none of us are."

She should have walked away. She knew the flavor of a fight in the air. She knew things between her and Ricky were so fragile they might not survive an argument like this one. But she didn't care anymore. She'd rather fight and lose than keep waiting for something to start.

"You're angry."

"You're damn right." He said it matter-of-factly, but his knuckles whitened around the mason jar. She wanted to pry his fingers from the glass and soften his grip just a little. "Should've stayed gone, Laurel. You coming back is the catalyst for all this, you know that? Home for a week and now there's bloodshed in my backyard. That's just how you are, though, ain't it?"

He didn't wait for her to answer. He set his water glass on the table and made for his room. She stood in the doorway and watched him kneel, fishing a shoebox out from under his bed.

"Really? You're smoking right now?"

"Yes," he said, shouldering past her, his voice twisted into something mocking and nasty. "Right now. I'm smoking the taste of blood out of my mouth. You are welcome to join me if you wish. If not, Garrett and Isaac are over there."

Laurel didn't smoke, but she didn't mind the acrid smell. It reminded her of summer nights in her Buick, familiar enough even under these alien circumstances. She could still salvage this.

She followed Ricky's shadow out the door and into the yard to the old trampoline where they'd played together as children. She slipped through the Velcro flap after him. They didn't talk for a while. She settled onto her back as he sat cross-legged next to her, packing a bowl. The spark of the lighter, the brightening glow as he inhaled, the cloud of smoke blotting out the stars above them. The night was all fire and shadow; bright, ephemeral flickers of light and long, blanketing stretches of dark. He took another deep inhale, his fingers dangling by his knee.

She reached out, barely managing to brush the tips of her fingers against his before he pulled away. "I still like you," she said.

"Of course you like me. We're friends. But you're not in love with me." He said it so simply, like it was something they'd talked about often as the weather.

"I could be." It fell from her lips like she was casting a spell, fervently hoping as she pushed each syllable out into the air that it would find some truth to latch on to, a place to grow.

But Ricky laughed. "You're scared of the future, so the past looks better in comparison. That's not love."

Laurel's face burned red. She closed her eyes to the stars above her; searching for the right words to say was like holding an injured bird in her hands. She had to work up the courage to say the thing that would snap the neck of whatever fragile casualty of fear lived between them.

Ricky's fingers traced her jaw, sweet. He ran his fingers through her hair, untangling some of the blond strands from the braid she'd worked them into. She let him, lying still, afraid any movement might frighten him away.

His voice was rough with smoke and sentiment. "I adore you, Laurel. Don't take offense, but I'd make a shitty farmwife, and that's all you seem to want."

"I'm not asking you to marry me," she spat, eyes fluttering open. There was something sharp in his expression as he looked down at her, eyes glittering like broken glass.

So, it was still a fight.

Good.

She wanted it this way. She didn't know how to be loved, petted into submission like one of his dogs. She only knew how to hold someone at arm's length. She'd already been cut open once today, and so had he. Shallow cuts scabbed his forearms where he'd thrown them up to protect himself. Fighting when already wounded was a good way to really get hurt. Laurel didn't care.

"You've got *American Gothic* in your eyes, sweetheart." He mimed holding a pitchfork, standing stock-still and serious. She pushed at his chest, hard, but he didn't bend.

"Fuck you. Stop deflecting every time I think you're starting to talk serious."

"I am talking serious. I've been trying to tell you as much since you came home. You don't want me. You want to fasten yourself to the matching half of your headstone and barrel toward death. I want to live." His voice cracked. "I've still got options. I've still got a future."

Her voice was hollow as a bird bone in her throat. She nearly choked on the words. "Well, all I've got is magic."

To her surprise, Ricky burst into laughter. He picked up the lighter and inhaled another lungful of smoke. As she stared up at him in shock, he looked down at her, still chuckling, releasing puffs of smoke as he laughed. "Magic," he said thickly. "Of course you do. You never played the princess, growing up. Always had to rescue yourself."

Laurel's nails dug into her wrists. She pulled herself up into a seated position. "Don't laugh at me. I'm scared out of my mind."

Ricky took a deep breath before speaking. "I've been scared this whole damn time. I'm helpless and can do nothing to save myself. Of course you're facing down magic with more magic. You're scared? You've got the solution. Buck up. Get brave."

"It's the same stuff that killed my mother," she hissed, her hands trembling as she raised them to her face. She rubbed at

147

her eyes before tears could fall. Her fingers stung with the salt she wiped away.

Ricky was angry now, angry that she was crying even though he was seconds away from it himself. His eyes were overbright as he leaned in, close enough that she could smell his aftershave under the smoke. "*Dry Valley* killed your mother. She had no way out and no way through. Magic didn't kill her; it wasn't enough to save her. Unless she had enough magic to raze the town to the ground, it never would have been."

Even through her fury, she knew the angle she'd have to turn to kiss him. He wouldn't forgive her if she did, if she ruined this by taking all the anger and fear and hatred and turning it physical. He'd rather she slapped him. "You weren't there to know her. You only know your parents' stories and what I've told you."

He didn't move an inch, frozen in place across from her while the bowl he packed burned itself out, his eyes locked on hers. "You never knew her either. But I know you. I see what's coming down the line for you. Have since the day you came back. But you're not your mother, Laurel. You won't be. I promise."

"I don't want promises you can't keep. I don't want to talk about my mother or the future you see for me. I wanna talk about us. Now. Something I can control. It's a simple question. Do you want me or not?"

Ricky sucked his teeth. He wiped his wet eyes with the heel of his hand. "Fuck, Laurel, I think I miss you. You used to have this insight, this hope, before you went away. Right now, all I've got is a double handful of your fear. I'm not sure what to do with it. There's enough of it in me to start with. I can't take more."

Laurel's mouth was a grim line. Her voice was cold when she said, "Well then, I'll go. I'll take my fear, and I'll leave." She scrambled up ungracefully to hop off the trampoline. Ricky cached the bowl and clambered after her, leaving the shoebox on the trampoline.

"Will you quit it?" he called after her. "This isn't me rejecting you!"

"Then what is it?" Laurel tossed over her shoulder. She gave them both the consideration of not waiting around for an answer he couldn't give.

She left him standing in the dark and made her way toward the fire.

CHAPTER
TWENTY-TWO

S omething was watching Isaac from the fields beyond the Mobley house. It didn't bother him. Twilight was a time for quiet observation, when creatures that slept through the day moved under the cover of darkness. The eyes upon him belonged to deer or maybe coyote prowling for field mice and rabbits in the tall grass.

Instinct instructed his eyes to fall into soft focus when the sun went down. Isaac knew if he tried to focus on the whispering shift of the waving grass, he'd see things that weren't there. Pale faces with long teeth and monstrous things moving through the encroaching shadows. So, he watched Garrett instead.

Garrett's face was another changed thing in the twilight. Instead of making him monstrous, the shifting light underscored a different side of him, a little too human. He'd cleaned his cuts in the bathroom but hadn't shaved, and the shadow on his face darkened by the hour. Twilight magnified the stubborn jut of his chin, the hollows of his cheeks, the furrow in his brow that fear had deepened, the smudges under his eyes from little, restless sleep. He seemed content to stay silent, gravel digging into the palm of his hand that had settled on the ground inches away from Isaac's. Garrett liked silence. He wouldn't try to fill the space with useless words.

Isaac sprawled on his stomach in the grass, resting his chin on his hands. The fire popped, sending a butterfly's wing of ash fluttering down into his hair. White clover tickled his nose, its perfume light and sweet. If necessary, Isaac could claim he was watching the lightning bugs sparkling along the dried-out creek bed behind the Mobley house, but he wouldn't need the excuse. In the twilight, Isaac could look as much as he liked. Garrett wouldn't notice, and if he did, he wouldn't mind.

By his estimation, Isaac had about five minutes left to be in love with Garrett Mobley before the sun set and the only light left was the dim red fire in the oil barrel. Depending on when Laurel and Ricky came back, he might have a little less. But if he could take a minute to let his heart fill up with the sentiment that he'd spend the rest of his life trying to purge, it would make the distance between their fingers a little more bearable, a little harder to cross.

He thought of how Garrett looked fourteen years ago, sun-flecked with a smear of reddish dust across the white knees of his uniform. He stood out in such contrast to the blur of other grass-stained, buzz-cut boys on the baseball field. Garrett had looked up at him with hard green eyes and a milk-sour scowl. To Isaac, it felt like coming upon an unexpected mirror the second before he recognized his own face. He and Garrett had the same stiff spines. They both knew, before they knew why, that life in Dry Valley would always be a fight for them.

Garrett had taken on the challenge as good-naturedly as he shouldered hard work and heavy lifting. Isaac had spent his whole life looking for the exit.

Garrett didn't look like the boy Isaac had grown up with anymore. He looked more like a man Isaac might never get to know. Isaac took the face he knew and tried to add another fourteen years of scars and sun damage, a life lived apart. He tried to think of the years ahead as kinder ones than he knew Dry Valley could offer, the work a little easier than it would be, the sun a little cooler, the liquor a little smoother than any Garrett had bothered to purchase before. He added laughter lines that would never form if Garrett spent those fourteen years alone, waiting for Isaac to come back. He wouldn't spend them alone. Isaac wouldn't come back.

A smile fluttered, barely there, across Garrett's face when he turned to see Isaac watching him. The palm Garrett had pressed into the gravel overturned, and his fingers flexed. An invitation, Isaac knew, to take or to overlook as he wanted.

Before he could move, Laurel stomped her way through the grass and up to the trash fire, fists clenched. Garrett pulled his hand back hastily to avoid being stepped on. "I need to go home," she said.

Alarm shot through Garrett. "Right now?"

She pressed her knuckles under her nose and bit at her fingernail. It struck Isaac as a childish thing to do, gnawing her nails to the quick. He looked away when she spat into the grass. "Given the conversation I just had with Ricky, it's probably best I don't sleep here."

Isaac shook his head. "I don't want you going back to the farm on your own."

"I don't want to leave without you, but I can't stay here with him." Laurel dropped cross-legged onto the ground next to him. Restless energy bowed her shoulders as she watched the fire.

"Can't you wait?" Garrett asked.

Laurel looked back at the house but didn't say anything. Isaac thought of Garrett's upturned palm and understood. "I know a place we can go. You won't like it, but it'll be somewhere to sleep tonight, and I can get a clean change of clothes."

Garrett caught on half a second before realization dawned on Laurel's face. "Absolutely not."

Isaac's stomach sank. Bringing up the apartment where he still lived with his father was like handing them a bomb and asking them to hold it for a moment. But he hadn't armed it against them; they'd just forgotten its ticking in the midst of new, more interesting terror.

Laurel dug her toe into the gravel, stubbing out the idea. "Garrett's right. We don't need to go there, not this late. We'll buy you another pair of jeans from Walmart. We don't mind if it'll tide you over."

Isaac bristled. It was thoughtless charity, dismissive of actual need. Something to handle the inconveniences he brought along with him. Mitigating fear and guilt. "*I* mind. I like my clothes. And it's not just clothes. I've got photographs, some letters. Some of my mom's things. My diploma. It's not like everything I keep there is a waste."

"That's not what she's saying," Garrett murmured. But it was.

Isaac shook his head. "He won't be there tonight, anyways. He's out with his girlfriend. Should be gone all weekend. Plenty of time to get what we need and get out. He won't even notice if he comes home to an empty apartment. And if he does, he won't care."

"So, what, we load the truck up and move you out to Cincinnati tonight?" Laurel said, her mouth a lipless line of irritation. She stared at the darkness behind him, shaking her head so minutely he didn't think she realized she was doing it.

Isaac's words were thin. When it came to the apartment and the shrinking, sad parts of his life that still dwelled there, explanations were delicate things that broke under his teeth. It was hard to talk without feeling the jagged pieces left over tearing at his tongue. "I don't know what I'm saying. This wasn't my plan. I don't want to leave right now. I just . . ."

"If you did, you wouldn't want to stay here," Garrett said. Between the twilight and the night ahead of him, Isaac knew that if Garrett offered, he might relent. But Garrett wouldn't.

"You could stay with me," Laurel said. "I'd help you pack. If Jay understood the whole of your situation, I'm sure—"

"Don't tell Jay anything!" Isaac snapped before she could finish, loud enough that she flinched.

"He knows enough already," Laurel suggested gently.

"I don't want to know that!" Isaac cut her off before she could say more. "I mean, I don't want him to know. I can't control what he thinks—I don't want to tell him anything."

The hot-cold wash of shame flooded his body as he imagined a look of soft pity on Jay's face. He'd rather take a punch.

It wouldn't be much worse than the way Garrett and Laurel were watching him, like he was spitting blood. He wanted to be like Laurel, to jut his chin out and glare the world down. *I've decided this. Deal with it.* Isaac stared at the collar of the shirt she was wearing rather than look at her face. It brushed the hollow of her throat.

"Fine," she murmured, like she was cornering a wounded animal. That was almost as bad. "I won't tell him anything. I'll just move you into the back bedroom, and if he has anything to say about it, I'll get into another shouting match with him. I'm getting pretty good at that."

"If I didn't have to, I never would," he said. It wasn't a promise, but it was as close as he could get to one. "Tomorrow, I could leave. But it's a place we can stay tonight."

"I'll stay there with you if you're certain," Laurel agreed, though she didn't sound certain herself. "And if you promise you'll let me help you leave tomorrow."

Garrett struggled to his feet, reaching for his truck keys. The twitch of his fingers over his pocket said no. The half second where his eyes flicked over the fire and past them into the darkness said, "Stop me." He was relying on Isaac to read him, to know him.

But he could read Isaac well enough to know that Isaac wouldn't give him the out. *Deal with it,* Isaac thought. It was easier to say. Garrett would take what he could get.

CHAPTER
TWENTY-THREE

L aurel's stomach dropped when she heard the snore. She would have turned around and backed out the door then and there if Garrett hadn't already torn out of the parking lot, leaving them stranded. She cast an alarmed glance at Isaac, who bit his lip hard, shook his head, and took a careful step into the apartment with all the certainty of a man walking to the gallows. With nowhere else to go, Laurel followed him into his personal hell.

Laurel had been allowed over before, a few rare times when Isaac knew his father wouldn't be around. She did not know the space well enough to lead the way toward Isaac's room, creeping past the couch on which Isaac's father had passed out, shirtless and snoring. Laurel tried to follow the path Isaac walked, trailing him through the dark kitchen into the questionable safety of his bedroom, a step behind as he settled one foot onto a floorboard he knew would not creak, then the next. The topography of safety was imprinted onto his mind. Laurel had never had to learn to fear the sound of her own footsteps.

Isaac turned on a lamp, illuminating a room that was spare, but not stark. His bed was made, a navy comforter tugged across its edges, and his shoes made a crooked line under its perimeter. Most of the books on the particleboard bookshelf were class assignments, hand-me-downs from Ricky's classes the year before. No framed pictures. Glass might shatter.

"What's he doing here?"

Isaac didn't meet her gaze. He moved slowly, lowered himself down on the floor by the bed and sat there stiffly, fiddling with the carpet. "Not sure, unless she's dumped him. They fight sometimes."

"So he's angrier than usual?" Laurel kept her voice at a whisper, even as she panicked.

"He won't wake up until midday, and the hangover should slow him down." His voice was smaller here, and she did not think it was entirely to prevent them from being overheard.

"Are you sure?"

Isaac didn't answer. He pulled a binder labeled ENGLISH 3 B:2 out from under his bed. "I've got some old pictures in here, if you want to look at them."

With nothing better to do, Laurel held the binder in her lap, thumbing listlessly through the pages, too wired from fear and the thought of magic to find sleep. Laurel let him narrate through memories they shared. It seemed to calm him. *Remember that time?*

Every Kodak print from the disposable camera was an obvious labor of love. The nearest drugstore was a mile's walk from the apartment complex, and his handwriting labeled the back of each photo with names and dates. Milk-white, red-eyed ghost children peered back at Laurel, gap-toothed grins stretched across their faces. Isaac with a sunfish, Garrett and Ricky tussling in the long grass, Laurel little more than a speck, floating down the river on a neon-pink blow-up raft. The next page was four blurry shots of a deer peering at the photographer from the edge of the woods, taken in the misty morning after a night at camp. There were a couple of Jay, camera tilted upward, the angle admiring.

This was home for Isaac. Not a bed, but a binder. His treasures captured in negatives and drugstore prints, a reminder that he could reach out and touch happy memories even when he couldn't conjure them in his mind.

His finger came to rest on a last photo, Isaac and Laurel, no more than eight or nine. They'd turned the disposable camera around to point at themselves, before selfie sticks and smartphones. The photo, a little blurry and overexposed, captured a piece of each of them: wide, flaring nostrils and laughing mouths, a tangle of Laurel's hair, the dusty freckles across Isaac's cheeks. Anyone else would have thrown away the accidental image. But with the same care as with the artful deer portraits, Isaac had labeled it "Laurel + Isaac, Summer '08!" in smeary, blue, left-handed scrawl.

There was no way to tell how much the children in that picture had lost. It was only evident what they stood to lose. There was joy there, love and family. How could he sleep with that under his bed every night and still think about leaving?

But Kevin's snoring in the next room was loud enough to remind her that Isaac still had something to lose. His father slept fitfully, drunk and dreamless. If his father woke to find her in his apartment, she didn't want to think about the confrontation that might ensue.

Isaac pulled the comforter off the twin bed and patted the mattress. "You sleep here, I'll crash on the floor."

"Trade you. I think the floor will be firmer on my back." It was a stupid excuse, but she wanted to put herself up like a wall between Isaac and his father.

Isaac was too tired to argue. He handed her a set of spare sheets he kept folded under his bed. She took them from him, wrapping them tightly around her so that they added some softness between her and the thin carpet covering a concrete floor.

"Get the light?" she asked, and he turned off the lamp. In the darkness, light from the street filtered in through a crack in the curtain. She could hear Isaac, the papery whisper of his cheap sheets, as he shifted on the mattress.

She wondered about his Cincinnati dreams. Maybe they would keep him safe. Maybe they would bring him happiness she couldn't foresee. But Laurel couldn't accept those dreams yet. If she truly needed to belong to the farm, to claim it as her own, she could not go back alone. Home was not home without Isaac Graves.

She woke a few hours later to her phone buzzing on the nightstand. The second call she'd missed from Jay flashed across the screen. She sent him a quick text message to put him off.

Am fine. Just woke up. Slept in Dry Valley. Isaac with me.

A minute later, her phone buzzed again.

When will you be home??

She didn't bother to answer. She shot off a quick text to Garrett, letting him know they'd need the truck as soon as he could spare it. Daylight was wasting.

Isaac was still asleep, snoring openmouthed with the sheet wrapped around his waist. He'd managed to get his shirt off, but Laurel could see the torn cuff of his jeans peeking out from under the comforter. *Gross.*

She knew she'd have to work quickly to get Isaac's things out of the house in one trip. She'd let him determine essentials from his bedroom while she checked the other room to see if there was anything he needed to take. Just a cursory glance, in and out, and they could leave. She let him sleep a second longer and stepped out into the kitchen.

She tried to re-create the path Isaac had taken the night before. In the daylight, she faltered, missing the marks Isaac knew so well. Each step sounded louder than the last, but Isaac's father didn't stir. *Probably too drunk,* she reassured herself.

As Laurel moved around the kitchen, looking for anything Isaac might need, she began to piece together an error in her thinking moments too late: She'd thought of his dad as a dysfunctional drunk. After all, that was the way Isaac described him if forced. She had imagined an empty fridge decorated sparsely with expired mustard and Miller Lites, but there were pizzas in the freezer and takeout in the fridge. She expected the cigarette-and-sweat scent of a perpetual hangover to bog down the room. Instead, the apartment smelled like trash just gone over and yesterday's coffee still sitting in the machine. She looked for evidence of a weekend bender but could only count two cans on the coffee table and three more at the bottom of the trash bin. He might have been a drunk, but he was not drunk enough to excuse the way Isaac flinched sometimes when she squeezed his shoulder.

Isaac was the only one who made excuses for his father, and drunkenness was always first to take the blame for any bruise Isaac wore. It was an easier monster, a television monster, to assume that Kevin Graves was wasted and wild, too drunk to be in control, too drunk to mean it. There was some forgiveness to the thought that this was the best he could do or that if he knew better, it might stop.

The more complicated monster went to work and church with folks who thought of him as an all right sort and then came home and beat his son because he thought hurt was something Isaac ought to inherit.

Which made the sound of his breathing shifting from sleep to wakefulness all the more dangerous.

"You're awful bold," he said from the couch.

"Would you like some coffee?" she offered, resisting the urge to turn around.

"Think that's supposed to be my line, given that you're standing in my house."

"I won't be for long," Laurel said. "Blink and I'm gone. Isaac with me. We don't want to disturb your weekend any more than we already have."

"You're awful bold," he said again. "But then, you think he's yours; why shouldn't you take him? Always moving that boy around like a chess piece. Y'all like him around when he's working for you, sure. When you decide you don't want him around anymore, though, you make him my problem again."

"Isaac's not a *problem*—" she began.

"Laurel." Isaac's voice sounded from the doorway to his bedroom. It should have been thick with sleep, but exhaustion wasn't a safe feeling in this house, so Isaac had shaken it off already. He was dressed and had his shoes on. "Can you go ahead and help me with the box under the bed? Truck's not five minutes out."

"What truck?" his father drawled. "That prissy little green one tearing through the parking lot at all hours, disturbing the hardworking people in this building trying to get some sleep?"

"Go on," Isaac told her. "I'll only be a minute."

"It's time to go," Laurel insisted.

"Take him with you when you leave," Isaac's father barked.
Laurel was tempted to whirl around and say something cutting.

"Don't," Isaac said, barely moving his mouth.

Laurel kept her back to the wall and her ear toward the door
as she returned to the bedroom. She picked up her phone, looking at her screen. Another text from Jay.

Weeding is waiting on you.

At that moment, she missed him terribly. He had only ever
offered her protection. He'd never been the source of a wound.

Laurel could hear the conversation through the cracked
door. "Yeah, I saw him dropping you off. Think I haven't figured you out yet, Isaac?" The way Kevin pronounced his name
sounded like a taunt. "That I haven't noticed you chasing after
him? Everybody in this town knows about Garrett Mobley.
Should have known you'd find a way to make yourself a part
of that. Should have known you'd bring it back here someday."

"I didn't bring him here," Isaac whispered, unwittingly ad-
mitting there'd been something with Garrett that he could take.

Kevin sighed like Isaac's voice exhausted him. "Figures. You've
never been a man, not really. Never acted like one. Sneaking out
to do God knows what, spending every cent you make a long
way from here, all while I work myself to death. What are you
doing?"

"I'm not doing anything," Isaac said.

In the bedroom, Laurel held her phone, unsure whether or
not to send another text to Garrett. She hoped Ricky was coming, too. That he was armed.

"You let that Early girl sleep on my floor last night. Waltzed in here like she owned the place, shuffling around my refrigerator for food my paycheck puts on this fuckin' table. She paying rent? You sure ain't. You're not even sorry."

Laurel sent the text.

HURRY

Isaac's chances of getting away were dwindling fast, but it seemed to slow him down. He was unpredictable around his father. He spoke a language of survival she didn't know. Every time she opened her mouth, she made it worse. She couldn't read his moods or watch his clenched frame for signs of violence. She had never had to fear a father. She'd never had to fear anyone in her life.

She didn't look to see if Garrett replied. She picked up her bag, aware that she had nothing to defend herself with. She usually liked having her LCP on her, but the real threat of violence permeating the room made her hand twitch. She wished she had it just in case.

When she came into the living room, Isaac's hand was covering his face. She hadn't heard a blow; he might have been anticipating one. His father was sitting on the couch, still as stone. He snarled a word that made Laurel blanch.

Laurel stepped between them. "You shut your mouth and lay off him, or—"

Kevin stood up. His presence swallowed up the cramped apartment. Laurel took a step back. He wasn't a giant, but he was a man. Bigger, muscled from work. Dangerous. He looked at Laurel but spoke to Isaac. "I'm the bad guy here. For taking you in and trying my best to raise you right, despite all the rotten shit inside of you that wasn't my doing in the first place."

"You're a fucking saint," Laurel spat.

"And you're not welcome in my home." Laurel marveled that even in his cold, alien face, she could see the shape of Isaac's nose and the warm brown of his eyes. But before he could touch her, Isaac was between them. He didn't say anything. Just stood there, staring at the carpet as though he could see through it.

His father smirked and took a small step back, hands up in mock surrender. "I don't ask for much. Only for you to act right. God knows I've given everything, and you've never had a problem taking from me."

"He was a kid!" Laurel shouted and Isaac clamped a hand around her arm.

"And now he's an adult, but he hasn't grown up. Never shown gratitude for the life I wasted on him."

"Some life," Isaac muttered, turning toward the bedroom.

His father slapped him. Open-handed and hard, the sick sound of skin connecting with flesh. Laurel had seen fistfights, bad ones, between boys with red in their eyes and girls just as willing to tear into someone as they were to walk away. Those were angry, brutal things, but there was always a little honor to them. She'd never really heard the sound a slap made when it was meant to break someone.

Her hand reached into her purse before she could think about it, before she could remember there was nothing there.

Neither of them knew that.

"Don't you dare, Laurel Early," Isaac hissed, his hand covering his jaw.

"You got a gun in there?" his father said with a laugh. He splayed his hands out, inviting her to try. An easy shot at center mass. "You gonna kill me in my own house?"

"We're going to leave, and we're not coming back. Any of us." She wondered if Isaac would argue, but he only stared at the oatmeal-colored carpet, his eyes unfocused. He was already gone. "We'll just get his stuff—"

But Kevin blocked her. His hand was on her shoulder, but his words were for Isaac. "Nothing here's his. You parasite. Get the fuck out."

Out on the street, Isaac rounded on her. "You were going to shoot him?"

"He hit you." She thought it would be all she'd need to say on the matter. *He hit you.*

But Isaac laughed. "Wouldn't be the first time he hit me. It would, however, be the first time you shot someone."

Laurel shook her head. "I wasn't armed."

"So, you threatened him without anything to back it up? Don't you think if you'd stayed inside the bedroom for another two minutes we might have gotten away?"

"I'm sorry," she whispered to the pavement.

"My things are still in there, and now I don't know how—"

"He hit you," Laurel insisted, spacing out each syllable as though she could get him to understand what it meant. He had to understand. After all, it had happened to him. "I wasn't thinking. I just decided—"

"You sure do make a lot of decisions," he said, exhausted. Laurel tried to speak, letting out a frustrated sound she couldn't form into a word. Isaac waved it away as Garrett's truck pulled into the parking lot. "It doesn't matter. It's like Christine said. You had to mean going home. I can't think of anywhere you'd rather be after this."

For all they call you the devil's daughter, you've got no idea what

165

it's like to be raised by one. Too late, the broken pieces of Isaac's moods and fears, the promises he hadn't made last night, and the future he hoped for solidified before her. She'd gone too far. She had to do something to make it right.

CHAPTER
TWENTY-FOUR

I saac remembered the last time he believed Laurel Early might be magic. They were nine or ten, and they'd snuck off behind a pine tree to hide and talk and do whatever the kids the class disliked did when they realized there was nothing to stop them from liking each other. Her hair was a rat's nest, always falling out of the thin braids she'd put in herself, and there were black moons of dirt and paint underneath her fingernails. She'd pulled a pair of safety scissors from her back pocket and brandished them at him in her excitement. "We're going to be blood brothers—siblings," she said, correcting herself. "Since we don't have any brothers or sisters of our own."

It seemed sound enough reasoning that they should be siblings without having to involve the scissors. After all, most kids in their school had a mess of siblings staggered throughout the elementary–middle–high school complex that served the whole county. Having someone who had your back had always been a dream of Isaac's. He had trouble saying no to Laurel, but could, upon occasion, work himself up to an uncertain-sounding "I guess . . ." that would at least put a momentary stop to her more outrageous plans, like a baby-bird-rehabilitation clinic under the pines behind the soccer field or a makeshift hair salon when his bangs started to fall in front of his eyes.

He was working up to just that, but Laurel already had the scissors poised over her index finger. She'd go first. Of course she would. "With this cut, we will mingle our blood together. My blood will run in your veins and yours in mine," she intoned in a low, mystical voice that she'd pulled from a television show or one of the weird paperback novels she kept hidden under her desk during math class. She dragged the blade of the scissors across her finger. A white streak of pressure bloomed in its wake, but it did not break the skin, no matter how many times she tried.

"Hmm," she muttered, testing the edge again. Too dull.

"I'm sure there's some broken glass in the sandbox if we dig," Isaac offered, though he hoped he was wrong. He did not particularly want to bleed. He wanted to be bound to someone who didn't want to cut him.

Laurel shook her head, dismissing the glass idea. She took his hand instead, looking with such focus into his eyes that Isaac was paralyzed. "With this vow, I promise to be your sister for as long as we both shall live."

"Yeah," Isaac agreed in a whisper, relieved as she tucked the scissors back into her pocket.

He tried to pull his hand away, but Laurel shook her head, so hard that the remains of her braid whipped around her head. "You've got to say it back," she whined. "It's already iffy without the blood."

Isaac was blushing so hard he could barely get his mouth to move. "With this vow," he said, "I promise to be your brother."

"For as long as we both shall live," Laurel finished with him, nodding encouragingly. "It's done." She squeezed his hand and let it go. Isaac watched a colony of ants crawling at the edge of the grass, so happy he wanted to hide.

He had never been wanted by anyone like that before—and hadn't been since. Not even Garrett loved him that way. He loved with reservations, with self-preservation. He could disengage if things got too spiky, but Isaac and Laurel were too entangled, blood flowing through each other's veins, if only through the tenuous, theoretical magic of childhood devotion.

But maybe that magic hadn't been so theoretical after all. Maybe there was a spell between them, something they'd managed to weave without knowing what it was they held. Now Laurel needed to go home if she had a chance of saving it. Isaac had to help her.

Her lips a thin white line, Laurel rested her hand on the door as though she might jump out of the truck to vomit. After a second, she pulled her hand away and set it limply on her lap. She took a deep breath and closed her eyes, settling back in her seat. Her hands twisted, palm up, palm down. She held them up toward the sky like she was praying, then dropped them to her knees, fingers pinching like she was trying to grasp at something none of them could see.

"I was just thinking how stupid I look," she muttered, her drawl as soft as the mullein leaves growing at the edge of the drive. They were steps away from her farm, but Garrett idled, waiting for her to make up her mind. "I don't think it did anything at all, coming home. Christine was wrong, or she was lying. This is just—"

The greenish sunlight filtering through the walnut leaves hit her cheeks in places that made her a little hard to recognize. Isaac stared, trying to reconcile this woman, strange and scared and a little bit magic, with Laurel Early, the skinny little girl he'd always known. The longer he looked, the easier it was.

There on her right index finger was the V-shaped scar she'd cut into it when they were teaching themselves to twirl knives, and there, peeking out from under the crew-neck collar of Ricky's shirt, was the edge of a sandblasted birthmark. Nobody else chewed their nails down until the edges were as ragged as the limestone ridges above the river. Those strange hands could be a witch's hands. Maybe they always had been.

"You said I could stay. Did you mean it? Because if you didn't—"

"I mean it," Laurel promised, threading their fingers together. Her hand was so much smaller than his, but her grip was firm and steady. "I mean it. But I haven't done it yet. Tell you what, you boys drive on down to the house. I'll walk behind you and see if I can't do it standing in the woods instead of sitting in a car."

It was a little more than a mile from the mailbox to Laurel's front door. Even if she walked briskly, Isaac didn't like the idea of her out there on her own with something evil hunting her down.

Garrett shook his head. "I don't think that's wise. You know what happened last time you were alone in these woods."

"I didn't know what I was doing then."

"And you know more now?" Garrett leveled back. His voice was mild but Isaac knew that tone. He'd heard Garrett use it this past fall to ask him, *Are you sure you don't?*

It said, *I know you're wrong. But I know you need to be right.*

It rattled in Isaac's head every time he wondered if maybe he ought to change his mind.

But Laurel didn't seem as swayed by Garrett's tone. Her hand flexed a little in Isaac's palm, like she was clenching her fist. "I do. I will. I have to."

"I'll stick with you," Isaac blurted before he could think better of it. Garrett muttered something like *The hell with this,* but he didn't lift his foot from the brake. His hand hovered over the gearshift like he was thinking about reversing out of the driveway.

"No, you won't," Laurel said, withdrawing her hand from his palm. "I've put you through enough this morning."

The anger and shame, so thick it had numbed him before, rushed in. He could feel it flare hot across his face. He started to argue, but Garrett mouthed, *Leave it,* and as quick as it had come, the fight drained from him. Isaac crossed his arms over his chest and said, "You've got twenty minutes before we come after you."

"I can do it in fifteen," Laurel said, and she slid off the bench seat and out of the truck, bouncing back on her heels as she landed. It was false confidence, cockiness, but Isaac wanted to believe her as much as she needed him to believe in her.

"See you then," he said.

Garrett lifted his foot off the brake, and the truck rolled forward down the sloping driveway to the farm. Isaac watched Laurel in the rearview mirror, shrinking behind them as she stood on the gravel path with her eyes closed, willing something into existence that he couldn't comprehend. Nothing seemed different. There was no impenetrable bubble of protection sloped down from the sky to encase the whole of the farm, nor were they sparkling with fairy light thick enough to repel the dust kicked up by the truck's tires. Isaac's breathing came a little easier, but that happened every time he set foot on the Early farm.

Maybe the only magic was in meaning it.

He knew he couldn't help her but decided to try, throwing up his own little intention, mingling with hers. *I'm home. I'm home.*

CHAPTER
TWENTY-FIVE

Laurel opened her eyes to nothing new. "Just me," she said aloud. The woods were no different than they'd been the previous morning. The only thing that had changed was her perception of what lurked within them. Her fear was not unwarranted. What was unwarranted was letting it get the better of her. The woods had never cared if she lived or died. They'd taken many and they'd take more. There had always been something at the edge of the tree line, watching her, and there would be so long as anything lived in them. When she was a child, had she stayed away from the shallow creeks that ran down to the river to avoid the copperheads cooling themselves in the water? Had the howl of coyotes at the edge of the woods kept her from looking up at the stars?

No. She'd be cautious. She'd stay alert. She'd use the tools she'd been given to find a way out of this. Buttercup and thistle sprouted from the gravel driveway. The gray dust scuffed under her boots as she wandered toward the house, looking for the right place to start. Sweat beaded her forehead and she struggled to breathe in the humid summer air. She'd have to get it done quickly, to keep the people on the farm safe, and get out of this heat without vomiting. She could smell it on the edge of the air; there'd be a storm soon enough. But there'd be no relief for her until this spell was cast. She just had to figure out how to cast it.

The south-facing hill behind the cemetery was the warmest place on the farm, a place where deer made their beds in the winter and raised their fawns in the summer. Tall fescue waved there, itchy and thick. A set of narrow paths that crossed the driveway and into the neighbor's property wove around the reddening blackberry brambles and blade-sharp honey locusts, all the way down the holler where Laurel had a deer stand and a trail camera attached to a tall red oak ready for fall bow-hunting.

Laurel's mind caught on the deer. She'd seen the devil go after them. If there was a place to hunt him down, it would be where she hunted most often.

But God, it was going to be a miserable little hike.

She swore softly under her breath as she cut off into the tick-infested fescue. Climbing back up the hill with the sun bearing down on her would be exhausting, though she supposed dying at the bottom of the holler would be even more of an inconvenience. She shuddered a little as the bite of brambles through her jeans tugged at her, begging her to stay or else carry a piece of them deeper into the waving grass. She could feel the sweat rolling down her back. Anything climbing up was likely a tick.

She paused for the barest second at a fork in the trail to either side of a narrow-leaf burdock plant when the first deer lit from the brush. She didn't see it, exactly, only the movement of the grass as it dove for cover in a copse of pine trees. A loud, huffing breath came from behind.

A second later, she was surrounded.

Deer blew to sound a warning. All around her, from so deep in the grass she could not see them, she heard the sound. They stomped in the underbrush and turned tail to escape. Everywhere she turned, she'd see a flash of white, a gangly limb, and hear another explosive breath.

Jay would get religion, in a grim way, like he'd already tasted the brimstone, every year the tobacco failed. In total, he'd been to church five times since Laurel's birth, but stopped searching for answers in the sermon every time his luck turned.

When she'd been young enough for white tights and Mary Janes, he'd tried to make sure she at least tried a taste of faith herself before she spat it back out. As was summer custom, the churches spilled out of their sanctuaries and packed white tents with people ready for a revival. She liked the singing but couldn't abide the talking. She'd squirmed in a hot metal chair for twenty minutes while the preacher warmed up, until Jay sent her to sit outside the tent to go "cool off" in the heat.

Laurel had spent the next hour and a half exactly the way she would have spent a Sunday at home, braiding grass and catching june bugs, waiting for Jay to bring her a paper plate and a Dixie cup of lemonade. The preacher's words filtered in and out of hearing, landing lightly as a cabbage butterfly out in the orange milkweed, beyond where the church mowed. But she'd heard a phrase once or twice that stuck with her, filtered through the fried speakers and the evangelist spit seeping into the mesh of the microphone: "the breath of God."

It surrounded her now, expelled through panicked lungs as God's creation judged her presence as a threat and bolted, leaving trampled blackberry brambles and flattened fescue in their wake.

Then, something cracked like a gunshot as it stepped out of the woods in front of her, and Laurel understood she had not been the threat the deer had run from.

The woods seemed to shudder around the figure escaping them. Tall enough that it brushed the tops of the elm saplings, the monster made of bones broke past the edge of the woods and started for Laurel. It seemed that some of its older, dried bones had given way and been replaced with newer flesh. In some places, it was hollow and desiccated, bones yellowed with age and sun or darkened with dried blood. In others, it was freshly skinned and inexpertly gutted, glistening black with old blood and the shimmer of fly wings on rotted flesh. Its grin a predator's smile out of a prey species' mouth and yes, she knew it was grinning, gleeful as it darted across the grass, right at her.

It's coming for my bones.

Hadn't the devil promised this fate for her? Here was the fight she knew was coming: protect herself or die. With every step it seemed faster than the night she'd run from it. She had no gun to save herself.

She considered vaguely what Christine had said about meaning it but found it didn't matter much. The voice in her head as it barreled toward her wasn't Christine's. It was her mother's, from a far-off dream.

The soil.

Seconds slipping away, she dropped to her knees, scratching her fingernails into the dry dirt. With her hand against the earth, she could feel a pulsing, like a heartbeat through thin skin. Had it always been pulsing, or had she summoned the sensation because she needed something to grab on to? In her body she could feel her breath, short in her chest, her heartbeat breaking down her ribs with fear and adrenaline, such a small and fluttering rhythm unsyncopated with the thrumming beneath her hand. She took a deep breath and felt the earth move, just a little, restless, like it was waiting for her cue.

It was a strange gift she didn't have time to puzzle out. Each pulse brought the monster closer, near enough that she could smell it in its rawness and rot, iron blood and salty decomposition. She could hear the cello strings of tight-drawn sinews caught in the mechanics of bone against bone, sawing across its rib cage. It was close enough that she could register the absence of heat and breath. There were engines with more life to them than this strange and silent creature.

The breath of God, she thought, remembering the warning the deer had left her with. She closed her eyes, scrunching them tight, and wished, "Keep us safe." Then, like blowing out candles, she let that prayer fall from her lips.

Wind roared around her, fast as a summer storm, and in its wake she saw a wash of pale petals, milkweed and blackberry and thorny foxtail seeds, whip across the clearing.

Under the force of the gust, the bones that made up the creature clattered and loosened, coming apart at the seams. They blew back across the clearing as though they were being tugged by an unseen force, recalled into the shadows of the woods on marionette strings. Laurel charged after them before she could decide whether that was wise. She nearly tripped over a tibia that had been left behind in the hasty retreat and saw more of the monster shed as she struggled past brambles to follow.

Yellowed bones remained, sprinkled liberally with petals like they'd been eulogized and tossed to the ground. She looked and looked, from the roots to the tops of the trees, but could not find the skull.

Still, there might be something in a withered rib that would let her know more about the origin of the monster.

When she held it, though, it was dead under her hands. The clearing was quiet as she waited for something to happen. Had she simply exhausted herself? Better to save it than let something else get its hands on the bone instead. Maybe it would not reassemble without all its original parts. Maybe she could buy herself some time.

She didn't understand the rules of this yet. She wasn't sure she believed her eyes.

"Magic," she breathed, and started to laugh, a startled shock coming from somewhere deep in her chest. She'd done it. How the hell had she done it? If it hadn't been for her mother's voice, she never would have thought . . . she scuffed the dirt with the toe of her boot, marveling. How much potential did the soil hold, after all? How much more did her mother know, buried beneath it?

In her back pocket, her phone buzzed.

Isaac texted:

Was that you?

She responded, breathless:

That was me. I did it.

Then come home, he said.

The walk down the hill was the most at ease she'd felt under the summer heat since coming home. She'd done it. She'd protected them all. What surprised her was how easy it had been.

CHAPTER
TWENTY-SIX

This is home now, Isaac thought. He didn't say it aloud. He didn't want to wake up the little back bedroom that had lain dormant for the better part of twenty years. He hadn't been able to bring anything with him, but there were things of his scattered throughout the house and the buildings beyond: a little money, a favored fiberglass fishing rod in Laurel's bedroom, a .22 rifle in the gun safe, his traps and lures in the shed, a few good knives where he could grab them if he needed. All valuable, all purposeful. Few sentimental. Nothing as practical as a pack of underwear or a box of dental floss.

None of the things in the room were his, and as such, he couldn't handle them like they were his things to move. Even the dust belonged to someone else. So, Isaac stood, a little at a loss, in the middle of the room, waiting for the dust to settle to the floor like he'd never been there.

The creak of the floorboards behind him said *Laurel in bare feet*. Her work boots stayed on the porch, their soles caked in dirt, their toes sprinkled with blood. Home was a place where her shoes had their place. Isaac's shoes stayed laced and on his feet. Ready to run.

"This was my room when I was a baby." She'd told him before, but it hadn't mattered then like it did now. The unspoken meaning: *I'm giving it to you*. Laurel ran a finger across the edge of the cast-iron crib that any contemporary parenting expert would immediately condemn. It had been hers. A truly startling arrangement of well-loved, long-forgotten dolls, belonging to several generations of Earlys, spread out across the crib mattress, with sunken plastic faces, half-lidded eyes teardrop blue, snarled twists of butter-yellow polyester hair glued to their scalps. "I know the mattress is a problem. And the dolls—" She frowned, brushing the coarse eyelashes of one open and shut. Her finger pad came away gray with dust. "I can take them to my room."

"You don't have to," he told her, but she shrugged. What was one more horror on her scorecard, really? At least this one was familiar, inherited. A product of love.

Isaac watched Laurel triage the room, measuring the work that needed to be done against the tired shadows of Isaac's eyes. She lifted up a corner of the blankets at the foot of the bed. Isaac craned his neck to see if there was still a mattress underneath. The comforter was really just a thick layer of dust resting upon a sedimentary stack of quilts, too old and valuable to throw away, but too thin to sleep under without them shredding like tissue paper. Who knew what was fossilized in between them?

"Let's get this bedding onto the laundry line. We can try to beat the dust out and let the sun take care of the rest."

Isaac cast a doubtful glance at the milky cellophane taped

across the windows, a vain attempt to prevent heat from leaking out in the wintertime. The light that filtered through it was cloudy white. He had an ache in the back of his head that promised rain.

"If we hurry," he said.

"What's the rush? Kick your shoes off; stay awhile. I've bought us some time." Laurel tapped his boot with her bare toes and turned from him, the tattling floorboard announcing her retreat. Isaac sighed, disturbing the dust. He didn't want to ask her how much time she thought she'd bought. He reached for his laces.

In the yard, Laurel brandished some sort of antique tennis racket she'd produced from the anachronistic piles of trash and treasure the Earlys housed in their disused upstairs attic. She beat showers of dust from the sheets while Isaac shifted from one foot to another with empty hands, grass tickling his bare ankles.

It was a relief to have a purpose when Garrett's truck returned from town, bearing Ricky, vast amounts of food, and jigsaw-puzzle pieces out of which Isaac was supposed to reassemble his life. Fresh towels and linens, a plastic dresser that once housed craft supplies but could now hold his clothes, a lamp he recognized from Garrett's nightstand, six or seven books that Ricky deemed interesting enough to lend out with no real worries about having them returned.

"Nice carpet beater, grandma," Ricky greeted Laurel.

"Nice to see you," Laurel replied, her tone so pointedly polite that Ricky flinched as though she'd pulled a knife on him.

With one eye on the carpet beater, he reached into the passenger seat and hefted a metal pan of fried chicken above another casserole tin that smelled warm and cheesy. Ricky shook the tins at her in offering. "I've got supper that needs setting up in the kitchen. Laurel?" he asked.

"I'll be right in." Laurel took another hard whack at the sheets, mostly, Isaac thought, for effect.

Ricky took a step back, careful to stay out of reach. "Won't you help me with some of this?" he asked like he was begging. Laurel huffed a sigh and handed Isaac the carpet beater.

Ricky seemed relieved. He turned to Isaac as though he was going to say something significant but swallowed it at the last moment. "Gonna be all right, huh?"

"Reckon I am," Isaac agreed. He wasn't sure he could say the same for Ricky.

Ricky gave a satisfied nod and ducked into the doorway of the farmhouse. Laurel was half a step behind, rolling her eyes the whole way. She had to squeeze past Garrett, an awkward dance with the tins of green beans and potato salad balanced in her arms.

Isaac's pulse beat in the palm of his hand. He didn't know if being alone with Garrett was a good idea. He knew there were questions, unanswered, between them. Every time he opened his mouth, he said the wrong thing. Eventually there would be a decision to make, to leave or not to leave. With every misspoken word, he came closer to Garrett making the decision for them both. They were very, very close to the edge of what their friendship could take.

His heart still quickened every time Garrett turned around.

It had been doing so for more than a year. Back then, Laurel had a scholarship offer, Ricky had half an associate's degree, and Garrett had a 1965 Ford F-250 that promised to roar to life before summer's end. Isaac started that summer with a black eye that faded into June. By July, he could have had Garrett but didn't know what to do with him. Isaac could read a map, knew that red and blue spots across the southern United States marked places he could and could not safely be. He was aware that he was living in enemy territory, born into it. His father was a bomb, primed to go off. His body held on to the shrapnel. Garrett flared up in unexpected moments, bright as lightning, hot as the sun.

He missed one moment that could have made them because he was afraid to move first, and another after that, stirring the dead embers of a campfire with his back to Garrett's voice as it spilled truth in the darkness. Then, his father broke his wrist over nothing, and Isaac realized that it didn't matter what rules he played by or broke. As long as he lived in that apartment, there was a good chance he wouldn't make it out alive. He wrote escape routes into every summer plan and saved back some money in an oil can in Jay's equipment barn instead of spending it on a college education. He stopped thinking about how kissing Garrett could kill him and started planning how to survive instead.

Now he was older, his plans were laid to waste, and there stood Garrett, an open invitation to burn.

Garrett cuffed him lightly on the shoulder. "Where are your shoes at, boy? Living up to stereotypes now that you're out of the big city?"

Isaac tapped his forearm lightly with the carpet beater. "Careful, I'm armed."

"Yeah, but with what?" Garrett disarmed him with a smile, turning over the strange old artifact and knocking its edge against the thick palm of his hand. "We playin' badminton after this?"

Isaac looked up at the thickening crop of clouds in the sky. They were not yet dark, but the western breeze heralded a downpour of rain before nightfall. "If the weather holds, we can do anything."

"Anything?"

Isaac had managed to bring something back from the apartment with him after all. It was something he'd carried for a while, a twisted sense of self-preservation, tamping down on the wild and reckless part of him that thrilled whenever Garrett smiled. He could give in to that tired old reflex that no longer served him. He could point at the sky, the darkening clouds highlighting the inevitability of a storm pouring through. The weather would not hold. They both knew.

"Anything," he agreed, settling into the comfortable safety net of home pulsing through the farm, not caring if it was a spell or just a state of mind.

He smacked Garrett on the hip with the carpet beater and dashed for the woods.

Isaac didn't make it far in bare feet. There were stalks sticking out of the grass, sharpened into splintered points where the lawn mower had cut them. As he hopped on one foot toward the road, his other foot landed hard on a sharp piece of gravel, and he swore, nearly tripping into a blackberry bramble and rolling down the holler. He could hear Garrett gaining on him, his boots stomping heavily across the yard and skidding across the gravel as he laughed. Another two steps and he was caught between putting a foot down in some Scottish thistle or slamming face-first into the oak tree. He stopped and turned.

Garrett caught him by the shoulder. "Should've worn shoes," he chided, "then I might never have caught you."

Isaac kissed him.

Garrett made a noise, small and surprised, against Isaac's

mouth. Isaac felt it in his chest. The goldenrod whispered around them as a breeze blew off the river. Isaac's hair lifted from his face at its touch and Garrett's fingers followed, careful as they alighted above his temple. A second stretched between them, all hot breath and blurred vision. Garrett stood still. Isaac pressed another kiss to the side of Garrett's mouth, encouraging him to move.

Garrett took two steps forward, careless of Isaac's bare feet, crowding him into a backward dance until the bark of the oak tree dug hard into his shoulder blades. Isaac's head knocked against the trunk.

The wrist that Garrett pinned back against the bark made a compelling point of interest on the map of their bodies. So did the press of a knee between Isaac's legs. The hand caught in Isaac's hair, Garrett's chest pinning him to the tree, the topography of everything Isaac wanted within his reach.

Usually Isaac lived a little to the left of his body, one eye on the exit sign, ready to leave the tangles of his nervous system behind and come back later to clean up the mess someone else had made of his skin. Kissing stood in stark contrast to the ever-present ache of work, the sudden shock of a punch. He recognized how tight his breath lay coiled from the way it loosened as Garrett's hand rested against his chest. This was easy. This was the easiest thing he'd done in years.

They were making a mistake.

The thought came abruptly, and Isaac couldn't shake it. His breath caught in his throat. Garrett's hands were too big; the sky above them was too wide. He'd only just gotten out of the cramped apartment, and now he was trapped between the oak tree and Garrett.

Isaac pushed at Garrett's chest. Garrett stepped back, his face swimming into Isaac's vision. "Isaac?"

"I—can't." Isaac sank to his knees.

Isaac had never known someone who died. His ghosts were living things, roaming out in the darkness. His mother was a living dead end, long out of reach. The horrors in Laurel's life had headstones and date markers, durations, ends. Isaac still flinched when he heard heavy footsteps, looked over his shoulder at the phantom feeling of someone standing behind him, hurt like he had hands around his neck even when no one was touching him. His body was the site of an active haunting. He could feel it rattling the bones inside his chest when he breathed sometimes, sucking the air from his lungs until he thought he might die.

But he didn't. His heart kept beating. The lights flickered on and life resumed.

Garrett's voice registered dimly from close by. "What's happening?"

They'd both felt a crack like the sky had opened up when Laurel had cast what she said was a protection spell. No one knew what she'd done or how long it would hold, least of all Laurel. Isaac felt as though the sky was falling. Garrett might gauge his reaction and fear it actually had.

"P-panic attack," Isaac articulated as he tried to stop it. After what felt like a decade, he forced himself to speak, words coming as short as his breath. "Nothing magic. Just me. So *stupid.*" Garrett flinched, but Isaac shook his head. "Not you."

Garrett's hand hovered above Isaac's thigh, but he pulled it back. Isaac shook his head, nose pointed toward the ground. He tried to slow his breathing, the treacherous pace of his heart.

They sat together until silence grew comfortable and Isaac could move. Embarrassment filled the place of panic eventually.

When it did, Garrett spoke. "So, I imagine that wasn't the way you wanted this to go," he said, scraping some grass seed up and watching it blow away in the wind.

A sharp exhale was all the laugh Isaac could manage. "You imagine right."

"I'd been imagining that kiss for a while."

"Oh, yeah?" Isaac asked, like he didn't already know. "Did it live up to your expectations?"

"You know it did. Don't get defensive." Garrett's voice was soft, blameless. Isaac could ignore the command within it if he chose. Garrett rolled onto his feet like he was going to get up and walk away, but instead he thought better of it and settled back onto the dirt in front of Isaac. He lightly tapped Isaac's ankle with the toe of his boot. "Look, I get this is delicate. I'm letting you call the shots here. But you've got to know I give a shit about you whether you decide to keep kissing me or not."

Isaac kicked back. "I know that."

Garrett caught his ankle, stilling him. Isaac met his eyes, green as the underside of an oak leaf. "Do you?" Garrett asked. "I don't think any of you do. The devil that's been after Laurel? I met it first, by the well next to the old shop. It was wearing your face. It told me it knew what I wanted, and it kissed me."

"Was that all that you imagined it would be, too?" Isaac snarled, shaking off the icy tremor of fear that climbed his spine. His fear made him furious. He wanted to get up and end the conversation he'd been trying not to have with Garrett for more than a year. He was leaving. Garrett wasn't. He hadn't done a thing to mitigate any of the hurt between them that leaving would cause. He'd just delayed it, then picked open the scab the second he remembered he was hurting. That kiss had been a cut, a nasty part of him thought. He'd sliced Garrett open in search of something to numb his fears.

For a second, Isaac was back there, caught between an oak tree on the Early farm and the pin of Garrett's body. When stuck between two impossible places, of course Garrett seemed like the softer option. If Isaac could just stay in that soft, still place for long enough, maybe the roaring fear in his heart would quiet.

A crow called overhead as Garrett said, "You don't have to keep hurting me to get me to let you go. I've been planning on it all along."

The landscape shifted on him again, and there was the path out of the woods he'd been looking for. He was so tired of being lost, but—

"You want me."

Garrett raised an eyebrow, but he nodded. "I do. I also want at least twenty acres within two counties of my parents and one of those kit houses with the green tin roofs. I want a Benelli M2 for duck hunting, a new outboard motor, and to keep most of the world out of my business. I want to be right where I am."

It was a pretty future, and if he'd wanted it anywhere else in the world, Isaac could have seen himself as part of it.

Garrett seemed to know. He added, "I also want you to be happy, safe, maybe even relaxed for once in your life. I don't see that happening anywhere near here, so I want you to get the hell out without a backwards glance."

Isaac had never been able to catalogue his own desires so precisely. He was used to not having. Self-denial was easy when it was status quo. "Stop wanting me and maybe I will."

"I think we just proved it doesn't work like that."

"Kevin knows." When Garrett didn't respond, Isaac clarified, "He knows how I feel about you. Maybe not all of it, but enough to guess. To use it against me."

Garrett shrugged. "He didn't kill you."

"He might yet."

"Any of them might."

Them. Bigots in Dry Valley were no different than straight people anywhere else. Garrett wasn't wrong. "Let's get out of here together. Living's easier other places."

"I don't want a different life. I'm fine with this one."

"I'm not."

Garrett shrugged, as if to say *That's your problem.* At the end of the day, it was. Nothing Garrett could do would help except letting go, and Isaac wasn't ready for him to do that just yet.

"So, until you get a new one, what are we doing in the meantime?"

Isaac wasn't sure. He'd blown his plan to hell and didn't want to go back to it anyway. He could feel a storm in the rising breeze and eyes on him from the shadows in the woods beyond. So, he pulled himself to his feet and pulled Garrett up after, standing next to him as close as gravity dictated they could. "Anything we want," he said.

CHAPTER
TWENTY-SEVEN

L aurel stopped outside the washhouse door to peer up at the sky. The wind whispered promises of a storm. "Don't hail," she whispered back, pointing a finger at a thunderhead. She had enough to worry about without factoring in losing the whole crop of tobacco.

July brought fat thunderhead clouds and huge lightning storms down on the tobacco fields, and there was no way to prevent the damage a hailstorm might do. They'd lose the crop and their livelihood for the year. Insurance might cover it, but nothing was certain. Laurel could hear the windows rattling as the breeze picked up. It wouldn't rain for a few hours yet, but a storm was ever more likely.

These summer storms were a reckless bunch, concerned only with their own expression. There was no stopping the rain once humidity and heat swelled into a fever pitch of blackening cumulonimbus clouds. They'd rain hail and thunder on any-thing below, not bothering to glance down at what grew in the fields they flooded or who was caught in them, winds whipping branches into the river and rain pummeling the tender leaves of growing things.

Above her the clouds churned and the breeze grew wild, a drunk and messy blast of humid air across her skin. The air hummed, charged with energy strong enough to make her eyes itch. Ozone tickled the back of her throat when she sucked in a breath. Humid heat made her stomach sick, damp on her skin as she pulled her hair over one shoulder. She had to pull in the maceration buckets before it started to pour. She couldn't do any-thing for the tobacco, but her bones, at least, she could protect.

The most difficult thing about hauling in the pickle buckets was keeping the washhouse door propped open as she lifted them inside, one after the other. The fetid liquid sloshed in the plastic containers. Laurel didn't even wrinkle her nose at the smell anymore. It meant nothing was about to explode on her. She'd learned her lesson long ago about trying to put an airtight seal on decomposition.

"Laurel," a strange voice sounded from beside the fireplace. It was as wet and rotten as the contents of the maceration buckets, electric as the distant rumble of thunder outside the window.

A shadow moved and resolved itself into the shape of Anna Early. She was nothing like the mother of Laurel's Polaroid-preserved dreams. The embalming fluid meant to hold her mother together had done its job long enough to keep Anna pretty for a funeral home visitation, but it hadn't held up much better than the stitches in her gum line and under her eyelids to hold her slack mouth closed and her eyes shut in fake sleep. They had long since dissolved. No—they'd been plucked away from softened skin. No longer firm and doll-like, her mother's body had yielded to the dirt. Much like Laurel's maceration buckets, no coffin was truly ever airproof. Once decay wormed its way in, there was no stopping it.

If Laurel was ashamed that her first thoughts regarding the woman standing before her were clinical, she was more ashamed that her second thoughts were tremulous, terrified. *A ghost. I'm looking at a ghost.*

A hand brushed Laurel's cheek, fingers as cold as the current. Laurel tried not to shudder. "Don't be sad," Anna said. Laurel followed the ghostly pattern on her skin. Had she been crying, or were her mother's fingers wet?

"You're really here?" Laurel murmured, wondering. Anna reached out again, but Laurel shook her head, taking a careful step back. "I'm not dreaming?"

"You're not dreaming. You've made it easy for me to manifest. What a strong spell you've cast. Keeps the monsters at bay but lets me move through. I'm proud of you."

"God," Laurel whispered. She wanted to thrill at her mother's pride, but she was overwhelmed by a wave of grief. Her heart was washed out with sorrow, held in the river's current until it was completely cleaned of blood. The wound she'd lived with all her life cried out for a mother even as her mother stood before her. It did not recognize the ghost flickering there. She wanted strength, vitality, life. Christine had described postmortem adrenaline. There was no life in the muscles working to lift the hand that stroked her cheek.

"Oh, sweetheart," her mother said, "I'm sorry I killed you."

Laurel blanched. "You didn't kill me," she said. The specter flickered uncertainly as a flame, then solidified once more.

"I've as good as killed you, and Jay, and everyone else. I killed everything in the world when I fell. Everything except the devil, still scrambling around there in the dark and the wet. Don't worry, baby. I'm going to get it right this time. I'm going to kill the devil and bring you back to life." Anna's hand reached out, skeletal and cold as the current.

Laurel didn't want to be held. "You're confused. You've been dead for twenty years. Even if the spell I've cast helps you appear, how long will it last? How can you do anything to stop the devil when you're dead?"

Her mother withdrew, shoving her withered hand into her mouth. "You need the bones to understand," she said around her finger. "I know that now. I'm learning more about you all the time. Your hobby—" She tried again. "Your *life*. I have a gift for you; hold out your hand."

It was the same wound singing out for her mother that forced Laurel to hold out her hands. Palms cupped to receive; an open wound was all she was.

Anna spat into Laurel's hand. Laurel's fingers closed reflexively around the small object in her palm, and Anna was gone.

The hot summer air froze around Laurel. Humidity crystallized; the temperature dropped fall-cold in an instant and sucked the warmth from her skin. With her next exhale she saw her breath clouding, peeling forth from lips that weren't hers. Her thin wrists and spider hands spread before her, blue-veined and long-fingered. Her mother's hands.

It was twilight. She was Anna Early, walking the crumbling remains of disused road to the equipment barn and the groundwater well beside it. She wasn't alone. The devil followed, a shadow at her shoulder.

He followed her everywhere.

It was the scent of fear on her skin that drew him to her. He'd imprinted on it like a child when she'd accidentally brought him into the world. She'd reeked of fear the first time she touched him, plunging her fingers into the swimming shadows where he lurked and yanking him into the sunlight.

It had been a dry year, and the people of the town blamed the sour turn of her frown for desiccating the creeks running across the county. She'd tried to conjure up a summer thunderstorm wild enough to wash them all away.

"You're not the storm I was trying to summon," she'd said, turning him over in her hands.

"I am so much more than that," he promised. He wriggled in her grasp, gape-mouthed with hunger. He'd wanted only to suck the taste of terror from her magic-stained fingers. But she'd brought him out of his crumbless world to a dinner plate piled high with meat and breath and could not stuff him back from where she'd drawn him. He'd come to life hungry for it.

She'd been an idiot to summon him. He was so much worse than the whispers of the town she'd called him to destroy. Everything withered in his mouth, and his mouth was always wide open. She'd pulled him into this world, but she couldn't command him. "Anything but the farm," she'd told him, but he'd replied, "Farm first."

He gorged himself. Even when the soil was flavorless in some places there was still more to taste. He sucked the green from the tobacco fields and grew as fat as the hornworms he licked off their broad leaves. He gnawed at the roots of the water maples growing along the river until their bark was skull-white like the sycamore trees.

As he grew, he'd donned the trappings of something monstrous, all shadows and claws and yellowed eyes. She took to calling him a devil. And he was, that or something more evil that man had not yet named. The slithering shadow at her shoulder reminded Anna what he'd looked like when she'd first pulled him from the earth, a worm slipped through a rotten spot in this apple of a world that wanted to eat through its core.

In truth, she preferred the worst he had to offer over the uncanny imitation of life he could conjure when it suited. She never feared ending up in his arms by mistake when he held out hands made of needles to catch her. At first, he appeared to her wearing the face of a man she loved. He'd been a near-perfect imitation, pale and quiet with the same pretty knuckles, but he wore the man's skin too tight over a mouth of sharp teeth, and where it wore thin she saw the monstrosity poking through. When he closed his eyes to kiss her, she'd stuffed a handful of exorcism herbs down his throat. He'd spat them, bloody, at her feet.

"If you don't love the faces I wear, I'll wear worse," he'd threatened.

"The sight of you doesn't scare me," she lied.

He chewed the falsehood from the marrow of her words and grinned, her lies sticking out from between his teeth. "Bring me something sweeter," he implored, singsong. "Something sweet like the baby you're hiding up in that house on the hill."

"What baby?" she asked, voice thin enough to be transparent.

"What baby?" it echoed, mimicking her voice. "The one behind the glass. I tap on her windows at night. I watch her little face turn red as she screams in her crib. Watch the door stay shut. Watch her sobbing in the dark."

There's no baby, she wanted to say, to deny it like she'd denied him for months. "The door doesn't stay shut," she whispered instead. "I always come for her."

It was a cold day, the scent of damp and plant rot heavy in the biting breeze. The time for storms had passed. The frost would fall soon enough. She wanted nothing more than to go home and shed her wet gloves, throw another log into the woodstove and warm the whole house up. Laurel would wake soon. She'd be hungry. Anna wanted to bury her face into the woodsmoke and baby smell of the soft hair on top of Laurel's head.

But instead of feeding her baby, she had to mother her.

Jay could warm a bottle. He loved tucking the baby's tiny body into the crook of his arm and watching her fall asleep nearly as soon as she started to drink. He could feed Laurel. Anna was the only one who could save her.

Tucked into the pocket of Anna's coat was one of her own teeth, roots and all. She'd pulled it this morning, hiding in the washhouse where her brother wouldn't see what horrible things magic was making his sister do.

It hadn't been easy. She'd stuck a pair of her father's iron pliers into the back of her mouth, clamping down on a molar she could do without. Desperation gave her strength she didn't know she possessed. She'd already let a baby move through her body like a car wreck. One missing tooth wasn't the worst she'd suffered for Laurel's life. In the split second where bravery overrode fear, she jerked up and out, and her tooth was in her palm. The metal-and-oil taste of the pliers turned to the metal-and-salt taste of blood dripping from her mouth.

When the pain erupted, she didn't scream, whimpering instead into the hand held over her mouth. She didn't want her brother to come running. She didn't want him to bring her back and pack her jaw with ice, to call that idiot doctor who'd frown about the trauma of her "situation," pregnant out of wedlock and birthing a baby alone, how it had broken her fragile little mind. Once she killed the devil, she'd be healthy and strong. Once she killed him, she'd be fine.

Now she had the weapon. Her tooth, a spot of her dried blood nestled in its crown. He wanted her body. She'd let him have a piece of it, poisoned with death. It ought to be enough to turn him inside out. It ought to be enough to kill him.

The old well by the equipment barn hadn't seen use since they'd gotten rid of the cattle ten years before. It was the only hole deep enough to bury him. If she could pin him in its depths, she could cover the wound she'd made pulling him out of the earth with scrap metal and barbed wire. She'd make his grave an uninhabitable place, a scour so ugly no one would ever think to let him loose. She'd trap him in a place already forgotten.

Prying the dry-rotted boards from the rim of the well took effort. "What are you doing?" he asked from where he lay at her feet, withering a patch of white clover as if looking for a lucky charm. She'd been unlucky for long enough. She worried about nothing but running out of time. The boredom in his voice ticked ever closer to another murder. Just this morning he'd dropped a dead nest of rabbits at her doorstep. Her weak spells could only hold for so long.

"Looking for an exit." She grimaced, prying free another board. Sunlight reflected in the black abyss of the well. There was enough water there, enough depth to pin him when he fell. She could do this. Casting aside the last board, she reached into the pocket of her coat, feeling around for the tooth. The metal taste of it still filled her mouth. She'd pulled him from the earth. She'd plunge him back in.

He crawled closer, claw over tooth over eye as he drew himself to his feet. The lichen of the well died under his hands. "You don't get an exit," he promised. "I'll stand at every door until you let me in."

"Then we'll cross this threshold together," she vowed. Her

mind was on the baby atop the hill when she took the tooth in hand and pushed the creature into the well.

Her hand made contact with the numbing cloud of his breath and her body went cold, frostbitten to the bone. She watched a trail of ice trace the veins up her forearms, racing toward her chest. The tooth slipped from the grasp of her frozen fingers and landed in the well, a hollow echo far below. She plunged in after.

Roots, rocks, water. Blood, splattered down the walls. There was something wrong with her neck. There was something wrong with a lot of her.

There was a shift beside her. The thinnest slice of shadow. She'd captured him but hadn't entirely killed him. "Finally," the devil breathed, "we're alone."

She could feel him licking her split lips. She couldn't stand to stop him, but she could take the dead parts of her she'd intended to use to kill him and turn them into a sacrifice that would. "You'll stay here as long as I stay dead," she swore, pulling all the magic seeping out of her into her core until she could make it come true.

She was still spitting blood when the world went black.

CHAPTER
TWENTY-EIGHT

Laurel burst through the front door, fist clenched around her mother's tooth. Jay, Ricky, Garrett, and Isaac stood around the kitchen table, filling their plates. Ricky gesticulated to Jay with his free hand, saying, "If we're lucky, the storm will miss us entirely, but I can't guarantee— Laurel, Christ, what happened to you?"

She slapped the tooth on the table. Garrett hastily pulled his plate away. "No teeth at the table. I feel like that should definitely be a rule."

"What is that?" Ricky asked, leaning forward to look at it. "Some kind of molar?"

"Human," she confirmed.

"Oh—nope!" Ricky pushed back from the table as quickly as he'd leaned in, knocking over a chair that went clattering to the floor.

"Jesus Christ!" Garrett exclaimed as Isaac cried, "Laurel, what on earth?"

"Where did you find it?" Jay asked. He kept his voice soft. His expression was difficult to read. He plucked the tooth from the table, holding it between his fingers.

"Mom gave it to me."

"You saw her?" Isaac asked, craning his neck to get a better look at the tooth. Garrett rested a hand on Isaac's elbow as though ready to pull him away quickly.

"I know what happened, the day she died. She didn't do it to herself," she insisted. "She didn't jump. She fell."

"Oh, Laurel," Ricky breathed, sickening sympathy in the sound.

Jay winced as he ran his fingertip down the long root of the molar, the pain of an old wound evident in his expression. "Laurel, don't do this, please."

But Laurel couldn't stop until he understood. "She only planned to undo the damage she'd done and come home in time for supper. To me. To both of us. She never planned to leave forever."

Jay's fingers trembled around the tooth, but it was only a dead bone in his grasp. He glanced between the tooth and the boys standing uncomfortably around the supper table. "Come into the living room, and let's talk about this."

"No, they need to hear it," Laurel protested. Now they could formulate a plan together and stop the devil before the hail hit.

But the boys obeyed Jay when he dismissed them with a gesture.

Laurel pointed to the door. "They care about this farm, too. They deserve to know."

Jay shook his head. His half-made plate sat on the table in front of him, going cold. "There's farm business and there's family business. They don't need to know about who your mother was or what she did. That's got nothing to do with the tobacco, or the soil, or anywhere their interests might lie."

"It does when there's magic involved." She glared, challenging him to dismiss her.

Jay's laugh was a sharp, mirthless noise, knifing through Laurel's resolve, as he put the tooth down. "Oh, magic again."

"Mom . . ." She faltered. "She must have said something to you."

Jay spoke to the table, unable to meet Laurel's gaze. "Your mother was sick, and I couldn't save her from it."

Tears welled up against her will. She stilled her hands by her sides, refusing to wipe her eyes. "You couldn't save her from a devil."

In the pre-storm light, the lines on his face were deep, worn paths cut over his lifetime by an ever-flowing river of sorrow. He let his eyes close and spoke without opening them, as if picking up the thread of a long-finished conversation. "Just because you don't like the answer doesn't mean you get to invent a new one. There is no devil, Laurel. There's choices, and illness, complications we can't blame on the supernatural."

Jay could not see what was right in front of him and wouldn't look. He hadn't trusted her fear when she'd run from the monster in the woods, he'd taken her guns away when she said she'd seen a ghost. Magic could not exist for Jay Early. If it did, it provided a tidy answer to every question he'd ever asked himself about his sister's death. It shifted blame and opened up a door to a softer universe in which there was a monster outside of Anna responsible for his family's suffering. Jay had lived with the harder answer this whole time. He could not accept the easier option.

It was going to get them killed.

Laurel slapped her hand on the table and snatched the tooth up from where it rattled in the aftermath. "I know my mother well enough to understand that she'd do everything to keep me safe. She'd fight anything, death included, to help me. And you won't even listen to me."

Jay scoffed. His coffee-dark eyes, the same shade as her own, glinted with fury. He tried to remain the stoic patriarch, the one in control. But his knuckles whitened as his fists clenched in an effort to quell his trembling hands. "Oh, I'm listening. You think you're the first woman on this farm to see visions and ghosts? Your mother saw things, for all the good it did her."

She felt dumbstruck, suddenly cold and remote. Her fingers prickled. Her mother *had* told Jay, probably begged him to believe her the way that Laurel did now. "And you still don't believe me?"

Jay shook his head. "I know better than to ever think like that again. What she thought she saw drove her to her death. If you're seeing what she did, close your eyes tight, or look in another direction."

"No," Laurel insisted. "She warned you. She warned you, and she still died."

"Don't you dare pin what she did on me!" Jay's voice cracked. Once, when Laurel was a child, she'd been running inside, her footsteps thundering through the living room. She'd knocked an old lamp full of kerosene onto the floor. It was just one of many heirlooms littered throughout their two-hundred-year-old house, an irreplaceable treasure she hadn't noticed until it shattered. Jay's voice in that terrible moment was the exact same pitch as the sound of that antique glass splintering into pieces.

Jay took a deep breath, settling down onto a chair as though he couldn't both stand and say what he needed to. "After Mom and Dad died, we were looking for answers. We didn't know much, only that there had to be some kind of explanation for all that tragedy. We were young; we still believed there were patterns to the world. Parents don't just *die* for no reason, right?"

Laurel nodded. She could feel it in the accelerated pace of her heart, knowledge that settled deep and true and right in her bones. Her mother had died to protect her. She'd sacrificed herself. Finally, the grief of not knowing why had dissolved and there was only the wound of wishing there had been another option.

Jay wasn't finished. "Senseless tragedy. That's how the coroner described it. Dad's heart attack, Mom's grief. They died too young, too close together. Used to doing everything together, leaving us to sort out what came after. Anna couldn't live with senseless. She'd been listening too long to the way other people blamed her for senseless things. Droughts and damnation. She couldn't handle being their monster any longer, so she invented something else, named it, blamed herself, and decided it was the reason for our troubles. A curse on our farm. A devil out to get us. That was when it got her. Wasn't long after that, she was gone, too."

Laurel twisted the tooth in her palm. "She was going to come back for me."

Her uncle gripped the edge of the table. "I'm the only person who's shared memories of your mother with you. It's unfair. I know that. When you were younger, I thought I could get by with only giving you the good things. I figured the bad things didn't matter anymore."

"What are you saying?" Laurel shot back. Someone had to love Anna Early, just like someone had to bury her. Speaking ill of their dead, especially one so badly maligned by the rest of Dry Valley, felt like laying a curse on their own name.

She thought Jay wouldn't dare say it, but his jaw tensed as he forced out the words that he'd been holding back for more than a decade. "Whatever ghost you've invented to make missing your mother easier, it's nothing like the real thing, and it's not telling you the truth. If your mother was still alive, you'd miss her just as much as you do now, I promise."

Laurel went stiff. Her stomach twisted, pushing against the thought, rejecting Jay's words before she could believe them. "She's fighting for me," she objected, her voice gravel as her jaw ached with tension. She would not cry. She would not let her voice crack. She'd keep repeating it, another protection spell woven over the loneliness of her life, until she meant it. Until she knew it to be true and the wound of doubt in her healed. "She loved me. She would never have left me if she had the choice."

Jay spread his hands, the wide stretch of his wingspan indicating the empty farmhouse around them, the empty fields beyond. "She left us both here, unprotected. And no devil ever came after me once she died. No monster. Nothing at all. It was just you and me on this farm together, alone. Stare into those woods all you want, Laurel, make a monster out of every tree branch and a ghost from every shadow, but there's no one around for miles," he said, standing up from the table. "That's the worst thing in them: all that empty space."

The door to his room shut with a clatter behind him. Laurel stared at the peeling white paint, ignoring the tears rolling down her cheeks. Her uncle couldn't be the hero she wanted. She'd have to do it for herself.

CHAPTER
TWENTY-NINE

After supper, Laurel surveyed the kitchen to keep from looking out the wide kitchen window at the backyard and the edge of the woods beyond. The day had stretched to its breaking point and night was coming, faster than the summer thunderstorm blackening the clouds overhead. Every movement in the warped glass made her flinch toward the shotgun propped up in the corner by the gas stove, but it was only orioles resting in the cherry tree by the smokehouse and squirrels gnawing pits on the ground. The gathering breeze from the coming storm shook the branches, but nothing emerged from behind the trees.

Isaac and Garrett sat next to each other on the couch, thighs touching, mouths twin grim lines, while Ricky had settled, cross-legged, into the La-Z-Boy, hand splayed across his face as he stared morosely into space. Laurel let the ice melt to slivers in her uncle's tea glass before dumping the remainder down the drain. Her stomach was half sick and her hands were restless, hovering over the pocket where she'd stored her mother's tooth. She set to work cleaning up supper.

She consolidated leftovers into Tupperware and rearranged the fridge before stacking up the aluminum containers by the sink. She filled the sink basin with rust-scented tap water and added a drizzle of blue soap before setting their plates and silverware to soaking. On the wall, the clock ticked closer to nine and a late sunset. Laurel let her eyes fall shut. The tooth in her pocket was a comforting shape, but it wouldn't be enough. She needed a weapon, not just a projectile. She couldn't very well hit a demon with a tooth and a slingshot. She'd need something heavier-grade to destroy him entirely.

But what did she have? A pocketknife with a thin steel blade and an antler hilt. The antler had once belonged to something living. But now, polished down as it was, would it be enough death to cut through the devil and banish him for good? She was a taxidermist. She had enough tools at her disposal. She could sharpen the tibia of a cow into a spear or plunge a sharpened arrow made of deer pelvis in his heart—if she just had the time.

She thought of the way the devil had first appeared, a grim, grinning illusion armored with the very thing that might kill it. Had it been offering up this easy secret all along, its heart, exposed on its sleeve for her to see? She thought of the rust red soaking stolen metacarpals. It hadn't abhorred death when it chased them through the night, stinking of it.

A shadow fell across the sink, but it was only Isaac. "I reckon I'm not a guest, so I'd might as well be useful," he said.

"I won't argue against extra help," she agreed, fetching a dish towel from a drawer. Isaac joined her, picking up the green-and-yellow sponge from the countertop and scrubbing off the leftovers stuck to the plates. They worked in silence, Isaac washing as she dried, eyes on their hands and minds in the shadows spreading at the edge of the woods.

This peace was uneasy. Not a cease-fire, but an eye in a storm that Laurel had pried open with no understanding of when or how it would slam shut.

Ricky slapped his hands against his knees, loud and sudden. Isaac winced, and the plate he held slipped back into the soapy water, hitting the bottom of the sink with a thud. "Forgot I brought dessert. Left it in the truck, but I reckon I could fetch it if y'all could eat."

"I couldn't think of eating more," Laurel groaned.

Isaac shook some suds from the tongs of a fork. "I could have a bite, depending on what it is."

"Lemon pies," Ricky said, before adding, "Oh, hush—"

"I didn't say anything, just made a face," Laurel said, arms crossed over her chest. "It's a lot of sugar."

"I could do with something sweet," Garrett said, stretching his arms above his head, "if one of you'd flick that coffeepot on?"

A smile flitted across Isaac's face, there and gone in an instant, but Laurel caught it. She raised an eyebrow, but he ducked to avoid her meaningful look. "Coffee'd be good," Isaac said, and went to measure some out.

"Might as well. Don't reckon we'll be sleeping much tonight," Laurel muttered. The after-dinner rhythm of dessert and dishes wouldn't solve a single problem they were facing, but there was comfort in the routine. She could steady herself in it.

Garrett stood watch by the window while Ricky went to retrieve dessert, slamming the door shut as he went only to open it, say "Oops," and shut it again more quietly. She glanced at the closed door of Jay's bedroom, but the sound wasn't enough to make him emerge. Nor was the smell of black coffee, or the slam of Garrett's truck door, or the curse Garrett let out in response.

"I know you're antsy, but you don't have to take it out on my truck," Garrett said as Ricky kicked his shoes off on the porch and padded back into the living room brandishing a tied plastic bag.

"You could always make yourself useful," Laurel said, motioning to the whitewashed cupboard where they stored the coffee mugs and dessert plates. Ricky tore a hole in the plastic bag with his fingers. He produced four small cardboard boxes, set them on the table, then ripped some paper towels off the roll. Isaac passed him a fistful of forks.

"Should I pour some coffee?" Isaac asked.

"Not yet," Laurel said, draining the sink basin. "I've got to take the scrap bowl out first." She dumped the contents of the sink drain into a steel bowl and went to find her boots.

Out on the porch, Laurel's fingers trembled as she double-knotted the laces. The oncoming storm was near, the wind rattling the screens that gave an illusion of safety and whipping strands of hair away from her head. She'd unlatched the old screen door when she heard the front door shut behind her. "I figured," Isaac said, a little short of breath—he must have jogged to get his boots from the back room—"I'd go with you, in case."

"It's just a short trek behind the rabbit hutch," Laurel pointed out, but she was glad for the company.

The Early farm was far enough outside Dry Valley's limits that there was no trash service to handle their leftovers, so they burned paper and plastic, sent what they could with friends heading back into the city, and dumped food scraps for the critters to dispose of. She'd cast the chicken bones behind the rabbit hutch, where the tall grass grew, and hope nothing reached out to grab her when she did. Isaac spent most of the journey in silence before a confession came bursting out.

"Garrett kissed me."

"Oh?" Laurel said, stopping long enough to give the information its due. "Sorry?"

Isaac looked bewildered. "What? Why?"

"I assumed you didn't want him to, what with the whole 'you'll get over it, same shoebox' talk you gave him in the fall." Isaac blinked, as though recalling a distant memory. "You haven't already forgotten your long list of reasons falling in love with him is a bad idea?"

The soft smile on his face faltered, but he shook his head. "I mean, it was all well and good before I knew the shoebox was stuffed full of ghosts that want us dead." Here he gave a little lopsided shrug to fit that growing grin. "So, I figure, why not have something nice before something horrible kills me?"

"Nothing's going to kill you," Laurel snarled, surprised by the vehemence in her tone. She spun on her heel and stalked away. Without ceremony she leaned over the electric fence marking the far edge of the yard and dumped the scraps out, holding her breath against the smell of pot likker and cheese sauce and coffee grounds.

"I believe you," Isaac said, catching up to her. "You don't have to get defensive. You're doing enough, and I'm grateful. For all of this. I am." His dark eyes were sincere. She was reminded of the games they'd played as children, the way he used to follow after her, waiting for her to do something magic.

"Takes death to kill the devil," she said, pointing at the chicken bones scattered across the ground. "Think this'll be enough?"

"As much as I understand about anything, I don't know that it will be," he said with a frown.

"I don't think I have what I need. In the vision, the tooth wasn't enough. I'm worried it might need to be . . ." She trailed off. "Fresher death," she said finally, because she didn't want to frame it the way her mind kept shaping it. Something sacrificial, something slaughtered. She could taste iron in the back of her throat, where her mother's pliers hadn't been enough.

Isaac considered this. "I could see that."

"We'll need to go hunting, but it'll have to wait. No sense in going out in this storm."

"Do we have that kind of time?" he asked.

Laurel looked up at the blackening sky, heavy clouds swallowing up the last dregs of sunlight. "I'll make sure we do."

CHAPTER THIRTY

When Laurel went to bed that night, Ricky caught the door before it could close, letting it fall shut behind him. The two of them stood inches apart in the dark until she moved to the center of the room, catching the light pull and tugging. The bare bulb glowed.

"We'll hunt for something big enough to kill the devil in the morning. Reckon you're staying with us tonight," Laurel said, nervous.

"Reckon so."

"We're about filled to capacity." Adding in Isaac, they had only the sleeper sofa and the front porch swing.

"We could share a bed."

Laurel whirled on him. "Jay will *kill you*—"

Ricky rolled his eyes, though she was certain he knew what he'd been insinuating. "I meant me and Garrett. Couch pulls out, right? And anyways, he lets Isaac hang out in your room all night long."

"He never had to worry about Isaac," she said. Ricky was something to worry about, even four paces away, standing close enough to the door to duck out before they could get into trouble.

"I used to worry about Isaac. The two of you." He knocked his knuckles against the doorframe, self-conscious. "I was afraid he might break your heart. At least, that's what I told myself at the time."

Neither of them had to acknowledge that Isaac had broken her heart already and would again. "What about now, with Garrett?" she asked.

Ricky shook his head. He wandered toward the window, its bloodless flower petals chipping off the glass. He lifted a finger as if to touch one, but seemed to decide it was too delicate. "Nah, Garrett's been gunning to get his heart broken for a while. Looks like he's finally on a good path to getting there."

And what about your heart? she thought. She couldn't look at him without thinking of him in the kitchen, the white of his knuckles wrapped around the water glass. There was already so much broken between where they were and where they wanted to be. Something else might shatter on the way to getting there. No matter what they did next, someone was going to get hurt.

What was it about those two? The Mobley brothers. Garrett had always been a bit of a daredevil. Ricky was a bit of a clown. She'd grown up alongside them, the same fields, the same schools, the same fifteen miles between county lines that made up the world they inhabited. All she'd learned from living there was to watch her step for scrap metal. Somewhere along the way, they'd learned different lessons.

Maybe it was the set they'd sprouted from, the complete

twosome of mother and father under one tin roof that held them so safely they felt no fear chasing down danger. All Laurel wanted was something settled, something true. A promise that she wouldn't be alone. She figured Ricky must have the answer. She thought even if he didn't, he might be able to give her a hint. But last night he'd been begging her to let him live, and now he was in her bedroom, saying he'd stay with her through danger.

Maybe he didn't know a damn thing.

"Why are you here? Is it because Garrett stayed?"

Ricky blinked. He'd been playing with something on her curio shelf. She watched him turn the little ceramic box with a painted hummingbird on its lid over in his hands. He hadn't opened it yet or he might have seen the sterling silver hummingbird skull pendant she kept there, a gift from an online friend that she never wore because she had no place to wear necklaces.

"Ricky?" she asked again when he didn't answer.

Laurel thought he might pick up another box from the curio shelf. But he bent down to unlace his boots. He padded over to the bed and dropped down onto it, patting the space next to him. "Come lie down," he said.

"Jay will—" but the withering glance he gave her shut her up. Clearly, he thought she was worth the risk.

"You're tired. I'm tired. We're both scared. Let's just . . . Come lie down."

Laurel pulled back the sheet, abruptly aware of how long it had been since she'd changed the linens on the bed. It smelled like sleep and her skin. She stood there, holding the sheet, waiting to be brave enough to lie down next to Ricky. He'd settled on top of the quilted coverlet, but she could feel the heat of his body next to her as she lay down. Awareness of their proximity prickled over her, sharp enough to make her shiver. It was not an unpleasant feeling.

Ricky's hand rested on the pillow behind her head, close enough to play with her hair. She lay stock-still, wanting him to, not knowing how to ask. He sighed, reaching out to snag a tendril, twirling it loosely around his finger as he thought. The gesture was casual, but she could barely breathe. "Stop that," she protested, reflexive, before she could think better of it.

He withdrew his hand. "Sorry, sorry." *Wait, no,* she thought, *I take it back.*

When he leaned away, it was easier to think. She needed to think. There were devils outside her door and everyone she loved trapped inside with her. If something were to knock . . . if something were to get in . . . "I still think you should go. It might be safe tonight, but who knows for how long? I don't know what I'm doing."

"Look, we don't know what's out there, what it'll take to stop it. What magic can even do."

"Do you believe in it?" she asked him, suddenly desperate for an answer.

He was quiet for a long moment, not as though he were at a loss for words, but as if he was measuring out the ones he had carefully. "I've always believed in something. Even when I thought it was stupid to attribute it to anything supernatural. There's this feeling that comes over you when you're in the woods, like you're part of it. Caught in the inhale and exhale of life everlasting, a split second in the eternal life cycle of being. You get to thinking you're entwined in it when you spend so much time growing and killing and watching things give birth. I've always wondered, here and there, if I couldn't move a couple of the pieces forward a little or bring them back. But I've never tried."

"So, you've got it too then?" she asked, quirking an eyebrow.

"What, haven't you always thought there was something special about me?" he teased, even as he shook his head.

In truth, she hadn't thought much of him. She'd thought he was all talk and bad habits, blowing billows of smoke to obscure that, behind it all, he was just another boy from Dry Valley. But that inner light in him, all that potential, wasn't the promise of success or an escape from the hole into which they'd been born. It was loyalty—pure, stubborn, and simple. Maybe she loved him, maybe she didn't. But they could abide with each other, two stubborn asses, through the worst of it without flinching. Here was the answer she'd been looking for: Ricky would stick around.

Instead of answering, she threaded her fingers through his. Maybe that was all the answer he needed. There was no teasing to the smile he gave her, no self-satisfied smirk. He looked happy. She wondered what her own must look like through his eyes. She lay there, watching him watch her.

She sank back onto her pillow, watching the shadows on the ceiling, hearing only Ricky's slow breathing. "I'm going to sleep soon." He hummed in agreement but didn't move. "That means you're going to crash on the pullout. You're not passing out here."

"Promise," he agreed, but his voice was thick and drowsy.

"Get up and be a gentleman."

He grunted in response. His warmth didn't leave her side. She tried to mind, but it comforted her as she started to drift off into a fitful sleep. The room changed before her closed eyes. She watched without sight as a warm, green light, ephemeral, rose up from the floorboards in tendrils. It sparkled below her and glittered above, crisscrossing like veins throughout the room.

This was the protection spell she'd cast, weaving its way

around the room, lazy like petals caught on the wind. But now she could see its mechanisms, and not just the things it moved.

It pooled in shallow streams, running across the dusty wooden floorboards and under the door. She knew without moving that it stretched farther than the farmhouse, all the way to the river-banks.

It was there, *right there,* a pretty glowing thing before her, a vine-like tendril curling above her head. She reached up to take hold of it . . .

Her fingers closed across Ricky's wrist, thumb pressed against the vein there, the pulse point running hot with dark blood. She could follow its course to the very core of him, fitting between the thick sheets of muscle as easily as if she were a vessel in his bloodstream, part of the mechanism moving his heart.

Her eyes snapped open, locking with Ricky's. His expression was blank with shock, mouth parted in a surprised *O.*

He might not have magic, but he felt it, too.

His fingers tangled in her hair before his lips met hers, a surprising spark of pain that thrilled through her, bright as starlight in her bones. Gravity was a heavy thing, and his body on top of hers was solid, not entirely comfortable but so very present that she could only urge him closer, inviting him to take up more space, to take more skin. She took the hand connected to the wrist she held and brought it to her waist. He slipped it beneath her shirt, large fingers splayed against the hot skin of her stomach.

Laurel's fingers fought Ricky's over the buckle of his leather belt, catching his laugh between her teeth as she surged up to capture his lips in another kiss. She managed, in spite of his clumsiness, to unfasten the buckle and the button beneath, roll his jeans off his tanned legs, and toss them to the ground. He struggled with his socks as she unfastened her bra without ceremony and dropped it in favor of pressing the newly bared expanses of their chests together. Her boldness was rewarded by hot skin and a messy kiss against her neck, inelegant, a little too much spit and desperation. She pinched her thoughts down to instinct and swallowed them with one of Ricky's moans.

Ricky's free hand pulled a strand of hair back from her face. He kept his hands high, long fingers splayed across her shoulder blades, farm-boy polite even after she pulled one of his thighs between her legs. When her hands trailed down the line of his spine, he kissed her so hard their teeth clacked together.

She dropped her head back onto the pillow to catch his gaze. "You can touch me," she told him. Some dark, wild force in his eyes called to something new unfurling within her, a young and hungry thing. His thighs tensed as her fingers trailed across him. "Or I could touch you."

She couldn't take everything she wanted, but she could take him in hand, her gaze never leaving his, even when his eyes fluttered shut and he groaned, loud enough that she hissed a warning through her teeth. He bit between his index finger and thumb to keep from crying out.

She could feel his pulse in her fingertips and the rise and fall of his chest sparking across her skin. She could feel the map of nerves across his body, the places where they bunched together, the need and ache coursing through them as desperate and visceral as if it lived in her own gut. She could feel the spreading warmth from every place their bodies connected.

Somewhere in between them was a whole vein of magic that she could trace down into the soil outside, so bright that she could see its glow stretching out from under the windowsill and into the night. Its light reflected in Ricky's eyes as they fluttered open, shut, open again. Wherever it touched, she vowed, was safe.

CHAPTER
THIRTY-ONE

I saac woke to the wet whisper of rain kissing the roof of an unfamiliar house. As he blinked into consciousness, he remembered that the farmhouse was his home now, that the sound of rain-splattered tin was supposed to soothe him, not put him on red alert. Garrett stirred next to him but settled back into sleep without opening his eyes. He didn't wake when Isaac left, padding across the cold wooden floor, past Laurel's closed door and into the bathroom.

Through the window he watched rain falling soft upon the garden beds, not much heavier than mist, as though God were doing midnight maintenance work and didn't want to disturb the sleeping occupants of the farmhouse. Maybe it had already thundered and this was the edge of the storm. Maybe they only had seconds before the downpour began.

The drip of the sink tap was almost as loud as the rainfall, unsynchronized with the patter of droplets against the roof. Isaac watched the curtain of rain shining in the moonlight, silver and wet. A bobbing gold light caught his eye.

At first, he thought someone was walking up the hill in the rain, a flashlight by their side, but the orb darted too quickly, climbed high and dipped low, more like the pattern of bird flight than of someone's steps. It glimmered under the stars, giving off a warm glow, nearly the size of the moon in the sky.

He wanted to be afraid. He should be. He'd seen what roamed these woods. But something about the glittering light and soft rain muted all sense beyond wonder. The cold whisper of fear tugging at his shirt didn't hold him back. Its grasp had been weak since he'd left his father's house and had slipped away entirely since he'd kissed Garrett.

Isaac zipped his fly and slipped on his shoes and socks in the living room. He grabbed the side-by-side twelve-gauge shotgun Jay kept sitting by the front door in case of emergency. The mist of rain against his skin did little to shake the strands of sleep still wrapped around his mind as he made his way into the damp night. The light bobbed past, almost teasing, as it continued up the hill.

"Hey!" he hollered. "Stop!"

He trudged on, mud squelching against his boots, shotgun smacking against his palm to the staccato rhythm of his footsteps as he chased it down. The light moved faster than it had before. It shimmered among the trees, occasionally climbing high above the canopy to sparkle like its own bright star.

Isaac was dimly aware that he ought to go back and alert someone that he'd left in case they woke to find him missing, but he was halfway to the old barn already. If he turned around, he might lose the light forever.

Something crackled behind him, as though someone had taken a deliberate step to alert him to their presence. Isaac swung his head around. *Please don't be bones,* he thought. But Laurel had pulled on a gray dress and followed after him, ten paces behind.

"Do you see this?" he called, voice a carrying whisper, hoping she would hear. She pointed at the glowing light above their heads. In response, the light quickened over the tree line and disappeared, only to reappear a moment later, weaving in and out of trees as it urged him deeper into the woods.

More confident with her close by, he dashed after it, as fast as he could. He was nearly to the trunk of the sycamore tree at the top of the hill, glowing bone-bright in the darkness, when he stopped cold. The light blinked out of sight.

He turned to see if Laurel had caught up.

A woman stood in the dark by Anna Early's gravestone, the hem of her gray dress stained with mud, her wet hair whipping in the wind. His breath hitched. It had never been Laurel.

"Are you Laurel's mother?"

"In the flesh."

Anna, the witch, the oracle straight out of Laurel's dreams. Was this a dream? It must be. She stood at the foot of her gravestone and turned her hand palm-up to reveal a sparkling little light.

He was strangely pleased, both to know this was a dream and to know that Anna had chosen him. It meant that there was something he could do to save the farm. He was a part of this journey. Isaac shivered. Her pruned fingertips, icy with rainwater, trailed across his cheek even though she had not moved. "What do you need me to do?" he asked.

"I didn't dare to assume you'd offer yourself up so easily."

But for Isaac it was an easy decision. "This is my world now. I want to be a part of it. I don't need visions to tell me that there's magic in it. I understand that now. Tell me what I can do."

"You've made your choice." Anna's smile was nothing like Laurel's. Laurel smiled to show she was happy. Anna smiled to remind you she had a skull.

There was a rustling from the woods, a horrifying click of bone on bone that Isaac remembered too well. Skull grinning, a twin of Anna's horrible smile, the bone monster peeled its way through the woods like bark from a sycamore tree, coming to stand by her graveside.

Cold terror pooled in the pit of Isaac's stomach. "Why would you let it into my dreams?" he whispered.

Anna's voice spilled out of the skeleton's mouth. "This is waking life."

Isaac shouldered the shotgun, his numb, wet fingers slipping across the trigger but unable to fire as the creature advanced. It knocked the gun from his trembling hands and splayed him across the ground. Mud forced its way into his mouth and blood spilled from his busted lip. His ears rang hollow as the monster bore down on him, scratching at him with coyote's claws, tearing his damp shirt and the skin underneath. Isaac's feet scraped the ground as he was hoisted high into the air, bruised in the cold, bony grasp of something he could not understand even as it held him in a death grip.

As the monster struck his head with supernatural strength, Isaac saw Anna's gravestone, abandoned as though she'd never been there at all. The grass had been torn up and the soil cast aside. The concrete vault was cracked and the casket was torn from its hinges. Her coffin spilled open. Something had dug up her grave.

CHAPTER
THIRTY-TWO

L aurel blinked awake from a dreamless sleep to someone tugging at her toe. Her hand came down to swat at it automatically, kicking free from the blankets. She was a little too hot, Ricky's arm loose around her waist. The farmhouse on a summer night had a feverish quality to it that all the box fans in the world couldn't blow away, like she'd fallen asleep with her face toward a fire. She needed a glass of water. She struggled out from under the sheet, forgetting what had pulled her from sleep in the first place.

The springs of the mattress creaked as she shifted her weight off the bed. Ricky's fingers flexed as though to catch her, but he did not open his eyes. He slept like he was safe, mouth soft and open.

She was awake enough to worry now, but she supposed they had been as safe as they could be. For all the jokes made about kids in the country with nothing to do, most of her knowledge was theoretical, categorized more under husbandry than romance. There'd been a lecture during freshman orientation that had covered a little beyond the basics. She hadn't had much chance to implement it before now.

Laurel regretted the way she studied him, clinical and curious instead of sentimental and sweet, as though she had not just learned a new way of looking at him. They'd both pulled their jeans back on afterward, and Laurel had refastened her bra, batting away his clumsy fingers as he'd tried to either help or hinder her. *Like it never happened,* she thought, though a darkening mark above her hip bone and a not-unpleasant ache in her ribs said otherwise.

It felt strange to sleep in denim under sheets, stranger still not to sleep alone. Laurel spent half the night turning over, trying to find her place in her own bed. She felt as though she ought to be a better hostess, to offer him another blanket or a little more space to sleep. Eventually, he'd wrapped his arms around her waist, fingers resting below her stomach at a place he'd learned she liked. It was odd and uncomfortable, but she'd managed to find peace in that position, her back to him, neck craned to catch a glimpse of his face once his breathing had evened out. She'd have to kick him out of bed before the morning light crawled over the horizon, but for now she let him lie there.

A hand tugged at her finger, insistent. For a second she thought Ricky was pulling her back to bed, but his hands were tangled in her bedsheets. When she felt the pull for a third insistent time, her gut lurched. Holding up her hand, she watched threads of light tense and loosen with the movement of her fingers. When she stilled them, one trembled like a taut fishing line dipping below the surface of the river. Something had caught on one of the lines of magic protecting the farm, and it was fighting back.

Neither Garrett nor Isaac was asleep on the couch. The door to Isaac's new room was shut. No one had bothered to keep up the appearance of having used the pullout mattress. But that was a problem for the morning. The tendrils of magic pulled at her, urging her out the door.

She stepped off the porch and onto a vein of light. Something about the magic encased her, arterial, and she could feel the thrum of the earth beneath her feet as she walked inside its glow, wide as a deer trail, down toward the rabbit hutch.

Laurel hadn't been the one to pick red paint for the rabbit hutch. Whichever long-deceased relative had built it to house chickens or carrier pigeons had. She'd kept up the tradition without thinking much about it, applying a new coat every few years when the paint flecked off enough to expose the weathered wood to the elements. The makeup of the paint had gone from lead to latex, but the message communicated by the color had always been the same: a warning. Stay away.

But coyotes were blind to the red spectrum. They couldn't read the warning in the red paint. They couldn't see the blood they spilled across the floor of the hutch when they dug past the chicken wire wrapped at the base and went after the albino New Zealand meat rabbits Laurel kept. Nor could they see the red light affixed to the front of the hunting rifle Laurel used on night hunts to illuminate them before she culled them.

Now the sky glowed red, sunrise red, hunting red. Laurel could taste the threat in its light as she wandered to the rabbit hutch. Her eye caught on a shadow in the window. A man's shape, too vague to belong to anything true. She saw the danger ahead, no warning sign necessary.

The door was closed but unlatched. *Predators could get in,* she thought distantly, reaching up to pull the latch and the door with it.

A predator already had.

Beyond the little door she could hear the scratch of claw, the soft flop of white rabbits loping across the wood floor of the hutch. The devil loomed over them, completely still against the shadowed black wall, an impression of a person's shape and nothing more.

His voice was a hiss of wood splintering into skin as he proclaimed, "Ah, Early magic. I can't see you. I can't smell you. But I know you, Laurel Early, beyond sense. You're right . . ." A claw-like shadow snaked out, moving like a dowsing rod until it sharpened to a point a hair's breadth away from her cheek. Laurel bit her tongue to keep from breathing. "There."

She didn't flinch, holding her ground even as fear settled heavy in her gut. "You hold no dominion here."

She thought of the sleeping bodies in the farmhouse, of Ricky lying there vulnerable with his open mouth. There had to be something more to the root-like magic under the ground. There had to be a reason she was the one holding it in her hands. What was it for if not for fighting back? Flowers had roots, too, and sometimes they had thorns. If she had to stick him in place, she could do it with something sharp.

Laurel shoved, pressing her will against where she thought the devil was. If she relied more on her fingers than her eyesight to carry her forward through the dark, she could feel the vague shape she needed to hold, stark and wrong against the soft shadows. If she pushed hard enough, maybe she could push him out of existence. It was a half-brained, half-asleep thought, the sort of plan that came from feeling power she couldn't understand. But it was what she had.

Laurel could not make out any other features clearly, leaning forward with the effort it took to hold the devil to the wall. She could feel the strain of the spell in her shoulders. She squinted to see what might have been an arm, a wrist, a hand still pointing from the darkness, but it could have been a loose nail sticking out from a board.

"Careful how sharp you make yourself," the devil warned, his voice labored. "You'll cut me an opening. There's holes enough in your defenses. Something nasty might slip through. Maybe it already has."

The shadow lunged forward. At once, the face Laurel had been looking for solidified before her, close enough to catch her between its teeth. Two yellowed, lidless eyes glinted bright with mischief. His smile stretched out like a row of old piano keys, ivory, the sort that echoed slaughter when pressed. Laurel fell backward onto the dirt in her haste to get away. Something shrieked from the floor, loud enough to wake the whole hillside.

The soft body of one of her rabbits fell at her feet. Its red eyes had gone pale and bloodless. Laurel recoiled as the devil's voice licked around the shell of her ear. "Fight me all you want, but you can't hold me down without holding me close. I'll be nearby when your guard slips, and then I'll slip inside you."

Laurel sat on the dirt long after the shadow faded. Her skin felt numb, prickling around her. She lost sight of the protection spell she'd woven. There was only the cold blue of the sky before sunrise. She reached for the rabbit's body with stiff, sore limbs. It was limp and warm in her hands; it had not been dead long enough for death's touch to make itself known. She held the tiny thing to her chest, her heartbeat against its still body. In the darkness, she cried.

Death had come to her farm again, a strange, unnatural shade of the death she knew. It had struck down one of her rabbits. The devil hadn't made his way into the farmhouse, but he'd opened a door and killed something she'd thought she kept safe. That meant no one was safe. She needed a new plan.

She could not stomach the thought of cleaning the carcass but couldn't stomach the waste of its life, either. It had to feed something living, not just the devil's appetite. She walked down the hillside to a little hollow place where she dumped food scraps for wildlife to eat. She laid its body down among the grease and potato peels. Before too long, scavengers would make use of what she could not.

She was not yet halfway up the hill when her phone began to vibrate.

CHAPTER
THIRTY-THREE

U NKNOWN CALLER, it said, but the voice was unmistakably Christine's on the other end of the line, hoarse with sleep. "You called?" she asked when Laurel answered.

Laurel blinked. "You called me," she said, frowning at her cell phone as she opened the screen door to the porch. She cast a nervous glance over her shoulder.

"Right. I'm horrible with the—" There was a pause in which Laurel could very nearly hear Christine gesticulating, possibly with a cigarette, to encompass the broad field neither of them seemed to want to call magic out loud. "Before my second cigarette."

It didn't matter who had called whom. Laurel knew why Christine was calling, even if Christine did not. "I saw him again."

"The devil?" Christine swore, a long and fluent stream of

words that made Laurel cringe. She held the phone away from her ear until it went silent.

"He was in my rabbit hutch. I don't know what to do."

Christine sighed, an exhale of smoke that Laurel could almost smell. "Listen. Bring a jar of dirt off your farm and pick me up a pack of Marlboro Lights on your way over. You're old enough to do that, right?"

"I'm old enough," Laurel snapped. Christine's laughter did nothing to ease her irritation. Laurel reminded herself that Christine was being helpful, in her way, and swallowed down the urge to repeat some of the ugly things Ricky had said. "But I don't have a car. I wrecked mine."

"Then you'll take one of theirs," Christine said. Laurel wasn't sure whether she was predicting the future or making a suggestion.

Laurel considered Garrett's truck, but his keys were probably stashed in the back pocket of his jeans, which were either on his person or on Isaac's floor. She didn't care to open the door to find out which. Jay's keys hung from a nail embedded in the wall by the front door, where he could grab them at a moment's notice.

"Anyone will forgive you if you save them," Christine insisted. "But you need to hurry."

Laurel hung up the phone and snatched the keys off the nail.

In the short time it took to drive to Baldridge Hill, the sun rose. There was a gas station at the bottom. There, the station attendant blinked sleepily when Laurel ordered a pack of Marlboros, as though considering IDing her, but he slid them over without argument.

The road curved past a golf course, one of the only establishments in the county where Laurel had never ventured. It did not belong to her nor any other local. Ohioans with time and money to spare rented carts for the day to drive up and down its slopes from one hole to the next. Its manicured green, dotted with small copses of uniform pine trees planted in neat lines, stood in stark contrast to the cow pastures and wooded ridges in the rest of the county. The effect was rather uncanny, especially when Laurel rounded another curve to the base of the hill where the trailers began.

Warm light glowed in the windows of a few trailers, decked with flags or Christmas lights, their yards dotted with painted concrete statues or rosebushes or hollow, rusted-out cars. Some trailers seemed as though they might be unoccupied, though it was easier to tell for sure in the winter, when thin blue trails of woodsmoke rose from their stovepipes. Two were nothing more than scorched remnants on abandoned lots, one for sale by owner. As Laurel slowed the truck, she heard a bark through her open window. A lean brindled mutt with sharp yellow eyes stretched against the chain-link fence of a dog run, fussing at her as she passed. She waved to it as the truck thundered up the drive.

The strangest trailer was the one that belonged to Christine. Situated at the top of the hill, it borrowed some aspects of its design from the other trailers. Creeper climbed its outer walls, but here the garden outside was lush and well tended. No light glowed in the windows, but the sparkling Christmas lights wrapped around the porch flashed gold. In the front yard, a circle of limestone rocks held a mound of ash from a left-over fire. Around it were three weathered Adirondack chairs, once painted white but now misted with green moss. Christine perched on one, legs crossed, sipping a cup of coffee. She gave a little wave as Laurel pulled into the gravel driveway.

"Did you bring my cigarettes?" she asked when Laurel hopped out of the truck. She wore a pair of bleach-stained pajama pants with chili peppers printed on them and a black tank top. Laurel pulled the pack of cigarettes from her purse.

"In that case, welcome," Christine said. She stretched, leaving her coffee mug on the chair. "Let's do this inside."

"Nice house," Laurel lied, peeking around the trailer. The laundry basket looked like it had been vulture-picked for clean clothes. A thin film of grease coated the dishwater in the sink. Nail polish bottles in every hue sat atop paperback novels and under the yellow spotted leaves of thirsty potted plants.

"House enough for me," Christine agreed cheerily, picking her way around a pile of newspapers to reach the coffee table, where twin towers of junk mail and unwashed dishes threatened to spill onto the floor. "Better inheritance than yours. I'm the only devil on my land."

Laurel, holding a jar of unholy dirt in one hand, could hardly argue. "How'd you know my number?" she asked instead.

Christine sniffed, but it was clear it was mostly for effect. "Ricky Mobley is trying to save your life and deigned to speak to me on that account."

Laurel turned to the sunken couch, picking a couple of newspapers off its surface to find a place to sit. "For what it's worth, I don't share his sentiments about you."

Christine shook her head. "No, you don't control him. He does enough all by himself. But enough about boys." She picked up a spray bottle labeled "cleansing" with blue painter's tape and Sharpie. She shook it hard, then sprayed it liberally throughout the dim room, aiming at the corners and a spot above their heads. Atomized droplets caught on a light source Laurel could not locate, smelling faintly of gin and neroli and Listerine.

"What's in the bottle?"

"Something to wipe out the negativity that I've no doubt filled my house with so we can get to the root of all that nasty hiding in your soil."

"I thought witches burnt sage?" Laurel picked a tangle out of her hair. She'd forgotten to brush it before rushing out of the house, but Christine was still in pajama pants, so it was clear magic did not require getting gussied up to work.

"If I wanted my house to smell like weed, I'd just light up a blunt and call the house cleansed." Christine motioned to an old cigar box sitting on her coffee table.

Laurel declined. "Better not add recreational drug use to grand theft auto."

"You're a troublemaker, Laurel Early. What would your mother say?" Christine lifted the coffeepot in offering, and Laurel nodded, willing to accept hospitality without intoxication. The mug of black coffee Christine handed her was printed with the address and phone number for the county credit union. Her own was a chipped anniversary gift from a local factory that shut down ten years prior, taking all the jobs and half the town with it.

Laurel swallowed a sip. "If I'd known you'd ask after her, I would have mentioned it when she appeared in my washhouse yesterday afternoon."

Christine stilled, setting the coffee pot down. "In person? You could touch her?"

Laurel spread her hands out, giving an awkward shrug. "The spell worked, like you said. I lifted a little bit of the pressure off her, and she appeared." Laurel explained the tooth, the feeling of falling into Anna's body, how Anna had summoned the devil. How she'd failed to banish it. Laurel had felt a thousand deaths in the bones of creatures she'd cleaned, but holding on to Anna's thoughts as she bled out at the bottom of a well was different. She rushed over the ending, afraid that if she lingered on the details, she might feel the loss.

When she finished, Christine sucked her teeth, shaking her head a little. "I don't blame her for wanting Dry Valley gone, but what a way to do it."

Laurel felt the blood drain from her face. She'd tried her hardest to banish the thought from her mind, that her mother had been the origin of the thing terrorizing her. "She didn't mean to, I don't think. Not really, not like that."

Christine raised an eyebrow at Laurel's thin excuse but did not tear it apart. Instead, she said, "It must have taken so much just to bind him. Lingering on after death to make sure he couldn't get out? That's strength. That's power."

No one had ever described Anna as powerful. If anyone spoke of her at all, they'd say she was sick or cursed. She'd killed herself, and to the people of Dry Valley that meant she was a waste. As the child Anna had left behind, Laurel was viewed at best as a victim of poor circumstance, and at worst, a victim of her mother's so-called selfishness.

But Anna's life meant something more than a curse to Laurel, even if she was rarely given more than a bad lens with which to view her. Anna had died protecting her. She'd managed to linger on past the limits of breath and body just to keep Laurel safe. It was the vindication Laurel had been hoping for her whole life, even if she couldn't tell the town. Anna had been powerful. She'd made a powerful choice, and as a result, Laurel had lived.

Laurel considered the coffee mug in her hands. Porcelain bright as the bones that had spoken to her long before she'd ever thought there was more power to magic than the last scream of a dying thing. "You said to do magic, I had to want it. But I never wanted what the bones would tell me. They just did."

When Christine responded after a long pause of consideration, it was not to Laurel, but to a cross-stitch on the door. HOME SWEET HOME. "You wanted to understand death. Magic was providing you an answer, the only way it knew how."

"That makes sense, I suppose. And now that she's not dead, there's more that she can show me—"

Christine's face twisted like she'd sucked up salt with her last sip of coffee. "She is dead, Laurel."

"She's not just bones anymore!" Laurel blurted. "She's not just one story of a swift end played on repeat each time I reach for her. She talks to me. She can touch me. I always wondered if there was anything more to death than dying. I always hoped . . ." For a mother. And if not that, some holy visitation, sun-bleached and glowing, sword-pierced by her daughter's suffering and shedding healing tears. A madonna. "This isn't what I hoped. But it's something."

"Oh, Laurel." She flinched at the pity in Christine's voice. But there wasn't more to it than that. Christine simply reached for the jar of dirt Laurel had brought and studied it with a frown. "She can't hold him off forever. We've got to work fast."

Laurel cocked her head, setting her mug down on the coffee table. Her mother's voice echoed in her ear. She felt the pulse of the earth in her throat. "What does the dirt do?"

"The dirt knows what I don't. Are you ready to find out what?"

Laurel tried to square herself up, to *mean it* like when she had faced down the bone monster across the clearing, trying to protect everything she loved with a spell she didn't know how to weave. She was afraid to root herself like she had the night before, in case reaching into the dirt meant pulling the devil out. "Is this like coming home, where if I don't say yes it won't work?"

Christine smirked. "I don't expect you to lie about it. I expect you to fetch me a seed from that drawer in my refrigerator. Get one of those lazy wife beans, they're an honest sort. Heirloom or whatever, none of that Monsanto shit mixed in with their blood."

"Beans don't have blood," Laurel said, reaching into the refrigerator and thumbing through seed bags.

"True," Christine said, stretching out the vowel as long as it would go. "Technically, neither does dirt. But when you're working with life force, think of it as blood. That way you've got something in common. All magic is blood magic. Nothing you do seems trivial."

Laurel could still feel the web of Ricky's veins against her fingertips and her own blood answering. She blushed red. "None of this seems trivial to me."

Christine raised an eyebrow, like she'd read something surprising over Laurel's shoulder. "It's good, ain't it?" she continued. "Even if it's rarely worth the price you pay to get involved."

"If it's not worth it, why do it?"

"Do what?" Christine asked, mock innocent.

Laurel scowled at her. "Magic."

Christine's fingers hovered over the lip of the jar. "Dirt and the overgrowth, life and death, it's all just God's muscles moving forward. But if offered the chance to be a part of it, how could you pass it up?"

Laurel's hand came up to her chest, fingers resting at her sternum. She could feel Ricky's breath lingering in her lungs.

It was a dangerous thing to hold, but Christine was right. She wouldn't give it up.

She pinched the bean between her fingers. There was nothing miraculous about it—its dried seed coat, envelope-colored body, a capsule of potential—root and plant a whisper just beneath what she could see. "God's muscle," Christine whispered. She dropped the bean into the jar.

It began to grow. First, a snaky white tendril of root plunged its way into the soil, branching and spreading throughout the jar until the whole tangled mess pressed against the glass. A curling green shoot shoved aside the dirt above. It spread into two heart-shaped green leaves and kept going. It trembled as it stretched upward, shaking out new leaf after new vine. In a final, bowing motion, blossoms unfurled like flags, white and pink-tinged. They leaned forward as if to whisper in Christine's ear.

Laurel felt light-headed with wonder. The joy of watching something blooming into life before her eyes shot across her body like sparks. There were fireworks in her heart as the leaves stretched toward the sun.

Christine closed her eyes and began to speak. "Blood spilled on the hillside, running toward the wound. Two hands doing the cutting—one dead, the other long outside of time. The plants don't like it. All they can do is root into the soil and try to hold on."

She tilted her head up to look at Laurel, as though expecting her to translate the meaning from a series of disjointed images.

"I don't speak dream."

Christine shrugged. "Different gifts." She frowned. The bean had slowed its growth, but as they spoke its leaves began to yellow, curling in on themselves.

"What's happening?" Laurel asked.

Christine pushed the front door of the trailer open with her hip, hoisting the mason jar as she stepped onto the porch. "Come on, into the garden. It's not her fault we don't understand the message she's relayed. Let's get her out of this demonic soil before it hurts her worse."

Laurel followed, nearly tripping over her own feet as she stumbled down the steps into the garden. Her thoughts tangled in the strange rhythm of life and death, dirt and growth, the carousel spin of the bean vines as its leaves unfurled from a tiny seed. God's muscle, but so few were privy to the machinations. She'd been granted a peek behind the curtain, the chance to watch the world at work.

Christine shook the dust of the Early farm from the roots of the bean plant. She buried her finger deep in her own dirt, then withdrew her finger and dropped the plant into the space she left behind. Like an infant's tiny fist, the plant wrapped around her pinky and allowed her to guide it toward a weather-beaten trellis above.

"You've got a wonderful garden," Laurel said, and the plants around her beamed. There was enough ripening there to feed a family. There was no blossom-end rot or pest-infested stem on any plants. The wine-dark okra plants fanned their leaves in the sunshine. The tomatoes hung red as rubies and gold as sunlight from their vines. Laurel didn't see a hoe or a bag of white, powdery fertilizer anywhere in sight. She'd farmed all her life and never seen a thing like it.

"It's just love," Christine said, shy but pleased at Laurel's compliment. "Start 'em out on the stuff and they can't help but come to life."

Laurel took a couple of steps back into the spring garden to look at the summer squash ripening under fat, prickly leaves. A peculiar expression crossed Christine's face, and she climbed to her feet. "Life and death. A hand outside of time. Where the rules don't apply, I wonder—"

"You're speaking dream again." Laurel patted the keys in her pocket, noting the warm light of the morning sun. She was running out of time.

"If I'm wrong, I'm wrong, but if I'm right ..." Christine pointed down at the withered patch of springtime lettuce in the garden. It had long since bolted and died back, and was waiting for the cool fall weather to be replanted. "You've got power I don't. You should try it."

"Try to do what?"

Christine grinned. "Bring it back to life."

"I can't do that." Laurel balked, staring at the dead stalks in front of her. "Bringing the dead back to life? No one can do that." *If I could, do you think I would have left my mother under that hill?*

Christine shook her head, responding to what Laurel couldn't say aloud. "There's seeds in the soil. You can't bring it back to life, but you can bring more life from it."

Laurel knelt down in the field of lettuce, running a hand over a withered leaf. It was wilted—soft and too dry, leaving a coating of dirt on her fingertips. But maybe the dirt beneath her fingertips held something more. "It's not like the bean. I don't know where they are."

"Root yourself down and feel it," Christine insisted, and she took Laurel's hand and shoved it into the dirt.

There was a disorienting moment where the only thing Laurel could feel was Christine, worn wax-paper thin from overwork but still desperate to try something that might save them all.

Then Laurel fell, fingers first, into the wet soil. She could feel the rain that lingered in the dirt, unabsorbed by dormant roots. And farther still, smaller than grains of rice, lettuce seeds sprinkled throughout the soil. She let her fingers run over them, coaxing shy roots from their hulls. They protested, afraid of the heat above, desperate for a cool breeze, but resistance gave way, and they began to bloom.

Above them, decomposition was king. Laurel could feel the pattern of the magic where the soil met the sun. The warp and weft of it was life and death. With one hand she could further rot the lettuce above, bringing up the new lettuce from underground.

"Life," Christine murmured, as Laurel pulled her hands out of the dirt. Laurel's lungs prickled, like she'd taken in a sharp breath of cold air. The lettuce bed, once sunburnt and moth-ridden, stood reaching for the sun, its leaves thrumming with chlorophyll.

"Or something like it," Laurel whispered. A laugh burst up from within her, as if the sunlight streaming through her fingers had been enough to melt something at her core. Laurel hadn't been happy like this in a long time.

"Laurel," Christine said, her voice cold as a sudden frost. "Your phone is ringing inside. There's bad news in the buzzing."

It wasn't her uncle on the line. It was Ricky.

"Well, Jay's fit to be tied, and Garrett wasn't too pleased, either, waking up to an empty bed at a time like this. My personal feelings on the matter aside, you and Isaac Graves better come on back before they come after you."

Laurel's stomach dropped like she'd stepped into a sinkhole. "I'm at Christine's, but I came alone."

Ricky was silent, and then Laurel heard him shout Garrett's name, mouth held away from the receiver. Laurel hung up.

"And there's your bad news," Christine said. "You'll need to hurry home. And Laurel?"

"Yeah?" Laurel asked, keys in hand.

"Remember the blood. You're going to need it."

CHAPTER THIRTY-FOUR

A body is a strange, miraculous thing. A clever mass of sinew and tissue, nerves and glands and organ meat. Boiled down to basic elements, there's nothing divine about it. Sugar here and acid there, carbon and oxygen and calcium in the bone, iron in the blood, nitrates and methane and metal and gas. A miracle of chemicals, prompted by electric shock and hormone surge to move forward, to keep synthesizing protein and consuming oxygen, to pump blood and plasma from vein to vein.

A body in crisis turns from chemical to magical when deliberating whether to live or die. More soul than substance for just a moment, the body compiles its resources, counts its cells, and decides from there whether or not the life inside the body is worth the effort it will take to perform the miracle of living beyond the impact; the accident. Human beings live in fear and awe of the primal spot in the back of their mind that weighs the worth of their life against the blow it has received. They worry they'll be found unworthy of their body's miracle.

Everyone knew the legends that grew out of the Dry Valley soil. Impossible encounters, where grown men lost their arms, but not their lives, to table saws and farming implements. Hunting accidents that shredded muscle and churned guts but left the heart intact and beating. Classmates who nearly drowned while drunk in the river but found themselves onshore, breathing in spite of their stupidity.

Surviving the impossible was a crowning glory in a piece of country where one wrong footfall could mean snakebite or a sinkhole in the frail limestone crust of their hollow earth. The stories were proof: Bodies were meant to survive, or no one would have settled in the South.

But more intimately than survival, people in town knew the stories of non-survival. The stories kept on bed rest in the back bedroom when it became clear that no home health nurse could get them to eat anymore. The great-grandfather, tired of being the only one left alive among the photographs and unfinished sewing projects. Those who took to drinking or kept refilling a prescription once their backs had snapped and they could no longer work. Those who undertook the slow process of dying from a broken heart.

Isaac's father was well on his way to becoming that kind of story when his girlfriend ran off weeks after giving birth to her son. Isaac grew up alongside the story of a man determined not to survive his own life. None of the rich growth blossoming on the Early farm could slough off the rot his father left in him. The black mold that clung to Isaac spoiled him from the inside out. Since childhood he'd been dying by proxy, an act that weakened the foundation of his body until he walked on hollow limbs, threatening to crack with every step out of the dark. Isaac had never thought of himself as someone who would survive, if his body were given the choice to save him.

This clearing was as peaceful a place to die as any. The body that tentatively belonged to Isaac hung from the sycamore branch by the cemetery. Clover in the grass brushed his bare feet, reminding him of a kiss he had received not long ago. A cool breeze stirred what strands of hair weren't matted with blood. Songbirds called to each other in the canopy above, their sound muted by the cotton of concussion and fuzzy feeling of blood loss. The pain he felt had numbed with shock. There was only the damp smell of soil after storm.

It was hard to think of a more pleasant way to die. Perhaps with wrists less raw from rope. Or more ribs intact. Perhaps after one last good stretch of his muscles, but that might bring back the unbearable sting of injury. The body attempted to flex the clumsy fingers he could barely feel. Even that small effort brought him closer to an exhaustion deeper than any he'd ever felt, an exhaustion that would lead to permanent sleep.

Isaac fought that feeling, slogging through syrupy thoughts to move the body beneath the sycamore tree. If he fell asleep, he might never wake. When consciousness was pain and sleep provided relief, some miraculous part of his body made the choice for him.

His heart had dreamed up escape routes, flourishing under the thought of sunlight someplace else. He'd made plans and mistakes from that hope, fashioned himself a way out of that dank apartment and onto better soil. He'd lived like living was a choice he could make. But his body knew the truth in the grass brushing his feet. He was not meant to survive Dry Valley. Boys like him never were.

He'd gotten so close to the escape he'd dreamed of before Anna snatched it from his grasp. He could hardly remember the taste around the blood staining his teeth pink. The ropes binding his wrists stung, but the hands above had gone numb. A mercy, one of Anna's few. She had not tied him in a way that showed she intended to untie him alive. He couldn't see her, only the hollowed-out grave she'd pulled herself from, but he could feel the pulsing anxiety washing off her spirit in waves. She was waiting for someone, or for something to begin, before she brought about Isaac's end.

The body's thoughts began to wander from the heat of the summer morning into a bright light above. The twine loosened its grip on the body's wrists but instead of gravity pulling him to the ground, unseen forces lifted him up, up, up . . .

The boy who called the body home did not think he was ready to leave just yet. Animal instinct drove him away from the source of pain that lay somewhere in his breathing. He was well aware that his rib cage was a collapsing cave and the slowing flood of his blood would soon drown him from the inside, but the pulse inside his chest was familiar. He was not certain how he would move forward without the reassuring beat of it.

The body hanging from the tree branch wheezed a shaking breath and swayed a little from the force of the movement, toes brushing the grass and clover beneath its feet. It was swollen and discolored and worse for the wear, but it was not a corpse. Not yet.

CHAPTER
THIRTY-FIVE

L aurel nearly flew back home, giddy with exhaustion and terror, new knowledge and new fear. Her gut twisted as she swallowed a bubble of wild, inappropriate laughter that stemmed from the pit of her stomach, where the worry she kept trying to swallow down lived. Isaac was fine. Isaac was okay. Isaac had probably risen early to check his traps. They'd put on a pot of coffee, and he'd be back before it filled, bitching about his bad luck like he had most other days that summer.

It was a stupid story, a lie, but it calmed her heart rate long enough for the tricky part of the drive home, back down the hill toward the highway. Over and over, the thunk of the rabbit's body at her feet played in her ears. The threat the devil had made, the promise there'd been holes in her defenses. The protective spell she'd woven had been strong but incomplete. The protection her mother had pasted to the window of the bedroom where Isaac slept had faded and crumbled to dust. She wasn't certain where the error lay, but she'd made a mistake. She could only pray it hadn't been fatal.

The spell had been real after all, hadn't it? Her mother had appeared. Those tendrils of energy, they'd been real, too. She had to hold on to that, the idea that she could do something *real*. Her entire heart was focused on the fleeting moment of clarity when she saw magic and understood it, when she'd held it in her grasp and felt its pulse thrumming through the living world, stronger than the hum of the pickup-truck engine in her ears. She'd slipped her fingers under the tissue of God's muscle and manipulated the hand, cupping the farm close and keeping safe the people within it. She'd brought life forward from dormant seeds. It was more than a magic trick. More than listening to a story told to her. She could tell one back and give it a new ending. One of breath and new life. One of survival.

The joy within her wilted as she parked the truck to see Garrett and Ricky standing at the end of the driveway, faces pale and flat with horror that edged into grief. Isaac hadn't come back.

She hopped out of the truck. "Any news?"

Ricky shook his head. Garrett kicked a walnut across the gravel, watching its trajectory instead of looking at Laurel.

"Keys," Jay demanded, and she handed them over without protest. "I'm gonna see if I can't find him on the road."

Laurel closed her small hand around his huge one as best she could. "Waste of time. He wasn't there or the highway. How long has he been missing?"

They all turned to Garrett, whose fists were clenched in the pockets of his jeans. His expression was utterly blank. "I don't know," he said, his voice dull. "I woke up and he was gone."

It had been nearly half an hour since Laurel had left Christine's. "He didn't go to check his traps?"

"I said he's gone," Garrett snarled at her. "Don't you think I'd know where to find him if he'd gone off on his own?"

"Calm down," Ricky murmured, doing nothing more than threaten to turn the rage bubbling inside Garrett on himself. "We'll find him."

There was the fear that they might not know how to find the person they knew best in this world. Laurel couldn't let it take root in her. She had to keep moving.

What do you do to find someone lost in the woods? Laurel tilted her head to the sky, praying something could offer her a bird's-eye view. If she shot a crow, like a bored teenager with a BB gun, would she be able to look through its eyes in its last moments if she reached into its rib cage? Would she see Isaac through the red glaze of betrayal before it plummeted to the ground?

The plant life in the woods far outnumbered any wildlife, and no bird or deer or fox would do for her what a plant might be able to sense with its nerve-like roots. Of course. It made sense now. To find someone lost in the woods, she needed to ask a tree.

A complex network of honey locust trees littered the farm. It was a pest of a tree, heavy-laden with thorns, but their shallow, expansive root system overlapped every other tree in the woods. Trees communicated with each other through their roots, a telegraph line informing of impending drought or fire, infection or infestation. The honey locusts had a reach farther than any wise old oak. If Isaac was within reach, they could point out where.

She didn't need to walk far. There were three in her line of vision alone, thin trunks mottled with lichen, branches blooming with thorns. She approached the one nearest to her. Its thorns beckoned her close, aimed at her chest, her neck, the lids of her eyes. Its roots urged her to trip.

She reached out, careful, and held its outstretched branch between two fingers. She closed her eyes, concentrating on Christine's words, remembering the veins in Ricky's wrists. *Find the blood in it.*

The tree hissed awake beneath her fingers, echoing a rasping thought into her mind, curious. *Blood?* Laurel could see into its core, the soft wood beyond the bark mottled with lichen and fungi. It was a young tree, fast-growing. One that hadn't been there when she'd been born. It was hungry for what pulsed beneath her skin.

Information, she corrected it.

Not without blood, it insisted, a whine that sparked across her skin like a dragging needle. She ought to have expected the request from a tree meant to wound.

If you confess, you can taste, Laurel thought.

Taste first, the tree cried, its red thorns bared.

The act of stabbing her finger onto a thorn was harder than she expected. It might have been easier to slice herself with her pocketknife than to offer herself up to the honey locust. But Isaac might be in danger. She had to find him.

She slapped the palm of her hand down onto the thorn. Blood bloomed in the puncture, quick and red, filling the space where skin had been. A trivial amount, but the wetness sickened her as it dripped down her palm. She smeared it on the branch.

You can't do anything with this blood. You are a tree. The climbing beans would have never asked so much of her. She hadn't seen them bite Christine's hand before they fed her the knowledge she needed.

The tree laughed, a susurrus of leaves that reminded her of

the skulls hanging from her washhouse wall. *Makes it all the sweeter. Unnecessary pain.*

Laurel bit her tongue. *Just tell me what you taste. Tell me where he is.*

We've tasted this blood before, blood that shares two sets of veins. Up the hill, it splatters the roots of a sycamore.

Laurel winced as the V-shaped scar on her finger that she'd earned one summer when she and Isaac taught themselves to twirl knives throbbed, one of a million little scrapes and scars they'd earned bleeding together. They'd been bonded by blood and by this town, maybe since before they were born. *Is he still alive?*

If the soil weren't so hungry, we might drain him dry, but the dripping slows with each beat of his heart, and by the time you put him into the ground where our roots might find him, he will be dead.

"Thank you," Laurel said, withdrawing her hand and mind from the dark heart of the honey locust. The blood from the wound had already scabbed and stopped. It was barely a wound at all.

Images lingered in the back of Laurel's mind, harder to scrub out than the blood in her palm. She spat into her hand, scraping the last traces off on her jeans. She could see the peeling white bark, the broad leaves. The sycamore in the cemetery, its roots spattered with red. There was no time to waste.

"Start the four-wheeler," she called to Jay. "He's in the grave-yard."

CHAPTER
THIRTY-SIX

W hat the hell happened to the gravestones?" Jay shouted over the roar of the engine. The lovely, quiet cemetery looked like a carcass picked at by scavengers. The gray slabs of weatherworn stone had been knocked over, some splintered in the grass. The dirt that had covered Anna's casket had been flung in huge clods to one side of the grave. Every piece of limestone stuck into the clay had been cast across the grass. The heavy seal of the concrete vault was broken, its cover flung aside. Laurel could see the wooden casket peeking out from the shadow of the grave.

She didn't have time to waste worrying about the dead. The honey locust hadn't lied. An old rope wrapped around the trunk of the sycamore, draped across the lowest branch. From its other edge, Isaac hung, pale and still. His hands were swollen and purple, his wrists rubbed raw by the tight bindings holding him in place. Blood stained his shirt and the roots of the tree, dried and rust colored. A sound of panic lodged in her throat.

Garrett leaped from the bed before Jay could shut the engine off. Not bothering to untangle the chain holding the bull gate closed, he cleared the fence, landing hard on the other side. He didn't stop moving as he reached into his back pocket for a knife. "One of you catch him. He's about to land hard."

Ricky was right behind his brother, throwing his lanky body over the gate, the soles of his boots imprinting in the drying earth. He reached the limb where Isaac was strung, craning upward to study the rope tied around his wrists. "He's bound really tight," he hissed. "He is breathing, but it's shallow."

"He's breathing," Garrett said. "That's enough. Here we go. Ricky?" He flicked open the knife blade, advancing toward the tree trunk.

The stirring wind in the trees transformed into the shriek of birds, and Laurel slowed to a stop where she had been quick behind them. The monster thundered into the cemetery clearing, a clattering framework of ligament and tendon, socket and sharp teeth hanging off it like talismans warding away the living. Its empty cranium swiveled back and forth, a manic grin plastered across its skeletal face. Its strength was not in its limbs or speed but in the space between its ribs. It was desiccated muscle and nerve-dead bones. It felt nothing as it cleared the wire fence, even as a piece of its arm caught and came off with a clatter.

"Devil," Laurel snarled. She understood this shoddy assemblage of bones. Dangling like ornaments from dried tendon, Laurel could see the threads of magic woven together, knotted with bones she had bleached herself and discarded. Her bone pile that had up and walked away was standing before its creator now. She could tear that spell apart. She could suck the devil from the hollow places where the marrow had withered. The only magic was in meaning it, and Laurel meant to end this.

Ricky's eyes widened with horror as the creature charged Garrett. "Look out!" he cried.

The monster plowed into Garrett, sending him flying onto the dirt, the knife knocked from his hands. He bounced to his feet as quickly as he could, scrambling to pick up the knife from where it had slid, perilously close to the open grave. He pressed a hand to his stinging ribs, wincing with obvious pain. "What the hell is that thing?"

The bone monster turned back to the sycamore tree, but this time, Laurel was ready. She threw herself between it and Garrett, forcing the mass of its body to halt rather than run her over. The hollow knock of dry bone on dry bone clattered as it slowed. The monster loomed over her, silent but for the creaking of the dried skeletal structure threatening to collapse under its own weight. Nothing reflected in the hollow sockets of its eyes but the back of its skull and the clover field below.

Garrett took the split second Laurel had given him. He darted back toward the rope at the sycamore trunk and began to saw at it with his thin knife blade. Ricky's outstretched arms were ready to catch Isaac as he fell.

The monster twisted, creaking with effort, but as its broken arm stretched to knock Ricky aside, Laurel reached out to shove the rancor of breathless bones away. Her fingers brushed its cold forearm, and a blast of rotten thought assaulted the inside of her skull. She seized the arm in a vise grip as her stomach heaved. Pain lit across her body, rocketing through her jaw and the back of her skull. Her neck snapped, her ribs crushed like chalk, the bone of her leg split through her skin. Her nostrils filled with wet mud and the scent of her own blood as she stared up at the sun setting around the rim of the well she'd fallen into.

This wasn't an animal's death.

Somehow, Anna had seeped into the pores of these old, dry bones.

"Mom?" Laurel asked.

Anna materialized in the space between her daughter and the bone monster, gray as her tombstone. She dripped well water onto the upturned ground.

Laurel hit the dirt hard as she fell, but the pain barely registered. She stared up in wonder. Anna reached a hand out to help her up. Laurel lay stunned, breath knocked from her lungs by the sight of her mother, her decayed flesh peeling from her face as she grinned, every tooth glinting in the mouth of the monster hovering at her shoulder.

"Mom," Laurel whispered. The word was a ghost in her mouth.

"Sweetheart," Anna said, "take my hand."

"That—that creature." Laurel spat onto the grass, trying to clear the taste of death from her tongue. "It's you. In the bones. You're controlling them."

Anna's voice was a coffin nail scraping against the glass of a bedroom window after dark. "They're meant to protect you. Let them go, and they'll do my will."

Laurel's legs felt like jelly, and her vision was blurred, sweat in her eyes and blood running from a cut across her forearm. "What, exactly, will they do?"

Anna Early had assembled this shoddy creature from Laurel's bone pile, desperation evident in the way it shambled forward, its hasty construction barely able to support its weight. Its supernatural strength had only ever been Anna pulling puppet strings. Had Anna been there the night Laurel wrecked the car?

When she'd sprinted with Isaac through the darkness, had she been running from her own mother?

There was a sickening thud as Isaac dropped from the tree and into Ricky's waiting arms. Isaac groaned against Ricky's shoulder, his eyelids fluttering. The knife slipped from Garrett's hands as he tripped in his haste to get to Isaac. Jay stood, mouth agape, seemingly unaware of the chaos around him. His gaze was fixated only on the ghost he'd sworn could never come back to haunt them, standing by the open grave he'd poured dirt on top of so many years ago.

If Anna noticed him, if she even recognized him, she gave no sign. Her clouded eyes pleaded with Laurel. "You know what they'll do. I showed you. The taste of death drives him away. Fresh bone, fresh blood drained from veins still screaming, struggling not to give in to the knife. You'd do well to coat yourself in it, so he can't touch you."

Several things occurred to Laurel at once. "The blood by the well. That was you?" Anna nodded. "The blood in the jugs?"

"To paint you head to toe. To hide you from him."

"That explosion could have killed us." Her mother had no answer. She moved her hand and the marionette strings of magic pulled the bone monster to attention. When it moved, the hideous noise startled Jay into action. He sprang toward the back of the four-wheeler, letting down the gate so that the boys could place Isaac in the bed.

"Put him down," Anna said through gritted teeth as the bone monster swung toward them. "We need his bones. We need his blood. It's the only way to stop the devil."

Laurel couldn't help but stare at her mother, a hideous, broken thing, imperfect and decaying, stuck in the same haunted patterns, trying to save herself the only way she knew how.

More death. "Is this the best you can do? A monster made out of the discarded quilt scraps of carcasses?"

"I can do better with you here. The knife. The boy. The spell needs love to work, someone who cares for you enough to keep you safe. He can do it when there's nothing left of me to keep it moving. He volunteered, but I need you to make the cuts."

"We're not going to taxidermy one of my friends!"

Anna smiled, sweet, water dripping from between broken teeth. "What's more death to you? You've seen too much already." Before Laurel could protest, bony fingers pinched her wrist, dragging her up out of the dirt. "No more arguing. No time. He sat at the bottom of that well for years, singing the same old song about my baby and her bones, how he'd lick them clean and step inside. He wants to wear you while he destroys everything I've ever touched, every place I've ever been. If you think I'll let him have you— Take the knife. Make the cuts. Do what you have to do to save yourself."

"You stay away from him," Garrett growled. His knife was far out of reach but he crouched, ready to take the first swing in a fight Laurel knew he'd lose.

Laurel looked at the monster before her, and the mother standing on the soil where Laurel's own grave would someday be. Rotting flesh and hands soaked with blood. There was no difference between the woman who brought her into this world and the horrific heap of bones haunting their woods. That was Anna's creation. Just like Laurel.

Her disgust must have shown. "Then *I'll* cut," Anna said, face grim. "Someone needs to mother you."

Laurel hadn't had much of a taste of mothering before, and it was quickly turning bitter on her tongue. The guardian angel she'd envisioned held a harp, not vengeance. Before she could wield the knife, Laurel grabbed her mother's hand, pulling herself to her feet. Anna stood before her, almost her height. She was young, wild-haired, and terrified. There was no pulse fluttering under Laurel's thumb, but there was terror in her mother's dead eyes. Terror had driven her far past reason. There was nothing she wouldn't do to save her child.

Laurel was young, too, just as scared and desperate. But she was not alone. She didn't need the love of dead things to protect her. Not when there was so much life.

She faced her mother, a warped mirror image of her face, a reminder that she would die one day, and placed her hand on Anna's shoulder. Pink skin against graying flesh, life against death, Laurel held her mother close enough to see through her into the cemetery beyond. Her heart thudded against her mother's empty ribs.

Time fizzled out as they embraced until they stood somewhere beyond it, beyond climbing light and sinking shadow, the meager markers humans used to count their time from living to dead. This embrace was a bridge Laurel needed to build, to take her mother from one side to the other. And there had only ever been one tool with which she could craft it. Her useless magic, her simple trick: Her hands knew death.

Laurel opened her hands and ears to the horrible crack of bones against the wall of the well, failure and blood loss, the pulp of her nerve in the bed of her gum, the last raw bit of pain Anna felt before everything ended.

The death she could feel emanating from those bones was putrid, guilty. She wanted to recoil from it. It was cruel and pointless, so violent, so early. A mother at the bottom of the well, a baby longing somewhere up above, without a goodbye, without any do-overs, without a true start. The pain of an orphaning slicing through them both, strong enough to sever the dead from the living world.

"You're dead," she whispered against her mother's ear. "You won't get to save me. You won't get to watch me grow up. You won't get the time we're meant to have together, because it was taken from us."

"Don't do this! It's hurting you." Anna writhed in Laurel's grasp. "It will break you apart. You'll never be whole without the love you bury with me."

"I know," Laurel said, pushing all the mortal pain her mother's bones emitted right back into their marrow. "That's what grief is."

She held one last gift at the tips of her fingers, the one that came after the pain and the panic of death. It wasn't a memory. It wasn't magic. It was the hopeful, constructed afterlife where her mother had lived in her head for as long as she could remember. A warm summer day, a blackberry day in the bottoms, with silken white cabbage butterflies fluttering around in the hazy heat. The sticky-sweet stain of berries on her fingers and mouth for an eternity, with the river to swim in and nowhere to be. It was simple but peaceful. It was where Laurel wanted to be herself someday.

The last thing Laurel saw before Anna broke apart under her hands were her own eyes, tearstained, an alien expression she'd never seen in them. They stared right through her until, at last, they closed. Laurel's hands held nothing. There was nothing more to hold.

CHAPTER
THIRTY-SEVEN

I killed my mother, Laurel thought. It echoed in her head like a ricocheting bullet, tearing through her every sense until it was the only thing Laurel knew. There was no more Anna Early, not where human hands could reach. There was a body in a casket, a name on a gravestone; but without the ghost, all that remained of Anna was organic matter and memories, and both would decompose with time.

The only stain of blood on Laurel's hands was her own, dried underneath her fingernails. Had Christine read this future for Laurel in her palms? Or did they only whisper promises of a long life and good fortune, with no trace of how many people Laurel would hurt, what she'd tear apart, who she would kill?

She'd stopped her, sure. But what price had she paid for their freedom, and how fleeting was that moment?

There was no sound. No birdsong or breeze or breath. Laurel's ears rang hollow, the sound as empty as her hands. Anna was dead. Laurel's work had brought about her second orphaning. The air around her grew cooler, the static of something big taking a breath large enough to pull the oxygen from the earth. Winter in the high heat of summer coming for every living thing. Unimpeded, it felt like a flood rising before her. They were on the highest ground the farm had to offer, but it wouldn't be enough to escape.

That was why the birdsong stopped, why the wind stilled, why silence coated her ears like wax.

The devil was free.

There was a grunt as Ricky and Garrett shifted Isaac into a more comfortable position on the bed of the four-wheeler.

"That's a lot of blood on his T-shirt," Ricky observed. His fingers hovered gingerly above the other boy's puffy wrists, afraid to settle on the raw skin there. "Christ, *Christ*, I don't know how to get him comfortable. There's so much blood."

Garrett slid into the bed of the truck, lifting Isaac so he could support his head on the drive back down to the farmhouse. He winced as his hands came away tinged with the blood soaking through Isaac's shirt. Unsure of where to put his hands that wouldn't cause more pain, he finally settled for wrapping an arm around Isaac's shoulders and resting a finger against the pulse point on Isaac's neck. Whatever he felt alarmed him. "His pulse is strange. He's not breathing right."

Ricky was almost as pale as Isaac. His hands hovered over the hem of Isaac's shirt. "We can't help him. I saw this before, when a table saw hit a guy in the chest with a two-by-four. He's bleeding on the inside."

"There's no time to waste," Laurel said, her voice raw and

strange. "Get him to a hospital. Go on, all of you, go. There's nothing more you can do here."

Ricky recovered from the shock, speaking up as Jay's expression turned from stunned to furious. "You're not coming?"

"She's coming," Jay said, resolute, a man used to his word being law on this land. But Laurel had to do what he couldn't, and Jay had to get Isaac to safety. Their roles had been decided for them, these desperate tasks that superseded his ability to parent her or even keep her safe. That was her responsibility now. His was to leave.

"I'm staying here," she insisted.

"Isaac would want you with him," Garrett said, his voice thin with terror.

"He'll have to settle for you," she replied. "There's nothing between the devil and the dirt now. I've got to do what Anna couldn't. I have to stop him."

Garrett protested, "But she—what was left of her; that was a creature. She was made of magic. You're just a girl."

This thought brought Laurel up short. She could still feel the pins-and-needles buzzing sensation of what she'd done under her skin. Trying to destroy a monster, Anna had warped herself into the very image of one. She'd been a girl once, too, before magic changed her. What did Laurel look like to them, after the awful thing she'd just done? Who would she be if she managed to survive what she had to do? It would be better to go it alone.

"I'll stay with you," Ricky volunteered, starting forward. She held up a hand to stop him.

"You'll go with them. I won't be far behind. Do me the favor of keeping yourself safe, or this won't mean anything at all."

He didn't mind her coming to stand before him. He pressed

a kiss to her forehead. She remembered her fingers tracing his wrists, the heat of his skin where it met hers. The look in his eyes was so vital, so sincere, she had to look away. "Laurel, you don't have to do this alone," he said.

"No more death," she said. "I just lost my mother again. I can't take any more. I need you to run and live."

"But—"

Jay seemed to understand what Ricky could not. Ever practical, he climbed into the four-wheeler. "Ricky, no more arguing. Isaac can't wait."

The expression crossing Ricky's face was mutinous, but he did as he was told. He watched Laurel, and she watched him, as the four-wheeler drove away.

The silence swallowed up the sound of the engine gunning down the hill long before it should have. She took one breath, then another, the only living thing in the cemetery. That was nothing new. Laurel didn't mind being alone in this place. She was alone here most mornings, with only the headstones for company. She wasn't afraid of anything the silence of the dead had to offer. The only thing that frightened her was what might happen to the living she loved.

The ozone scent of the air prickled across her skin like little teeth. The first bite of fall had come too early, winter in the next breath. Roots spreading deep into the soil around her shriveled, reeling back from the poison pulsating through the groundwater. They couldn't escape the onslaught of silence. The devil wanted his due. Anna's deftly woven protection spells fell to earth like stars blinking out of the sky. He was coming for them, unimpeded. But she'd be faster. She'd be cleverer. She'd end him, once and for all.

CHAPTER
THIRTY-EIGHT

The four-wheeler engine whined as Jay accelerated down the hill. All Garrett's attention was focused on the arm he had wrapped around Isaac's body, hoping he wasn't squeezing too tightly, hoping the ride hadn't jostled something vital, hoping the warning against carrying passengers in the bed of the four-wheeler wouldn't see itself realized today. Under the hum of the engine and the labored sound of Isaac's breath, there was nothing. The dead silence emanating from the woods made his stomach sick. The animal part of his brain begged him to escape.

The farmhouse was close now. They'd have to maneuver Isaac into the backseat of Jay's truck to take him to the hospital. There wasn't room in his own truck for the four of them, and time was of the essence. The hospital twenty minutes away was a good place to die, so they'd have to drive the extra half hour into the city if they didn't want to gamble with the time a helicopter might take to land. It was a delicate balancing act, measuring time against the blood sticking to Garrett's palms. Garrett wasn't good with delicate.

He hadn't planned to wake up alone this morning. He thought he'd have more time before he had to let Isaac go. He'd thought, after falling asleep with Isaac's arm thrown heavy over his chest, his breathing easy and even in his ear, that they were finished keeping each other at arm's length. But the next morning, it might as well have been a dream.

Garrett regretted those first moments spent orienting himself as he stared up at the yellowing painted ceiling, taking stock of the state of the sheets, the sounds outside the door. He regretted the confusion as he slid his jeans on and the anger he bit back as he padded into an empty living room. He regretted the seconds spent hesitating before he knocked at Laurel's bedroom door to see if Isaac was behind it. He'd been jealous. Laurel and Isaac were a matched set. They had an easy intimacy, a suffocating, all-consuming friendship that could squelch the new flame between himself and Isaac he was trying to ignite. Of course they'd gone off together, twin heroes, to rustle up whatever evil had left them alone while they slept.

But they hadn't been spared.

All Garrett could think was that he should have been faster. He should have been more alert, or trusting, or brave. He should have been smarter or made different decisions.

He squeezed Ricky's hand tight enough that he felt his knuckles crack. Ricky held on until they parked at the bottom of the hill. Then he let go only long enough to lift Isaac, sliding him into the backseat of Jay's truck. Garrett settled Isaac's head in his lap, fingers tentatively combing through some of the bloody hair matted to his scalp. "Well, come on," Jay said to Ricky, who was hesitating outside the door. "Get in. We've got to go."

But Ricky didn't get in. He squeezed Garrett's hand again, hard, and Garrett understood. "No," Garrett said, as Ricky pulled away.

"'Fraid so." Ricky shrugged as though it were nothing.

"I need you with me," Garrett said, blood seeping through Isaac's T-shirt onto his hands. This was a hopeless situation that he was trying, *trying* to believe would work out well. Ricky, hand on the doorframe, refused to meet his eyes. There'd be forms to sign at the hospital. Insurance he wasn't sure that Isaac still had. His hands were coated in blood. He didn't think he could sign anything. He didn't think he could get them to stop shaking.

Ricky shouldered open the truck door. "Get out of here with him. I've got to help her."

Garrett scoffed. "You're not going to save her. You're just going to break her heart."

Ricky leaned closer, resting a finger on Isaac's faint pulse. "Isaac hasn't got long. You haven't got a chance if he takes her. If he takes me first, she's the one with the power to stop him."

"Idiot." The word snarled from Garrett, sharper than he intended it.

"I know."

"Ricky, we've got to go," Jay insisted, turning the key in the ignition.

The earth warped around them like the sound of a distant gunshot. The next breath Garrett took felt short, empty of oxygen, full of panic. There was a dry, crackling texture to the silent woods, prime kindling for a fire.

"I've got to get moving, or I'll run out of time," Ricky murmured. He rapped on the roof of the truck with his knuckles in lieu of a goodbye and turned to go.

"Wait!" Garrett shifted Isaac across his hips as he reached into his back pocket for his truck keys. He offered them to Ricky, palm flat. "If you get the chance to run, take it."

Ricky was stunned, mouth agape in the thinning air. "But, your truck. You're just leaving it with me?"

"Use it. Wreck it. I don't care. But get out of here alive."

Ricky didn't say anything beyond offering a weak smile as he snatched the keys from Garrett's hand. He squared his shoulders and headed for the woods without so much as a backward glance. Garrett wanted to call him back, but his voice was weak with panic. He couldn't get the words out. He closed the door, and Jay started their ascent up the driveway. Garrett pressed his forehead to the window and watched as his brother disappeared into the trees.

It was so easy to lose the things you loved.

Garrett had spent months preparing for a world in which he had no hope of being with Isaac Graves. That morning, it had been so easy to give in to that resignation once more. But fear solidified his priorities in a way that months of overthinking couldn't: He wanted Isaac. Safe, happy, and far away from here.

Garrett threaded his fingers through Isaac's as the truck rolled up the hill, his forehead pressed hard into the glass. He held Isaac's hand tight enough for them both and hoped that even if he woke up next to a hospital bed tomorrow, he wouldn't wake up alone again.

CHAPTER
THIRTY-NINE

I nstead of following the driveway back toward the bottoms, Laurel half scrambled, half slid down the steep, wooded ridge from the top of the hill to the fields below. She could sense the eerie silence emanating from its source: the well where her mother had drowned. Cold stillness wound its way up the hill, suspending animation of everything living in the woods and crumbling it to ash. She'd find the devil where it all began.

Close to the equipment barn, the landscape before her was alien. Monochrome as an old tintype picture of the farm over one hundred years prior, but instead of young growth and new buildings, the apocalyptic landscape before her was dry with un-natural death. The devil at the height of his power did not just kill, he consumed. There was no decomposition, only a chill lack of it. Without rot, nothing could grow. The soil was flat under her feet.

Icy light filtered through the branches of dead trees, emanating sterile white from the strange sun hanging off-center in the sky. Where it caught on dust motes, they glittered like broken pixels. The dirt path fell somewhere between static and snow. It did not hold Laurel's footprints as she wandered farther on, looking up at the branches for any signs of life.

There was the old pin oak, its pointed leaves scattered in the snowy ground. The ash tree had fallen, splintered across the road. She picked her way over its pieces, dead as plastic in her hands. She'd never seen a tree fall without something new growing from its stump. It housed no mushroom spore or snake hole. No poison ivy crept across its trunk. No ants gnawed busily under its bark, and no centipedes crawled across its rough surface.

She passed the place she'd first faced the devil down, the rough ridge where she'd fallen attempting to escape him. He'd had only a sliver of the power he had now, yet he'd managed to bring her to her knees. She wouldn't be taken unawares again, and she wasn't powerless anymore. She understood the world she was working with intimately. She knew the names of the flowers withered under her feet, the broad bull thistle and the delicate wood sorrel blossoms alike. The vicious thorns of the honey locust and the strength of the red oak. Her hands remembered what it was like to call life from the soil. But could she call life back from this?

Down the path, the scentless air caught on something foul. Sharp and musky, the scent of death was comforting to Laurel even as she choked from how it overwhelmed her, filthy in comparison to the chemical-clean scent of the devil's hunger. The dead doe she'd found the other day with the boys was draped over the maple branch still. Under her hanging flesh, there were patches of untouched earth, like melted snow showing forth signs of spring.

Her mother had been right; the dead weren't to the devil's taste. Rot repulsed him. Laurel bent down to the tufts of moss underneath the doe's feet, pressing her ear to the earth. She could hear, barely a whisper, the beat of life. It pulsed against her cheek for a second of warmth, a sacrifice of oxygen and energy. Then it crumpled into black dust, staining her skin. She cried out, fingers pricked with the feeling of frostbite. She wiped the sensation off on her jeans and moved on. There was no time to mourn. There was no time to think. She had to keep going.

She stepped onto the lot, the only living thing among the dust and rusted skeletons of old cars. The menacing cover of scrap metal and old wood that barred any childhood exploration of the old well had been cast aside, a scab of rust peeled away to let the devil free.

A headache crept from her temples across her skull as she stared, half snow-blind, into the heart of the devil's destruction.

A voice from the well called to her: "Laurel!"

Ricky, hip cocked against the stone side of the well. His Colgate smile sparkled even in the ashen landscape. His green eyes glowed with mischief against the backdrop of wilted tobacco leaf and dead wildflowers. All swagger and spit, immortal in his youth and arrogance. He was a man made for the apocalypse.

"I told you not to follow me!" she snapped. "Get away from here!"

But Ricky did not move. The wicked grin on his face split into something sinister. "Laurel Early." The devil's bloody voice burbled out of Ricky's mouth, smile stretching wider than his teeth could contain.

"Christ," she whispered, almost falling over herself in her haste to get away from him. The sharp slice of a rusted fender pressed against her back.

"Not quite," he drawled.

"What have you done?" Nausea burned through her core, illuminating the shredded place where only seconds ago her heart had beaten. Ache spread through her ribs as she heaved another breath. There wasn't enough oxygen in the air left to scream.

"He sacrificed himself." The devil stretched out his hands as wide as they could go and let his wrists drop, mocking. "Aren't you proud? He thought you would be. It's what the land cries for, whispering into your deaf ears as you bend low to serve it. *Sacrifice.*"

Laurel's throat clenched and she bit back another wave of nausea. The devil had Ricky's body, maneuvering it like a puppet to torture Laurel. Was this the possession he'd threatened her with? Was Ricky's soul suspended somewhere high above them, lost in the poisonous satisfaction of being separate from his body? How could she free him? "You've taken him instead of me. That wasn't the deal you tried to make."

The devil shook Ricky's head, his grin all mouth and alien on Ricky's face. "He was proud of himself, of how much weaker he was than you. He thought his weakness was a strength, cunning enough to buy you time and solve this puzzle. But you and I both know, don't we? Strength is strength. You're strong. So am I. The two of us, together, wouldn't that be something?"

Laurel kicked a cloud of dust at the well, snarling and utterly dismissive like she knew Ricky could be. If she could just reach some part of him, maybe she had a chance at freeing him. Desperate to stall long enough to come up with a plan, she said,

"That won't happen. I'll end you or die trying like my mother so you can't have me."

"Your mother," the devil said with a chuckle, a sound like clotted blood. "You've picked off her protection spells, stripping yourself naked of her love. Why, if not to give your bones to me like I asked?"

"I won't give up that easily." Laurel stared hard at Ricky's face, searching for some miracle, some sign of life.

The devil huffed, an exaggerated pout on an endless, hungry mouth. "Then I will chase you until you tire of running."

"I'll be excellent prey," Laurel promised, "if you let Ricky go. Leave him and you can come try to destroy me."

"Okay," he agreed.

Just like that, the devil cut the puppet strings and Ricky's body fell, sending up a puff of static and snow as it hit the ground hard.

Laurel whimpered. Her knees stung, an afterthought. She did not remember falling onto them, but there she was, crawling toward where Ricky lay collapsed at a weird angle. Her breath caught around a gulp of odorless air. It choked her, and she heaved a cough, trying to spit onto the dirt. Saliva clung to the dry inside of her mouth, dribbling across her chin. She wiped her face. There wasn't enough oxygen. Air escaped her lungs, but no replacement came to fill each space her breath emptied.

The body in front of her was cold beneath her fingers. Her hands understood what her eyes saw but couldn't comprehend: faded tie-dye, dust on blond hair, milky eyes, and still breath.

The devil had not possessed Ricky; he had killed him.

CHAPTER FORTY

Laurel lay defeated next to Ricky's corpse. The whole of her world was poisoned, crisp and odorless and strange where the Kentucky humidity should have saturated Ricky's cold body with warmth and sunlight. Her hand rested on the gnarled twist of Ricky's leg, and though it did nothing to warm her, there was some comfort in holding him, the last familiar thing in an unrecognizable world. She held him like a child holding a doll, burying her face against his stomach to hide from the sight of everything destroyed.

There was something in his pocket, small, and unlikely to be useful. She reached anyway. Her fingers closed around something familiar. The keys to Garrett's truck. "No," she whispered. Maybe Ricky hadn't been the only one caught on the farm.

"Laurel," the devil said, "I'm tired of waiting."

"Did you kill them?" she asked, rolling onto her back, blinking in the toxic light. The devil had abandoned the dedicated imitation of Ricky and adopted the shape of something more horrific, an occasional flicker of Ricky's smile or hands or swaggering walk caught up in something bigger, darker, more deadly. The sharp shadow that had killed her rabbit reached towards her with Ricky's hands.

"I'll kill them all," he promised sweetly, "but if you let me inside you, you won't have to watch."

Laurel's fists clenched. She wanted to push him back into the well where all the other nightmares lived and drown him in its depths.

"This is my land," she told him.

She'd been cut by its many stalks and thorn trees, scraped herself raw across the sharp stones at the bottom of its river. With blood and sweat and desperation she'd set her claim. He would not have it, or her.

The devil shrugged. "The trees recognize no master until you carve them into fence posts. You are simply a servant, tending to the soil that will one day own you."

"Better it than you," Laurel said.

The devil sneered. His fingers closed around the edge of her soul, a touch so light she could hardly feel it. He stood very still above her, an imitation of Ricky's arms stretched out in offering and ending in claws. "If you just took a taste of my power, nothing would ever own you. Creator, destroyer. You could eat the world."

She could taste the promise in the devil's whisper: chocolate cake, sweet tea, smoked duck on Christmas and banana pudding for Isaac's birthday. Her hand twitched. She felt the soul-crushing weight of boredom, the monotony in work that pulled at her back and threatened to break it. The lettuce seeds under her fingers had opened up everything to her. Would it ever be enough to tend to the earth after she'd used magic to control it?

With that power at her fingertips, she'd never be bored again. She tasted banana pudding on her tongue.

All she had to do was to bite down.

She pushed herself up on her elbows and spat at the devil instead.

He scoffed. "Well then. Remember, I did offer nicely."

He administered a swift kick to her sternum, knocking her into the soil. She was reminded of Christine's hand on the back of her neck, pushing her down into the dirt. From that vantage point she could feel every seed humming under the soil, waiting for her to bring them to life. All she had to do was reach out. There were veins of magic somewhere far beneath her, untapped by the devil's thirst. If she could only touch them.

The pressure on her chest increased. A foot, a hand, a claw. The devil peered down at her, Ricky's face distorting with glee until it melted away entirely. It wasn't a face any more than the shapes in the shadows of the rabbit hutch had been. One second he was the red stain of dead leaves across the forest floor; the next, the flashing jaws of a fox swallowing silvery fish skin. His mouth stank of fertilizer in a stream, runoff from a meatpacking plant. He was an expanse of fungi coating the thin skin of a young box elm, a tangle of plastic wrapped tight around a turtle's neck. He was a wolf at the door, his many teeth raring for blood. His foot dug into her chest. His hand reached to grasp her throat.

Laurel's fingers struggled for purchase in the ashy soil. Deeper beneath the devil's waste, some seeds remained, so small they might have been missed in the gluttonous spread of his feasting. With her hands down in the dirt, Laurel could see that his consumption was expansive, but not total. Here and there, like patches of melting snow, life struggled on.

Laurel reached into the clay with beggar's hands, and the seeds came alive. She was still the farmer, even if she had done more to destroy than to cultivate these hungry roots.

"Live for me."

The words felt hollow in her mouth. She was undeserving of a miracle. Still, whether or not she deserved it, she felt one coursing within her hands. A clean, green tendril of bindweed burst from the soil by her hand, wrapping around the devil's foot.

The devil looked down at the new life, perplexed. Almost elegantly, he plucked the shoot from the ground, stuffing it into his mouth. "Is that all the fight you've got?" he asked, talking with his mouth full.

But she did have fight, and it crept down the hillside toward him. A flood of climbing things, bindweed and creeper, relentless in its approach. It carried bits of dead things to her, offering them up as the woods always had. It pulled the doe's carcass from the tree branch. It tugged along a coyote's den of deer and possum and raccoon bones, some sucked of their marrow, some with wet flesh still clinging to their sides. It knocked over her pickle buckets of macerated bone and brought those along. There had always been enough death in the woods to satisfy Laurel's art before, and what she created now would be no different. She could see the bones taking shape in her mind, binding together a new creature at the bottom of the hill.

She gave it hands where hers were pinned down, claws where she could not fight for herself. Teeth like her mother had, sharp enough to bite all the devil's rot from the world. She tied it together with the very exorcism herbs her mother had pasted to her window as a baby, plantain and violet leaf. Muscle that had desiccated long ago fused with growing greenery, flourishing robust across the yellowed radial bone of a deer, flexing with the strength of a new joint.

In the clearing, the devil stared, slack-jawed, as a marionette string of vines pulled the new monster to its feet. A bruise-colored trillium blossomed in its chest, velvet petals peeking out from its sternum. The creature opened its coneflower eyes, blinking awake in the sick white light.

The devil let Laurel go, rounding on the creature in the clearing. Fear flickered in and out of the shape he tried to hold. The white underbelly of an Asian carp flashed in Laurel's vision. She could strike now and gut him. The monster moved, blowing in like a breeze of sweet milkweed scent.

The devil lurched toward it, a momentary reprieve Laurel used to fill her lungs with oxygen before his jaw unhinged and he sucked the air from the world, withering the trailing tendrils of bindweed dripping from the creature's claws. But more sprouted up in place of what he killed. It grew and overgrew, reincarnating faster than he could kill it. Seasons passed in the blink of an eye as new growth darkened, hardened, and withered away. Casings split open and whimsical tufts of seeds spilled forth into the soil, springing to new life, all of it stretching toward the devil's open mouth as though it were the sun.

Just as she couldn't hack away every weed encroaching on the tobacco field, the devil couldn't eat the overgrowth as fast as it grew up against him. Another shooting tendril of new growth sprouted in place of every plant he cut down. His jaw extended wider and wider to control it, but he was losing the battle. That was the overgrowth's promise. No matter who tried to cut down the woods, shaping buildings from the mud and bulldozing clearings of wildflowers into urban sprawl, the overgrowth would sprout through the concrete and turn every field fallow once more. So many old houses dotting the county, their foundations crumbling under the weight of creeper, already knew what the devil was learning.

Appetite and endless greed were no match for the life of the woods.

His gaping mouth, now stretched over half the sky, was the target. Laurel readied herself and the bone monster, struggling to her feet. She took a deep breath, slowing her pounding heart. She wouldn't miss. She never missed.

Reaching out her dirt-blackened hands, she let them fold together like a thunderclap, every streaming channel of energy she'd picked from the earth focused on her target. At the sound, the bone monster sprang straight into the maw of the devil. One gulp and it was gone. Death, not to the devil's taste, would do the poison work that jimsonweed could not.

The devil's mouth stretched thin, foam speckled. He choked, a sticky sound that echoed through the bottoms. He spat onto the ground, a tangle of bloodroot, its tiny white flowers splashing across the dead earth. Clawed hands came up to his mouth, trying to fish the bones from his throat. A long, viperous tongue flashed like a whip across the landscape before his needle fingers disappeared into his mouth. The tongue followed after, curling in on itself as the devil gave another sick cough. His yellow eyes flashed with fear as he sucked them in, each tombstone tooth toppling like a domino into the endless black. With a hot blast of fetid air, the devil's death rattle knocked Laurel back into the dirt. She buried her nose in the humid smell of earth and waited. When she lifted her eyes, the world was still.

CHAPTER
FORTY-ONE

L aurel took a breath and another, head aching, lungs burning. There wasn't enough oxygen in the air. The trees
weren't breathing. In the silent field beyond the hollow, rusted-
out skeletons of cars, she saw nothing but withered tobacco
leaf and flattened grass. No cycle of decomposition and growth
moved the world forward in this flat, lifeless place. No mito-
chondria stirred within the cells of the dead things sprinkled
across the ground. What sugar the devil left behind lay dormant
in desiccated skin. The only muscles she could move were hers,
and they ached so badly she'd rather set them down next to
Ricky and sleep.

She couldn't bring her eyes to focus on his face. It hurt too
much to look at him, his still body unnaturally chilled. She
rubbed her hands against the denim of his jeans, trying to spark
heat from the friction. She'd pulled those jeans off him the

night before, hands on hot skin. But there was no warmth left. His body was as cold as the woods.

Some fragile part of her had gone icy in answer when he fell, and she realized what the devil had done to him. When Laurel forced herself to look at his face, the ice shattered. Tears rolled down her cheeks, fast, ugly, hot, alive. Her lagging, grieving mind forced her through the steps of checking vital signs.

Breathless body.

He's gone.

Central pulse absent.

He's gone.

Laurel had kissed these pale lips last night, flush and pink with life. The body before her was sallow and bruised, skin settled, his green eyes cloudy. The devil's unnatural power had drained him, so dead it seemed as though he'd been that way for days, though she'd just seen him alive not an hour before. Already into the process of decomposition, his muscles would not take to compressions, his lungs would not hold her breath. His heart would not beat. She could not bring him back.

Say it.

"He's dead," she whispered.

Like the spread of tangled vines and split seed casings scattered across the ground, their tufted seeds falling to the earth like snow. He was dead as the dirt beneath her hands and the trees in the woods, her mother on the hill. The devil's handiwork was all around. What had once been a verdant river valley was a lifeless ruin.

She held Ricky's stiff hand, her thumb rubbing circles in his palm in a futile effort to get him warm. It wasn't fair. This wasn't the future she had planned.

Still, the heat of magic pooled in her palms, itching for more work. The devil's magic worked only to ruin; the death it caused was unnatural. She could pull life out of the seeds around her. Why couldn't she push life back into Ricky?

What life should look like didn't matter anymore. She needed to get him warm.

She could turn the death around her into life if she worked the right way. If she could command the seeds, couldn't she wake the bacteria in the soil? Couldn't she call forth the decomposers and warm the dirt around her with their flurry of activity? And if she warmed Ricky's body, maybe she could pull his soul back into it.

"Rot," she whispered, spreading her fingers out as far as they would go.

From its death, the ground listened. The spray of bloodroot browned, petals withered, and leaves grew thin as gossamer dragonfly wing, breaking into veins and then into dust, sprinkling the dirt black. A few scattered bones that hadn't followed the monster into the devil's mouth yellowed and broke apart, slivering like melting soap before they sank into nothing.

Laurel laughed as summer sunlight broke through the strange, sterile light the devil left behind. New wind stirred through the dead trees, stripping leaves from their bare branches to be subsumed. The world smelled of humus and falltime, even in the heat of summer. The soil beneath her burned hot against her skin. She could hear it, the whisper running just under the earth of breaking down and building up.

Seeds off the flag leaves scattered on the slow breeze. They hit the new black dirt and broke apart, capillary-thin roots cutting down in search of food. Decomposers buzzed up from underground, worm eggs and beetle grubs, black fly nymphs and gnat larvae. Cool relief came and went as the tender white crowns of grass blossomed into jade-green blades and faded golden above her, spreading seeds and crashing back to earth once more. Their shadows crested like waves following the inhale, exhale rhythm of a thousand springs and falls.

From the splintered trunks of dead trees came tender green saplings, sprouting sturdy trunks, encroaching from the tangle of woods into the prairie blooming through the bottoms. They flowered and fruited and spoiled over, ripening and rotting on the forest floor.

No deer foraged under their spreading branches and no squirrels scurried up their trunks, but Laurel could hear birdsong in the distance. Animals would return to fill the places they'd vacated, guided back down ancestral paths by metals and magnets under the earth. There was only one soul she needed to guide home.

Satisfied with the pace of growth from the woods, she turned back to Ricky's body. It was time to bring him back to life.

He was gone.

Laurel looked up, startled, expecting to find him standing. When she looked back down, a guilty twist of morning glory handed her a torn piece of T-shirt. Cold horror climbed her spine. An encroachment of brambles had sprouted up from near the well water, and they'd pulled Ricky's body halfway under them.

Laurel picked bramble shoots as fast as they could grow, swearing as she swatted them away. "Not him!" They cut, uncaring, into the flesh of her palms and kept coming.

She could not stop what she started. The devil hadn't lied; she was not the master of the earth around her. She could only tend it, push it here and there, and send it the way it knew to go already. But she could not trim back every flower in the forest or tell them where to grow.

Thorns cut into his flesh. They grew from everywhere, above his head and under him, splitting his skin and cutting up through his rib cage. He was dead; the earth wanted its due from him. It did not understand human sentiment, only that it was right to bury the dead. It wanted him underground.

"No," Laurel commanded, yanking her hands from the stove-hot soil. "Stop!" She tried to cut off the growth she'd started but she could not untangle her hands from the very plants that were eating Ricky.

She was foolish to have protested unfair outcomes. Decomposition was the only fair thing this farm had ever known. The overgrowth cared so little for any one life. Its only job was to make way for more life. Laurel had traded one hungry monster for another, and it demanded one hollow body to feed a forest of trees. Surely that was fair.

Laurel would not accept it. Instead, she burned. Magic thrummed through her fingers. She cut back the vines she'd called up, letting wet, gray smoke peel forth. She coughed, her throat raw from the fire, her core scorched hollow, too much magic in the palms of her hands, blistering them clean.

But new growth loved wildfire; as it smothered the flames, more grew from the ashes.

"Stop," she cried until her voice was burnt to coals. "Stop!"

How foolish she'd been to think she was any better than her mother, messing with a storm she could never have hoped to control. She had to flee the farm. She had to take what she could of Ricky, gathering his ribs against her own like she could hope to hold what was left of him. His parents, they'd gone on vacation for the summer, how would she explain to them that their son—

Grief bit her again, and she almost lost her footing, knocking loose soil down toward the scalding flames she was running from. The air was thick and hot; she could feel a sheen of sweat across the burnt skin of her forehead. She clung to what was left of Ricky as hard as she could, her boots weighing down each step as she struggled up the ridge.

She had his brother's keys. If the truck was still at the house, maybe she could escape.

She should escape.

Even if her dreams of cabbage butterflies and blackberry fantasies were ash. Ricky was gone, her mother was gone, and those were just the dead she'd touched. She did not know if Jay and Garrett had made it off the farm. She did not know if Isaac had survived her mother's torture. Even still, her feet carried her upward. Her body understood survival. It was making the decision for her, even as her mind turned over and over, looking for a way to escape the knowledge that nothing would ever be the same.

The good was gone, but Laurel was still standing on the same ground where it had grown. And she'd made things grow there before. Some of that good she'd cultivated. Her hands had to be good for something more than telling death stories.

This time when the limestone tripped her, she let it carry her to the ground, blistered palms stinging with the impact. The bones clattered onto the dry dirt before her, yellowed and brittle. She knew this soil. She knew these bones. She knew better than to do what suddenly seemed so obvious. The burn marks across her skin would scar, a permanent reminder of the lesson the overgrowth had tried to teach her. She tore the blisters open on hot bone. Let them scar deeper. She stroked her thumb across the mandible before her, teeth once hidden behind lips she'd kissed. She knew better.

She plunged her hands into the earth anyway.

CHAPTER
FORTY-TWO

C hristine hadn't decided if she was chasing fate or trying to outrun her guilt, even as she maneuvered her beaten-up '99 Corolla into the hospital parking garage. She could smell piss and peeling paint and desperate prayers in the elevator up to the lobby. The uninterested administrator at the front desk let her sign in and peel a sticker off without much more than a brief pause to search for the room number. She was grateful to skip past unnecessary scrutiny. She hadn't announced her intentions to visit, during her last, short phone call with Laurel to confirm: *Yes, he's still alive, yes, they say he's stable, he's been awake off and on, and yes, we hope he might pull through.* She was afraid Laurel would say no if she asked. So, forgiveness versus permission: She'd weighed the pros and cons of each and decided to show up uninvited, the way she often did.

She was hoping it would provide relief. After a week and

a half of shivering every time the heat of summer so much as touched her skin, after a morning that had ended with splinters in her hand and all the bindweed ripped from the back of her trailer to keep it from creeping in, after the taste of ash and mint toothpaste in the back of her mouth made her retch when she awoke from uneasy dreams of finger bones scratching the glass of her bedroom window, Christine did something she hardly ever did: She called in sick to work. She took a whole day off and used a quarter of a tank of gas. In her defense, she hadn't been well since Laurel's truck had pulled out of her driveway, and it was getting worse.

Sitting guard when she arrived at Isaac's hospital room was Garrett, one leg crossed over his knee as he fished ice chips out of a Styrofoam cup and scrolled through his phone. Not quite the dragon she'd feared. Garrett Mobley had never been a welcome sight to her before. Usually, he sneered a little whenever they crossed paths. But though exhaustion weighed at the corners of his mouth, the smile he gave her seemed genuine enough.

He stood when she approached, ice rattling, and she could smell at once the sticky sweetness of Sprite in the bottom of the cup, Irish Spring soap on his skin, Tide detergent in his T-shirt. He hadn't been here long. Maybe he and Laurel had just switched shifts, and she'd caught him at a good moment. He'd have more of them now that Isaac was stable and on the mend. Garrett could rest, if he remembered how to. But beyond the shuffle of every uncertain second, he'd have time to think about what had happened and Christine's inability to stop it. The blame would settle, and the sneer would return.

But all he said when she waved to him was, "Do you want to see him?"

Definitely a good moment.

"He'll sleep right through your visit, I'm afraid," Garrett said, his voice low. "They've got him on some meds. I wish they'd give me some. The way they're always in and out checking this and fiddling with that, I can't catch a wink of sleep the nights I stay here." It was dark in the room, but Christine could see Isaac asleep in the bed. He seemed smaller than she'd ever seen him, even when he'd habitually tried to shrink himself in anyone's field of vision. He'd lost some weight and his muscles had atrophied from a sudden withdrawal from farmwork. He hadn't shaved or had anyone do it for him, and the dark shadow of hair across his face magnified his hollowed-out cheeks, but his breath was slow and even, if not deep.

Christine wasn't a doctor. She was a psychic. Psychics, as a rule, did poorly in hospitals. She could barely manage a double shift at a small-town diner without drowning in other people's desperation. But there were high notes that she could cling to; the wail of a newborn baby, relief as a grandmother stabilized and blinked her eyes open to see her family surrounding her, the grim determination of someone certain they could beat the odds they'd been given.

And then there was Isaac Graves, breathing shallow but steady in a hospital bed. What she couldn't tell by looking at him, the monitors reflected, and what the monitors didn't show, Christine knew like her own lungs. She could smell it: a future. For so long, Christine had stayed away from Laurel because the scent of destiny made her sick. It was a rare perfume in Dry Valley, with its wild notes of possibility and base of uncertainty. It lingered long after the person who wore it walked away and it changed those exposed, like some strange radiation that brought them back to life. Most people didn't want one or denied what they had until they smothered out its light. But here it was again, after all this time.

She caught a whisper of motor oil and Ivory soap in one of the pillows she moved as she sat down in the chair placed by his side. Isaac's wrists were blotched with fading bruises. His hand faced upward as if waiting for her to take it. She hesitated to hold it, but she needed some point of connection to let her magic work.

No sooner had she reached out when Garrett blurted, "What are you—?"

There it was; the fear she'd been expecting. Christine snatched her hand away, apologetic, as Garrett continued, "No, don't stop, I was just wondering how you . . ." He trailed off, waving his hand a little to indicate magic, however it was he understood it.

"How I . . . ?" Christine echoed, trying to keep any semblance of mocking from her voice, her hand hovering above Isaac's skin as she waited for permission. She bit back a nervous peal of laughter. The heart monitor and Isaac's strange breath were the only sounds in the room. Garrett had been generous, even allowing her to see Isaac. And as she inwardly railed against having to explain her magic to someone who'd once reviled her for it, she reminded herself that people changed their minds all the time.

Garrett shifted uncomfortably before muttering, "Do what you want. I trust your . . . whatever. I just wanted you to know that I do."

It was what she needed. He had no reason to trust her magic or anyone else's. He had the results of magic before him: Isaac barely breathing—*still breathing*, she corrected herself. But he trusted her.

"I won't hurt him," she assured him, and pressed a hand against the roughness of Isaac's cheek instead. Her mind skipped right into the familiar path it always wandered down: *What happens next?*

What she touched was time, in thick fistfuls, more than she could grasp in one go. There were nights with dimmer stars and mornings that broke through blackout blinds and spilled thick across the carpet, golden as stabbed yolk in a hot pan. Fat, fried breakfasts and cereal in thin skim milk, blue as a faded bruise. A secondhand supper table creaked under the weight of years where they'd have to stretch each meal with rice and flour just to keep that table set. Memories that stuck to the ribs but hurt a little when they hugged tight the old, bruised cage that held his heart. But old wounds always would. He'd learn to live with it.

She'd never suspected Isaac Graves possessed much innate magic, and if he had at some point, she figured something in his life had killed it before she'd ever gotten a chance to look. Now, she considered, his survival drive seemed aided by supernatural forces. Perhaps his instinct to hide had kept her from looking too hard. He'd kept that flame cupped close. Everything in his environment seemed primed to fail him and yet, stubborn as pokeweed, he'd thrived. His ribs had punctured his lung and he was still breathing. And resting in a hospital bed in Cincinnati— no one could deny—he'd made it out of Dry Valley just as he'd intended.

Christine shook her fingers free when she withdrew her hand. It was his future, not hers, and she wouldn't keep a second of it from him. Isaac sighed in his sleep and might have opened his eyes if she'd whispered his name. Instead, she let him rest. There'd be plenty to do when he woke.

"I figure I owe you lunch," Garrett told her as she started to say her goodbyes out in the hallway, not ready to go home right yet.

"I figure you do," she said with a grin she only had to force a little. Christine couldn't help it. She jumped at the chance he offered her to figure out why she couldn't seem to walk away. "Lord knows I've put half that weight on you, as often as y'all are in my store."

"It ain't your store," he said with a roll of his eyes, but there wasn't any meanness to it. "Let me treat you to something better than the slop y'all dish out."

The food was palatable, but hers was better, and from the wry twist of Garrett's mouth as he lifted a green bean with his fork, he knew it, too. They were both too polite to comment on it while eating, and instead chewed in silence. It was not uncomfortable, sitting across from him at a table by the window, shifting sour mashed potatoes around on her tray. "It certainly is well priced," she said after a long moment.

"What a deal," he agreed tonelessly, taking a heavy swig from a bottle of tea. Then he pushed his tray back and said, "Listen, Christine, I owe you an apology as well as a thank-you, and I'm not good at giving either."

"I'm no good at taking them," she said, cutting him off quickly, "and I don't want them either way."

"Well, what do you want, then?" he asked. He sat back in the hard plastic chair as though it were a comfortable place to wait for her answer. She had all the time she wanted to come up with something worth saying out loud to someone she'd only just begun to trust. She could feel the remnants of Isaac's future under her fingertips. Hers was always harder to grasp.

She knew in an abstract, animal way what she wanted: True

rest, not just sleep, hours of time to spend on nothing impor-
tant, minutes not dictated by cost as they ticked away. A bottle of
nail polish in the verdant green of bruised mullein that coated
the inside of her eyelids every time she closed them. Orthopedic
shoes to dull the ache of the bone spur in her right foot. The
taste of food someone else had cooked for her might be nice for
a change.

When had she gotten so *boring*? When had her thoughts
shrunk to fit the size of the town she lived in? The thought
crystallized like sudden frost across the forefront of her mind:
The options offered to her were no different than the ones Isaac
had, or Garrett, or Laurel. Only the details were different. To
change herself, she'd have to either change Dry Valley or leave
it behind.

Laurel would stay. The love story between her and that patch
of unruly earth was womb to tomb. Ricky had his aspirations,
and he had Laurel. He'd stay, too. Isaac and Garrett were already gone, though she wasn't sure they knew it yet. She'd never
fit herself into their group, not when it was stretched so thin.
Wanting to be a part of them didn't make sense. Under those
circumstances, what was there left to want?

Christine scraped the last of her mashed potatoes from her
tray, and said, "I want you to fix my car."

CHAPTER FORTY-THREE

Isaac was alive. At least, he was pretty sure he was. The doctors had patched over the torn knit of his muscles and straightened every broken bone. There'd been a surgery and stitches, a few snatched seconds of memory between doses of medication, vomiting in the PACU, rustling movement by his bed, and cool hands on his brow, eventually solidifying into a morning as dusky violet as the dull ache of pain in his ribs when he woke up into some clarity and saw Garrett Mobley asleep next to him, propped up between two chairs with a folded pillow crammed under his neck and a thin blanket across his chest. He'd watched the rise and fall until the world around him turned blue, more aware with every breath that they'd survived.

There'd been hasty decisions, hospital decisions, made in the precious seconds snatched between codeine and sleep. One had led to this: them, a new city, together.

"I can't go back." Garrett had been the first one to voice what they were both thinking. He said it through his fingers as he held his face in his hands. It was after he'd ignored his ringing phone for a third time. After he'd thrown it under the hospital bed, but before he'd bent to retrieve it.

Isaac, bone-tired of the woods and waking from nightmares about them, had said, "Come with me."

"Where are we going to go?"

"Anywhere, together."

Anywhere hadn't been far from the hospital, but it had been far enough from the woods. Garrett had made most of the plans, while Isaac was still confused and cloudy and mean with hurt. He'd tried apologizing afterward, into the dark of the bedroom they shared, for the things he'd said and couldn't remember. Garrett had untangled himself from Isaac's grasp and said to the ceiling, "We've had enough regret for one lifetime, haven't we?"

Isaac hadn't been the only angry one, after all. But these days the sun was peeking back out of Garrett's smile. They were going to be okay.

They rented an apartment near the north side of the city. It wasn't much to look at, inside or out, just a second-story walk-up on a side street. One in a quadrant of housing occupied mostly by college students, an old brick building with the name GRIFFIN ARMS embedded in the cement block over the front doors. Rickety Juliet balconies made from prison-like iron bars housed dead plants and framed windows shaded with printed sheets and patterned flags, sports teams and mandalas and rainbows. Years of incense and pot smoke had settled like powdery ash into the cheap, plasticky carpeting. Tacky layers of white paint covered the cracked plaster walls.

Climbing the stairs to the apartment required some caution.

The boards were warped in the center from years of coed comings and goings. They creaked under their feet, but did not give, as they hauled up a couch they'd rescued from the curb, arguing about who could or should shoulder the weight, bickering about navigating it into the one-bedroom, utilities-included home they were making together.

Isaac wasn't broken by what had happened or fragile like he feared he would be after. He'd done more healing, asleep in the hospital bed, than he'd thought, though he felt sore before rainfall. He kept score of the weather in his body better now than he ever had in the fields. Still, there was a distraction to match every dull ache that overcame him. At first, it had been a trick, balancing a new budget on two thin incomes, made easier when Garrett picked up a job at one of those franchise oil-change places. He'd come home after a long shift, smelling the way he had that summer in the garage when Isaac had only wanted him but hadn't had him yet, and Isaac would hold him because he could. Garrett would fall asleep first and would still be asleep that next morning when Isaac woke and watched him.

The days were longer without work to break them up, and Isaac was working on it, he was, but there were so many steps and so much future, bright and blue above his head. There was so much life to live, and every choice he made changed it a little. So, he didn't move much at first. The medical bills piled up, a cost of living he couldn't pay without a birth certificate, a license, the Social Security card his father had used to rack up debt in his name and wouldn't return. He could get them replaced, if he filed for them. He could prosecute his father for their unlawful use, if he went to the law. But he could barely leave the house. There was so much paperwork snowing him in.

"Maybe you could go back to school," Garrett suggested, just once, in the tone of someone who'd never considered going to school in the first place.

"*Mm*, maybe," Isaac had agreed, burying his face in the crook of Garrett's neck, hiding his eyes as he pushed the jumbling steps of a project that big out of his thoughts. Gasoline and motor oil and radiator fluid, and when that wasn't enough to wash out the worry in his throat, he thought about dinner, about slicing up onions with one of the good knives Garrett's parents had given them, frying them in a pan with butter, and then— and then—

It was easier to take things a step at a time.

Ricky and Laurel had been by, so often at first that Isaac wondered if they should have rented a two-bedroom. He'd suggested it once to Laurel just to watch her laugh. Ricky and Garrett were trying to hang a framed poster in the bedroom. Laurel and Isaac hadn't even bothered to invent a chore to justify hanging out. They sat, shoulders touching, on the kitchen floor by the refrigerator, sharing a sleeve of cookies she'd brought as some sort of hostess gift.

Laurel showed up regularly and never empty-handed, with little things, homey things, things that wouldn't last forever. Cookies and jam and, once or twice, flowers that wilted in their vase. "It was a dumb idea," she said after the second time she'd tossed molded stems into the garbage, draining green water into the sink. "I just thought they might help." A piece of her, a piece of home, snipped at the stems and crammed into a washed-out jelly jar to wither out of the sun's view.

Help what, Isaac wasn't certain. Laurel wasn't much for assuaging her own guilt. She made gifts of it instead, time and snacks and flowers, not to even the score but to show she still remembered its weight. He hadn't heard much about what had happened beyond the initial horror story he'd finally pulled from Ricky in sputtering sentences when no one else could stand the bruising on his face long enough to tell it. The tree, her mother, the monsters, everything ending in a riot of green overgrowing the waste the devil had made of her fields. Her mother had been the start of it all, and when Laurel had ended it, the only legacy she had left to inherit was the guilt and blame for every drop of blood spilled. She was a good steward of those things. She'd keep the farm and the graveyard both and grow new things on that same patch of land. Flowers were probably the best of it, but the brush of ironweed and lacy wild carrot still made him flinch.

"I hate it when they die," Laurel said, echoing thoughts he hadn't realized he'd voiced. "Watching them wither like that. I've had enough rot for one lifetime."

He supposed, technically, she didn't have to watch them rot. She could just grow them again, even in the snow. She'd explained what she'd done, over and over until he could almost believe it had really happened. He'd seen her burned palms and watched them heal again.

"It's just," Laurel muttered around a mouthful of cookie, "that coffee table looks like shit. I thought it could use a touch of something and flowers are all I've got most days."

Isaac had to laugh. The cheap veneer of the coffee table was bubbling and water-stained when they bought it for three dollars from a yard sale. Even a month more of wear had put a notable strain on it, as had the junk mail, pamphlets, and coffee mugs piled on it. Isaac could almost forget it. "Doesn't it? I keep telling Garrett we should drag it out and spray-paint it."

Laurel shook her head. "Don't do that. It's where you eat half your food. You'll get flecks of paint in your supper."

"Is that true?" Isaac frowned, shaking out the last two cookies from the sleeve. He offered one to Laurel, but she declined.

"Does it have to be true? It's cautious. It's good sense."

Isaac rolled his eyes, mouthing *good sense* at her before he popped the last cookie in his mouth. "I'm tired of being cautious."

"Well, get brave about something other than eating paint," she muttered, trashing the empty sleeve of cookies in the bin under the sink.

Isaac whistled low under his breath. "Harsh."

"Sorry," she said immediately, hand darting back to her side like she was afraid she'd hurt him when she hadn't even touched him. She settled back onto the floor across from him, examining a water stain on the ceiling.

He tapped the toe of her sock with his foot. In the bedroom, he could hear Ricky cussing out a screw as Garrett cackled. "What's going on with you?" he asked her.

"Ran into Christine Maynard at the beauty supply store when I was picking up some peroxide," she said. "For the first time since, you know."

"What'd she say?"

"Asked after you. I'm never sure what she sees and what she has to be told. I think you're a frequency she's not picking up anymore. She's glad you didn't die."

"I'm glad I didn't die, too," he said.

"I've been thinking about ghosts," she said in a rush, "and what they're made of, really, more than magic. It's guilt, isn't it, that pins someone into place like that?"

Ghosts. Like Isaac could think of much else anymore. "Sure," he said, bewildered. "Guilt."

"But not always their own, I think." She took a long breath

through her nose, letting her head fall back against the refrigerator door. "She's leaving, too, soon enough."

"I know," he said.

Laurel raised an eyebrow at him. "How is it you only start paying attention to town gossip after you leave?"

"Garrett helped her out with some car repairs, free of charge. Not sure if it was a thank-you or an apology, but she's got wheels, will travel." Sometimes it took a boost like that, to get someone unstuck. Isaac was still waiting for his.

"Right," she said.

They let the quiet between them stretch, while in the bedroom, Garrett and Ricky hammered away. A sharp peal of laughter cut off with a muttered "fuck" just as Laurel said, "I might want—"

Ricky came tearing out of the bedroom, hand cupping his closed fist. "I smashed my fucking thumb with a hammer," he swore.

Laurel was already on her feet. "I'd better get him home," she said, snatching up her shoes from under the coffee table.

"Shake it off," Garrett said from the doorway. "Think we've still got a full ice tray in the freezer if it worries you."

Ricky kept his thumb clenched in his fist. "Laurel's right. Time for us to go."

Garrett laughed, confused. "Oh, come on!" But Laurel swept her purse from the floor and pressed a kiss to Isaac's cheek.

"See you soon enough," she promised, ducking out the front door, halfway down the steps before Isaac could ask her to wait long enough to finish her sentence. He wanted to know what she wanted. But he was sure, when she figured it out, she'd let him know. He should do her the courtesy of figuring out his own answer.

CHAPTER
FORTY-FOUR

They sat in the Buick for a long time before Laurel turned the engine over. From the street she could see the sheet hanging in Isaac's window rustle then fall still. Ricky held his injured hand cupped close to his chest, staring out the opposite window. "Come on," Laurel said. "Let me see. How bad is it this time?"

Ricky sighed and stuck his hand out. She turned it over, examining the scarred fingers for injury. A delicate cloverleaf of sour sorrel bloomed from his bleeding nail, green where red should have been.

It wasn't bad. Not like the tansy that spilled from his palm when his knife slipped as he was gutting fish last week. Not sharp as the bull thistle that had sprouted from his thigh a month prior when he'd called Laurel over and asked her, astutely, what the hell she'd done to him.

"You'll live," she said, and he laughed, dry and humorless.

Ricky bit his thumbnail, then pulled the curling stem of sorrel out of his mouth. "I don't bleed anymore. I bloom." He sounded sick as he said it, scraping bits of green out from under his nails.

"We'll have to tell them eventually, you know," Laurel said to the dashboard. *What happened. What he did. What I did.*

Ricky examined his nails. "We don't know what to tell them. Best to keep my mouth shut. Just in case . . ."

"In case what?"

He spat a yellow blossom onto his palm. "In case I break my arm and a pin oak grows from the wound. In case I pull jimsonweed out of my windpipe after a bad cough or spit love-lies-bleeding into the sink when I'm brushing my teeth. In case I don't last the winter because I've wilted," he said, turning the blossom over in his palm before crushing it between his fingers and flicking it out the window. "Like I said, we don't exactly know what to tell them. We don't know what you did."

"If you hadn't done what *you* did, I wouldn't have had to do anything," Laurel snapped.

Ricky's laugh was humorless. "Don't I regret it."

"I don't regret a thing I did," Laurel insisted, starting the car. She turned her head to look back over her shoulder, away from him.

"I'm a farmer, which means I'm going to bleed and keep bleeding. Someone's going to see."

Laurel turned onto the road, drumming her fingers on the dash. "Then we'd better decide what to tell them."

They both knew they needed to come up with a plan. They should offer up the truth before someone scratched the surface of their flimsy lie and flowers bloomed from its wound. But what would they say? The truth was this: Whatever life Laurel had forced into Ricky's bones didn't fit right under his skin. His eyes were too green in the summer sun, vibrant with a life that wasn't human. His stare was as deep as the woods, and in his kiss, she could taste sweet blackberry and bitter walnut where before there'd been only boy.

How could they explain what was inside him when they didn't understand it themselves? Sometimes Laurel had him in her arms and couldn't fight off the alien urge to dissect him, to find the place inside of him where the roots turned to veins, where the flowering stopped and the bleeding began. She wanted to know for certain if there was any charred bone left or if that had been overgrown by the wild, green heart of the woods she could hear beating when she pressed her ear to his thin skin. She wasn't sure he'd stop her from cutting to the core. Sometimes she was certain that all she had to do was ask and he'd open his rib cage just to satisfy her curiosity. But if she hurt him, Laurel wasn't sure that something stranger still wouldn't bloom from the places she'd sliced.

Was he Ricky? Or was he something that had slid under Ricky's skin? She didn't know. Neither, she thought, did he. They were too afraid to find out.

She had to touch him gently as the leaves in the field, afraid to bruise him in case his capillaries spat out smartweed from the places they'd been crushed. She'd forgotten herself more than once and had to pick bleeding heart from scratches that hadn't scabbed over. Sometimes she'd take the flowers that spilled from him and preserve them in resin as though they were a gift he'd presented to her in a jam jar instead of something she'd grown from his skin. She treasured them no matter their origin, a reminder of a summer when, in spite of everything, they were young and in love.

They kept their silence the whole drive home. Ricky fiddled with the radio for a while, then, three minutes from their exit, turned it off entirely. Laurel waited for him to say something, but he didn't until they were parked in his driveway with the car turned off. "I don't think I'm going to wilt this winter," he said finally, one hand on the door. "It's like the opposite. The feeling in my chest since I woke up on the ground. It's all sunshine. It doesn't feel dangerous. It feels right."

It was hard to talk about, even still. Laurel felt her breath catching around dead air every time she tried to explain what had happened on the farm, but she forced it out. "When I did it, I was thinking of summer. I was thinking of the way your eyes go all hot and river-green, and the fields in mid-July, and the summer storms. The plants were just what was there at that time. If you weren't who you are, if you weren't made so much of summer, I don't know if I could have brought you back at all."

Ricky's face was pensive. He was searching for something in her eyes that she couldn't give him. There was little assurance, mostly fear. "But did you bring me back? Are you sure?"

"I'm not sure of anything," she said, "but I hope . . ."

He pressed a kiss to her lips—short, soft, and sweet. "Then that's enough for now."

It would keep, at least until the snowfall.

In the washhouse, Lauren unloaded the bottle of hydrogen peroxide she'd purchased from the beauty supply store, but she didn't linger to check on the coyote skull she had degreasing in a tub. The four-wheeler was parked outside the farmhouse, but she wasn't ready to go in and catch Jay up on how everyone was just yet. Instead, she climbed the deer path up to the graveyard.

When she reached the top of the hill, she looked down at the fields, hazy purple with ironweed. There'd been no tobacco to sell this year, but the neighbor up the hill with a cattle farm had helped them bale the roughage growing in the fields. It would save them a bad tax bill, at least. Next year—well, Jay wanted to talk to her about next year. About tobacco. About growing other things instead. The last time they'd talked, he'd said, "You'll have to come back at some point, but right now you don't have to *stay.*" She wasn't sure what he'd say this time.

It was new soil and a whole new world, besides. Maybe the devil had destroyed something crucial, turned the lands that Anna Early had roamed into something new and unrecognizable after all. The graveyard was the only thing that looked like it had before. Jay had spent the better part of the summer resetting the gravestones and filling in the soil that Anna had shifted off herself before she'd fallen back down into her grave.

Laurel didn't talk to the grave anymore on her frequent visits. There were no ghosts to hear her. But she did visit that lonely spot from time to time when she needed to think clearly. It was the place where she could see the whole of her world without having to do more than turn her head.

She rested on the yellowing grass of the graveyard, palms upturned. They were numb from scarring, the deep lines scalded off by the fire in the bottoms. "That means it's your own," Christine had said. "Your future, yours to do with what you will."

"What should I do with it?" Laurel had asked, watching the light catch on the glitter glossing Christine's nails.

"The lines don't work like that."

"But what do you think I should do with it?"

Christine snorted, looking down at her worn-out shoes. "I'm not much of a role model in that regard."

Laurel disagreed. She thought of the heaving garden that

Christine grew, of the kindness she couldn't seem to shake no matter how roughly she was treated by the world. Dry Valley didn't deserve Christine, but it was strange to think of it without her. What would grow without her there to guide it?

"I'm not asking for another favor. I'm asking as a friend."

"I can't tell you what you should do, either way," she'd said, but she'd smiled and given Laurel's hand a squeeze before she let her go. "But maybe come visit me, wherever I go next. Don't make yourself choose anything. Just let yourself see."

Now, Laurel had two open doors that led anywhere but where she was. It was a convenient choice that could paralyze her for years if she let it build and linger. There was magic in knowing just how wide the world was before you. It could curse you, stuck to your spot, for the rest of your life.

It was like she'd tried to tell Isaac. She didn't want to get stuck here. She wanted the blank page, the future yet to be written. But what she had were these fields, this cemetery, the people on the soil, the people under the ground. She was needed, she was wanted, she was expected right where she was. She had so much. She'd taken so much more than she ever should have taken. Could she demand more?

Some stirring in her fingers, the same that remembered how it had felt to knit skin from memory and love and growing things, said she could. That stirring was awfully close to the memory of missing her mother. Sometimes the wires crossed, and she wanted to act.

It was strange, this new grief that patched the old grief strong. Sometimes she could feel it knifing through her when she moved too fast. Better to sit still, here at the top of the hill, until the aching passed. Better not to let her hands clench or give in.

So, here was Laurel: standing at the top of her world, mother-less, wanting, her hands a blank road map that she could follow anywhere she pleased.

When she stood, the breeze stilled for a long, terrible moment. Then a bird in the sycamore tree called to another in the air, and the world moved into motion, another inhale in an endless pattern of life and death. Laurel climbed over the bull gate once more and started her long trek down the hill. She'd join the bones in the graveyard in due time, but for now, she was headed home.

ACKNOWLEDGMENTS

Before this book had a title, I called it the big grief book. It was heavy, at times, to write, and letting it into the world has been the lightest thing I've ever done. I am grateful for the many hands uplifting me along the way. Writing is often said to be a lonely endeavor, so I feel blessed that I've found home, family, and community through the creation of this novel.

To my agent, Erin Clyburn, I cannot thank you enough for your tireless dedication to championing this story. The world has been wild these past couple of years, but you have been steadfast and supportive of making all my dreams come true. The team at Jennifer De Chiara Literary Agency are wonderful negotiators and advocates. Thank you for all you've done for me now and in the future.

To my editor, Vicki Lame. I'll never forget how excited I was during our first phone call and how immediately we clicked.

I love your vision and genius, your ability to shape and revise what's on the page to make me sound even more like myself. Thank you so much for taking this story on and helping it bloom.

I am so grateful to the team at Wednesday Books: Vanessa Aguirre, Jonathan Bennett, Kerri Resnick, Rivka Holler, Brant Janeway, Melanie Sanders, Lena Shekhter, and Mary Moates. Wednesday has felt like family since the start, and I'm so grateful for the incredible attention to detail and love that brought this book to life in such a beautiful way.

Thank you to Mary Knight for taking this book in its earliest stages and all the wild energy that came with it and helping me harness it into the story it has become. To Jason Sizemore, who is awesome, for his keen editorial eye and constant support of this book. To Cara Coppola for her music, her magic, and her way with words. To Samantha Puc for cheering this book along since its earliest stages, misplaced commas and all. To Serena Devi, Reed Puc, Katie Noble, and Blake Glass for beta reading, and to Saint Gibson and Kit Mayquist for every late-night porch Discord call that got me through to today.

Thank you to the Carnegie Center for encouraging me to follow this dream since I was small. You are truly home to me. Thank you to the Lexington Writer's Room, both its members for such a lively and supportive community, and all its ghosts for keeping the atmosphere spooky during late-night revision sessions. Thank you to the Moonscribers for bringing my writing back to life.

To my family, who first taught me the magic of words when you used stories as a salve to pull a thorn from my knee, and who never said no to reading me a book when I asked. You've never flinched at the weird ways I've decided to use that magic since you shared it with me. To Caroline, my love, for believing in me from the start, and for the life we've built that's made this possible. To Stella, who was there from this draft's first page and who motivated me to finish by leaning over my shoulder and sounding out the words. You are a wonder and I'm so proud of you. To Elliot, who came along at the end of this story's journey, your brilliant smile lights up my whole life. I can't wait to see what happens next.